HEALING *Hazel*

OTHER BOOKS AND AUDIOBOOKS BY JENNIFER MOORE

Regency Romance

Becoming Lady Lockwood

Lady Emma's Campaign

Miss Burton Unmasks a Prince

Simply Anna

Lady Helen Finds Her Song

A Place for Miss Snow

Miss Whitaker Opens Her Heart

Miss Leslie's Secret

The War of 1812

My Dearest Enemy

The Shipbuilder's Wife

Charlotte's Promise

The Blue Orchid Society

Emmeline

Solving Sophronia

Inventing Vivian

Healing Hazel

Stand-Alone Novellas

"The Perfect Christmas" in *Christmas Treasures*

"Let Nothing You Dismay" in *Christmas Grace*

"Love and Joy Come to You" in *A Christmas Courting*

HEALING
Hazel

A Victorian Romance

Covenant Communications, Inc.

Covenant

Cover image: *Victorian Woman Running in Snow* © LEE AVISON / Trevillion Images

Cover design by Christina Marcano © 2022 by Covenant Communications, Inc.

Published by Covenant Communications, Inc.
American Fork, Utah

Printed in Mexico
First Printing: September 2022

28 27 26 25 24 23 22 10 9 8 7 6 5 4 3 2 1

ISBN 978-1-52442-218-9

For Julie Daines,
adventurer, Anglophile, bird-watcher, candlemaker, K-pop fan,
lover of duck-fat chips, and appreciator of a good barrow mound

PRAISE FOR JENNIFER MOORE

Healing Hazel

"There's complex artistry to historical romance, balancing modern sensibilities and ideals of the modern reader against the societal conventions in the period in which the book is set. Jennifer More demonstrates a mastery of this art, staying authentic to the period in which [the novel] is set whilst using modern ideas of feminism to create a wonderful leading lady in the form of Hazel Thornton. Her determination to use her unexpected new opportunity to pursue her dreams makes her an admirable and relatable hero. As her journey toward this fulfillment slowly starts to be realized, [her] interactions with Dr. Jackson serve as a beautiful foil for her determination and hope as his viewpoint is wisely grounded in the harsh reality in which he lives. Their chemistry is palpable, and as their interactions continued throughout *Healing Hazel,* I found myself on the edge of my seat, wondering where their journey would take them next."

—Readers' Favorite five-star review

The Blue Orchid Society Series

"Moore (*Charlotte's Promise*) launches her vivid Victorian-era Blue Orchid Society series with this romantic murder mystery that sees a gutsy upper-class Londoner defying the rigid expectations of her time . . . The detailed descriptions and gentle push and pull between the couple will please readers looking for chaste historical romance. A plucky heroine and engrossing mystery make [*Solving Sophronia*] a treat."

—*Publishers Weekly*

"Moore has done an excellent job moving her story forward from the Regency period to the Victorian by using or mentioning some of the inventions or innovations of the late 1800s while showing the lingering social class distinctions. The story moves at a comfortable pace and leaves just a hint of the pending stories to come in this series while giving [*Solving Sophronia*] a satisfying ending."

—*Meridian Magazine*

"This charming and somewhat unexpected Victorian romance includes hints of mystery. Moore has created an endearing and unusual heroine and hero, both of whom bring a breath of fresh air to her well-researched depiction of Victorian London [in *Inventing Vivian*]. The settings feel accurate, and I got a good sense of the era and location. This is a truly enjoyable read with memorable characters and is recommended for all lovers of sweet historical romance."

—Historical Novel Society

"[*Emmeline*] was a good read, and I can easily recommend this if you're looking for an enjoyable afternoon diversion."

—Carolyn Twede Frank, author of the Craig, Colorado, series

"A twisty mystery with sweet romance!"

—Samantha Hastings, author of *Secret of the Sonnets* (coming 2023)

"Having never read anything from this author before, I was excited to find her writing witty, romantic, and suspenseful. As a teenager who fell in love with biology and dissections, I can relate to Vivian's passion for science and learning. She is a marvelous character and great role model. I can't imagine the opposition she had to withstand growing up during the Industrial Revolution. I loved how the author talked about wanting to write about the supportive relationship between women. As someone who is a third-generation Chinese-American, I was also interested in how she portrayed Chinese immigrants during that time. I felt she was respectful and well researched."

—Inside the Wong Mind

ACKNOWLEDGMENTS

Thank you to everyone who helped me get this book written. I am so grateful for Frank and my boys, who let me imagine and read and write and totally shut everything out for hours at a time while I stared at the computer screen and tried to make a story.

As always, I thank my critique group. Nancy Allen, Josi Kilpack, Margot Hovley, Cory Andersen, and Amanda Taylor, what would I do without your support and friendship?

Thank you to carpoolers, neighbors, and dog-sitters who took care of those little things that freed me up to get my writing done.

Thank you to the people who helped me in an expert capacity:

Dr. Jeff Gardner, MD, and Tiffany Lee, RN, thank you for answering medical questions.

Magen Francis, thank you for helping me understand head trauma and what kind of lasting effects a survivor can have.

Graham Bradley, thank you for your help with the Basque language. And, Carla Kelly, thanks for the research-book recommendations.

Thanks to the world's best editor, Kami Hancock, for your help and patience and encouraging words.

And thank you to Christina Marcano for this gorgeous cover.

PROLOGUE

November 30, 1873

The grand front door swung open, and Miss Hazel Thornton stepped into the entryway of the Lancasters' London home.

"Good evening, miss," Jameson, the butler, greeted her, a twinkle in his eye in spite of his formal manner. "The young ladies are in the sitting room." He took her wrap, gloves, and hat.

"Thank you, Jameson," Hazel said, pleased to be spending an evening with the other members of the Blue Orchid Society. She glanced at her gown in the entry hall mirror. It was—as requested in Dahlia's invitation—Hazel's most "festive" gown. She believed it was, anyway. Made of deep-green taffeta, this gown had the most ribbons, flounces, and silk flowers of any of Hazel's clothing. There was even a train, which made a swishing noise as she walked down the passageway.

Hearing the voices of her friends, she entered the sitting room, but just as she opened her mouth to greet them, Hazel stopped, staring around her in astonishment. Pine boughs and holly tied with velvet ribbons decorated every window, doorway, and mantel. A dining table had been arranged on one side of the room, covered with a rich red tablecloth and adorned with greenery, displays of fruit, and even more candles. But what made Hazel put her hand to her mouth and gasp was an enormous pine tree festooned with bows, ribbons, candles, and glass balls that glittered in the light of the flames. Her four friends watched her reaction with wide smiles.

"What is all this?" Hazel asked, her gaze traveling around the room as she took it all in.

"It's a Christmas party, dear." Dahlia kissed her cheek. Dahlia, as usual, looked stunning, her hair perfectly coiffed, her gown the height of fashion, jewels glittering at her neck. Hazel had no doubt the decor was her doing, as Dahlia had an excellent eye for embellishments.

"But Christmas is not for another month yet," Hazel protested.

"I know what you're thinking," Sophie said. She put an arm around Hazel's waist, drawing her closer to admire the tree. "Some consider holiday decor before the season to be bad luck. But we wanted to celebrate Christmas all together before you leave us. And we wanted to do it properly."

Hazel didn't know what to say. Her eyes prickled at their thoughtfulness. "This is all . . . it's all so . . ."

"Extreme?" Elizabeth said, taking Hazel's hands in greeting. "I know." She gave a dramatic sigh and then a smirk. "My cousin does tend to get carried away."

Hazel glanced at the cousin in question and saw that Dahlia shrugged good-naturedly at Elizabeth's appraisal.

"Happy early Christmas, Hazel," Vivian said by way of greeting. "I'll have you know the turkey has been cooked to an inner temperature of 165 degrees Fahrenheit. I made certain myself." Hazel stifled a smile, imagining how Dahlia's cook must have reacted to a scientific thermometer in the kitchen. "You know," Vivian continued, "bacteria in undercooked poultry has been known to cause sickness, often resulting in abdominal pain, vomiting, diarrhea, and fever."

"Of course she knows," Sophie said. "She is a nurse trainee. She knows all about bacteria and illness." Sophie was not the least repelled by Vivian's inappropriate dining room conversation. The young ladies were used to it by now, and while Vivian's observations might be considered improper or, more often, embarrassing, the Blue Orchid Society never discouraged her from speaking what was on her mind, and they never allowed anyone else to do it either. That loyalty was one of the things Hazel loved most about her friends.

Dinner was served: a veritable feast of ham, potatoes, meat pies, various breads, soups, gravies, vegetables and fruit, and a sufficiently cooked turkey. And just when Hazel thought she could not take one more bite, an enormous selection of desserts was brought in.

Once the meal was concluded, the women gathered on the sofas and chairs at the other side of the room.

"We shall miss you dreadfully, Hazel," Sophie said from her spot on the sofa beside her.

Hazel adjusted the train on her gown, not wanting to smash it while she sat. "I will be away for only a short while."

"Things won't be the same without you here," Dahlia said.

"I think you will all be far too busy with your various obligations to even notice." Hazel spoke in a cheerful voice that was at odds with the emotions inside her. Although she was extremely proud of her friends' accomplishments over the last several months, she felt an immense shame at her own failure to achieve what she'd hoped for. Months earlier, the five women had vowed together to achieve a goal, their own dearest wish, and Hazel had watched her friends do just that. Her personal ambition, to finish nursing school, had started out well-intended, but in the end, she'd been forced to abandon the endeavor. Unfortunately, she'd learned, there was more to nursing school than caring for patients and studying anatomy books. One must attend lectures in crowded halls and lessons in small classrooms, and for Hazel, being pressed into a small area without immediate means for escape had brought on panic spells that made it impossible to continue her schooling.

"Are you nervous, Hazel?" Vivian asked. "You will be traveling quite a distance. And I believe you said your father is unable to escort you the entire way to the Canary Islands?"

"He cannot be spared from the Gold Coast of Africa for the extra weeks it would require to travel to England and return with me," Hazel confirmed. "Taking weeks of leave for the holiday has already proven difficult enough. He'd proposed sending an officer to accompany me to Cádiz, but I was not inclined to travel with a stranger, and in the end, we found a suitable compromise. Pernella Westbrook is one of the instructors at the Florence Nightingale School of Nursing." Hazel blushed as she mentioned her former school. "Miss Westbrook is happy for the opportunity to travel, and I enjoyed her company quite a lot."

"A sensible choice," Elizabeth said, perhaps mistaking Hazel's blush for unease at the unconventionality of the situation. "Two competent women are entirely capable of making the journey together without having to worry about a man to escort them."

"And she's been excellent with my . . . spells," Hazel said. "I feel very comfortable with her."

"As she should be," Vivian said, frowning. "One would think if anyone would be understanding of your ailment, it would be those committed to healing the sick."

"And they call themselves caretakers." Elizabeth frowned as well, folding her arms.

Hazel felt warm at her friends' support. She was glad that, with them, she didn't have to hide the truth or minimize it. They were interested and never made her feel as if she were defective. The only other person who had been so generous with his compassion was her dear uncle Archibald, with whom she'd lived in London for the past three months.

"You seem to be doing better," Dahlia said. "It's been quite some time since a panic spell came upon you, hasn't it?"

"Weeks," Hazel said. Having friends who understood the cause of her spells and took steps to prevent them had cut down the incidents significantly. "Not since the dinner party at Lord Hastings's." Remembering her reaction to the stuffy room and her inability to move through the crowd to the exit started her fingers tingling. She balled her hands into fists and breathed deeply.

"His sitting room is terribly small, isn't it?" Sophie said gently, setting her hand over Hazel's. "And he invited far too many people for a comfortable gathering."

"Once we reach France, Father made certain Miss Westbrook and I will travel in a private train carriage for the entire journey," Hazel said, "so I don't need to worry about crowds or feeling trapped." It was extremely freeing to be able to discuss her condition so openly. Most people acted as if the panic episodes were something to be ashamed of. They certainly never asked how she was feeling or learned how the spells could be managed.

Jameson brought a bottle of wine and poured for the women.

Elizabeth raised her glass high. "Here's to Hazel and the exotic adventure awaiting her in the Canary Islands."

The others raised their glasses as well.

"And please say you have packed at least one set of trousers," Elizabeth continued, winking as Dahlia gasped. "You will find they are so much more practical when it comes to riding a bicycle or, I imagine, exploring a beach."

"I have not," Hazel admitted, thinking her father would likely suffer an apoplexy should he see his daughter wearing trousers.

"Pity," Elizabeth muttered.

The ladies continued talking well into the night. And when the hour came to bid farewell, Sophie, Elizabeth, Vivian, and Dahlia had each presented Hazel with a wrapped gift and strict orders not to open them until she was happily celebrating Christmas with her father in the officers' private villa in the Canary Islands.

When she returned home to her uncle's house, Hazel packed the parcels carefully into her trunk. After spending the evening with the Blue Orchid Society, her worries about the journey were nearly nonexistent, and a feeling of excitement had taken their place. She had her father's company and a holiday at the seaside to look forward to, and with her friends' encouragement, she felt as if she could do anything.

CHAPTER 1

Hazel watched through the window as the train wove through the Spanish countryside. They should have arrived at Cádiz hours ago, but she had learned that timetables were only approximations in this part of the world. There were always unexpected delays or repairs to contend with. What should have been a six-day journey had taken eight.

Across from her, Miss Westbrook—or Nella, as she insisted upon being called now that they were traveling companions and not student and teacher—let out a snore and shifted in her sleep. The knitting slipped from her lap, sending the ball of yarn rolling. Hazel stopped it with her foot and leaned forward to set it on the seat. A partly knitted stocking hung from the needles in the woman's hands. Nella was a middle-aged spinster with round cheeks and a puff of hair that was neither blonde nor brown but a dull in-between color that sparkled with hints of silver in the sunlight. She seemed, by all accounts, to be a respectable matron, but underneath her proper exterior, she possessed a jolly sense of humor with just a hint of irreverence. The older woman had made the long journey anything but dull. She was witty and good-humored, and Hazel had already decided that when they returned, she would introduce Nella to the Blue Orchid Society. They would love her.

Hazel touched the blue-orchid brooch at her neck, feeling its familiar filigree edges. She missed her friends. Though it had been only ten days since Dahlia's Christmas party, it seemed so much longer. Hazel sighed. So far, the trip was not the adventure she'd hoped for. The train journey through France had been fraught with delays and stopovers in nearly every little town between Paris and Bayonne. When they'd reached the Spanish border, she and Nella had retrieved their trunks and travel bags and engaged a carriage to take them to San Sebastián. The ride through the rock-covered mountains had taken an entire day, but it was necessary since the Spanish, always wary of a French invasion, used a different track gauge for their trains than did the rest of Europe.

The train slowed, brakes screeching. Nella jerked awake and groaned. "Oh my. Are we still on this train?"

"Not for much longer," Hazel said, pointing through the window. Ahead was a walled city surrounded on three sides by water. "That must be Cádiz."

"Thank goodness," Nella said. "I fear my bottom might be permanently fused to this seat."

Hazel smiled to hide her shock at Nella's indiscretion. But, if she were to be honest, her own bottom was suffering the effects of sitting for so long as well. She would be glad to get off the train and onto the steamship. At least then she could walk around and enjoy the fresh air and the view of the ocean. She looked forward to the sea voyage almost as much as she did the destination itself.

The train came to a stop, and the conductor opened their compartment door. "Cádiz, senoritas."

"Gracias," Hazel said, using one of the few Spanish words she had learned before the trip.

The women gathered their things, put on their gloves, straightened their hats, and left the compartment. The moment they stepped out of the train's shade, Hazel squinted in the bright sun. She closed her eyes and tipped back her head, loving the feel of the heat on her face. She raised and lowered her shoulders, wanting to stretch her back, but her corset made it next to impossible.

Nella dug through her bag, pulled out a fan, and wafted it in front of her face. "My goodness, it's warm."

Hazel agreed. It was warm but nowhere near as hot as an Indian summer. And with the sea breeze, it felt very comfortable. She had hardly ever been warm in England. The weather was always so damp and muggy, and one could go weeks without seeing the sun. But the Canary Islands would be warm and bright. She could hardly wait to walk along the beach or eat tropical fruit beneath an umbrella on a veranda overlooking the sea. The weeks at the villa would well make up for the uncomfortable travel.

They walked along the platform to the station, and Hazel's heart picked up, beating happily. She hadn't seen her father for almost five years. Not since she had turned sixteen and the major general had decided that a young lady needed to be among Society.

"Miss Thornton?" A man wearing the red coat of an English officer stepped into Hazel's path. She estimated his age to be near to thirty. His face was tanned and weathered, his back straight.

Her gaze moved to the epaulet at his shoulder. "Yes, Captain . . . ?" She glanced behind him. He must have accompanied her father to Cádiz.

"Bryant." He gave a sharp bow. "Captain Edgar Bryant."

"How do you do? And this is my companion, Miss Westbrook." Hazel glanced behind the captain again.

"A pleasure." Captain Bryant spoke in the efficient clipped tones Hazel associated with military men.

"You have come with my father?" she asked, feeling impatient. Why were they standing here on the train platform?

Captain Bryant cleared his throat. "The major general sends his regrets. Things are very active right now in the region, as you no doubt are aware. A missionary family was kidnapped by the Ashanti, and the Corps of Engineers is even now building roads to transport our armies for a rescue. Your father sent me to accompany you back to England."

Hazel's throat got tight as she listened, trying to make sense of the captain's words. "My father isn't here?"

A shadow of sympathy crossed the captain's face. "No, miss. I'm sorry."

Hazel swallowed hard. She glanced around for a place to sit but saw nothing. Her mind struggled to grasp the implications. He hadn't come. The disappointment was so heavy that she felt weak.

Nella put an arm around her waist. "I'm sorry, dear. I know you were looking forward to Christmas with your father."

Hazel's thoughts simply would not make sense of what was happening. All the planning over the past months, all the traveling for the past eight days. It was all . . . over. A waste. And now the idea of making a new plan, of going back to . . . Her shoulders slumped, and she hadn't the energy to straighten her posture. She felt like a child, helpless to manage her own situation. There would be no Christmas with her father, no warm sun on the beach.

And now what would she do? Return to England to spend Christmas with Uncle Archibald and her cousins? The thought of the parties and crowds nearly made her break down. She closed her eyes and rubbed her temples.

"Miss Thornton, if you please"—Captain Bryant's voice broke through her bout of self-pity—"the train to Madrid leaves tomorrow morning. I've arranged rooms for you, and I imagine you've not yet had supper."

Hazel looked up at him, not knowing what to say. Of course, a thank-you was in order, but she couldn't bring herself to speak. Not when she couldn't trust that her words wouldn't come in a flurry of weeping.

"That's very thoughtful of you, Captain," Nella said. "We'll all feel better after we've washed up and had a nice supper."

Captain Bryant nodded, looking uncomfortable, probably because he could see Hazel was hovering close to tears. "Would you like to see the city before we leave? The cathedral is magnificent."

Hazel stood, feeling suddenly resolved. Wallowing would do no good. And she would not wish for Captain Bryant to think his commander's daughter fell apart when things became uncomfortable. "Perhaps later, Captain. As Miss Westbrook said, we are very tired. Will you please take us to the hotel?"

"Yes, miss. If you would wait for a moment while I arrange for your luggage."

"Very well." She held herself straight, shoulders down. "And, Captain, I believe you said you intend to accompany us on our return journey. There is no need. We managed perfectly well getting here."

"Your father insisted, miss. There has been recent unrest with the Carlist rebels."

"I thought that was all in the past. Besides, we are not traveling near Catalonia."

Sophie had raised concerns about the Carlist rebels as well, but Hazel wasn't worried. Her father was fully aware of this type of situation, and he would never have allowed her to make the journey if it were not perfectly safe.

"Nevertheless, miss, I have my orders. I am to watch over you as I would my own sister."

Hazel waited as the captain made arrangements for the luggage, and then he accompanied them to the hotel. Voices around her spoke in what she assumed was Spanish. Palm trees stood tall against whitewashed stone buildings with red-tiled roofs. They followed narrow winding roads filled with exotic smells, but Hazel barely noticed any of it. Once again, a decision was made for her, and she felt familiar frustration at the lack of control she had over her own life. She had come so far, but it was all for nothing.

Three days later, Hazel sat back in her seat in the train compartment, feeling numb with boredom. Although it was not the same train, everything felt exactly the same as it had for nearly two weeks, the countryside moving past the windows, the gentle rocking of the locomotive lulling her into a stupor. Click, clack. Click, clack. The only difference was the new member of their party.

Captain Bryant had become much more personable during their journey. He did watch over Hazel like a brother, and she felt a sisterly affection for him. The three played cards, and he spent long hours telling the ladies about his childhood in Northumberland and making them laugh with stories about his father's sheep. It seemed the closer they drew to England, the less he acted like a stiff soldier and the more excited he became to return home.

The train had left Madrid the evening before, and the scenery had become more mountainous throughout the morning, the air cooler. Around noon, the squeak of a trolley's wheels indicated a steward had arrived with their luncheon.

Nella put away her knitting, and Captain Bryant lifted the ladies' travel bags onto the rack above. Knowing Nella would want a nap as soon as the meal was finished, Hazel moved to sit beside Captain Bryant and the older woman sat across from them. It was all a well-rehearsed routine at this point. The others seemed to take it for granted that Hazel would sit near the door, and she was glad. She'd been worried the small compartment would lead to a panic spell, but if the feeling of being closed in came upon her, she could easily slip out into the train's passageway and walk until her panic settled.

The steward unfastened the tabletop from the wall and raised it in place between the compartment's benches. He set the table quickly with practiced hands, arranging plates, glasses, and cutlery over a clean cloth. He filled their glasses, sliced warm bread, and scooped up steaming bowls of soup and plates of paella. After making sure they were comfortably settled with their meal, he closed the door, pushing his trolley down to the next compartment.

Hazel took a bite of the fish and flavored rice, wondering if this was the last meal she'd eat in Spain. The thought brought back the disappointment of her failed plans.

"In spite of all the delays," Nella said, sliding a piece of fish onto her plate, "I estimate we'll arrive in England before or perhaps on Christmas Eve."

"This will be my first Christmas in England in five years," Captain Bryant said. He took a sip of sherry. "I've nearly forgotten what snow looks like. And the taste of my mum's Yorkshire pudding."

"And how will you celebrate?" Hazel asked, glad for a distraction from her discouraging thoughts.

"Same as anyone, I imagine," he said. "Church in the morning, roast goose for supper. Mum will insist on singing carols. Da will eat too much and fall asleep in front of the fire."

Nella speared a bit of fish with her fork. "Your family must have changed since you saw them last."

He nodded, taking a drink. "My sister's children will hardly recognize me. They were all wee ones when I left. My brother manages the farm now. It will be different, I suppose, but we're still family."

Hazel blinked at the stinging in her eyes, angry at herself for feeling an emotion as petty as jealousy. She was happy for this man, pleased that he had something wonderful to look forward to. She only wished she did too but said nothing as she wiped her napkin over her lips and set it back on her lap.

"I believe we'll have some time in Paris between trains," Captain Bryant said, lifting his glass. "Thought I might do a bit of Christmas shopping. Maybe you ladies could help me find some fancy perfume for m—"

A crash threw Hazel forward. She fell hard onto the table, hitting her forearms, then was thrown back against the wall, sending a spike of pain through her shoulder. The bags from the upper rack spilled down, falling around her. Captain Bryant moved to shield her as the car tipped, but he was knocked back against the compartment wall. Dishes, bags, and people slid, crashing to the floor and flying against the walls and windows. Hazel fell to the side, landing hard on an uneven surface that seemed to be swaying. The noise was so loud that it left a ringing in her ears that was matched in intensity only by the sound of her heart pounding. Dust filled the compartment, obscuring her sight, and she lay dazed, trying to piece together what had happened.

When she was able to make sense of her surroundings, Hazel was lying against the compartment door. All around her was the detritus of what had a moment earlier been their luncheon. She pushed Nella's travel bag off her face and moved carefully, testing her body for pain. Aside from the aching in her shoulder, she hadn't been injured. She sat up, looking around, still confused as to what she was seeing.

The train car tilted at an angle, creaking as it settled. It must have come off the track. One of the windows was shattered, and a long crack stretched over the other. The luggage rack had broken away on one side and hung there, bumping against the wall with the swaying of the carriage. Her ears rang, making everything seem unnaturally silent. A bench pressed her against the door, and she struggled to right herself in the small space. Sounds reached her ears—a scream, a child's cry—and without warning, Hazel was back there, in the cold room beneath the fort, huddled behind her mother as cannons and guns were fired outside. She was trapped.

A spike of energy surged through her, spreading cold fire as it shot to her fingertips and toes. In her panic, she was blind. Tears filled her eyes, and she couldn't draw breath into her lungs.

"Hazel!" Nella's voice broke through the panic. "Hazel, listen to me."

Hazel pressed her fingertips against her eyelids. "I'm . . . trying."

Nella was one of the only nurses who'd understood the intensity of Hazel's spells, and she could typically help calm them. "Hazel." She spoke in a commanding voice. "You must breathe."

"Nella." Hazel whispered her friend's name. "I—"

"Breathe, Hazel." Nella's voice tightened, growing softer. "You are needed."

Hazel's panic did not fully abate, but she heard something in Nella's voice that shook her out of the depths of her fear and gave her a purpose. Nella was in pain. And Hazel had heard nothing from Captain Bryant, which was even more worrying. She gathered herself together and moved, dislodging a mess of dishes and food, and brought herself into a kneeling position to feel around through the settling dust. What she'd assumed to be part of the bench was, in fact, Captain Bryant's torso. Carefully, she brushed bits of glass off him with the wadded tablecloth and rolled him onto his back. "Captain Bryant, can you hear me?"

He was terribly still. Blood from a gash on his head covered one side of his face. She used a napkin to wipe it away, but it welled up again.

On the other side of the cabin, Nella groaned.

Hazel crawled through the wreckage, climbing over a bench that was dislodged from the wall. Pain shot through her hand as she pressed down on a bit of glass. She removed it, wincing at the blood that welled up in her palm. She was impeded by her layers of skirts but grateful that they protected her knees from the shards of glass that littered the floor. Scrambling to her feet, she lifted the folding table off her friend and saw that Nella's leg was crushed between the broken bench and the compartment wall.

Nella's face was white, a small cut slashing across her cheek. She grabbed on to Hazel's hand.

"You're hurt," Hazel said. She found another napkin and wiped blood from Nella's face with trembling hands.

Nella nodded, closing her eyes. "And you?

"I'm unharmed."

"The captain?" Nella's voice was raspy and quiet. Her earlier admonishment must have expended her strength.

"He suffered an injury to his forehead. I can't wake him," Hazel responded, falling naturally into her role as student.

"Does he have a pulse?"

Hazel moved toward Nella's trapped leg, meaning to pull away the bench, but Nella stopped her with a hand on her arm. "Check his pulse."

Hazel pushed back through the debris and knelt at the captain's side. She touched her fingers to his neck, wishing she'd thought to check before. She felt a soft beating. "He has a pulse." She wiped at his forehead. "And the wound is still bleeding."

"Bleeding is good," Nella said. Hazel could just see her over the bench and the broken table. "It means his heart still beats." She drew in a shaky breath. "But you must stop it before too much blood is lost."

"Apply pressure," Hazel muttered, remembering what she'd learned in nurse training. She pulled open Nella's travel bag, taking out the scarf Nella had been knitting. She pressed folded napkins against the captain's wound and tied the scarf around his head to hold them in place. The captain still did not move.

Hazel patted his face gently. "Captain . . ." She looked across the compartment to Nella. "I still can't wake him."

"He needs a hospital," Nella said. Her voice was quiet, and in it Hazel could hear pain. She moved back to the bench that trapped Nella's leg to the wall, grabbing on to it and pulling.

It slid just a bit.

Nella sucked in a breath through her teeth. She cried out as Hazel pulled again, moving the bench farther away and making the train car creak with the shifted weight.

When Hazel returned back around the bench, her friend was leaning forward, holding her ankle and breathing heavily.

With slow movements, Hazel loosed the strings and pulled off her friend's boot and stocking. Nella's ankle was purple with one large lump on the side. Her foot bent at an unnatural angle. "Oh, Nella."

Nella readjusted her skirts, covering her feet. She dabbed at her face with the napkin. "Check on the captain's bleeding again," she said. "Then you must go for help."

The bleeding had slowed but hadn't stopped completely. Hazel applied fresh napkins to the captain's head wound and retied the scarf. "What happened?" she asked Nella even though of course her friend had no more idea than she.

"I don't know," Nella said. "Did you elevate his head?"

Hazel put the bag beneath the captain's head. She stood, brushing herself off, and braced herself against the wall as the compartment tilted. She paused at the door, peeking through the window into the passageway and holding herself tightly. Passengers stumbled through the corridor, trying to walk along the slanting floor. Some held injuries; others looked dazed. Would she be safe outside?

The hesitation lasted only an instant. Her friends needed help. She pulled the door, managing to slide it only partway because of the debris.

Hazel squeezed through the opening, stepped along the tilting passageway, bracing her hands against the walls, and climbed down out of the train. She was immediately surrounded by chaos.

Children cried and women screamed words she didn't understand. Some just sat staring. Hazel turned in a slow circle, unsure of where to go or what to do. She felt lost and overwhelmed. Smoke hung in the air, and her ears were still ringing. The train car was indeed off the track and leaned on damaged wheels.

Hazel stumbled along the track, staring at the damage and the other passengers, who looked around them with the same blank confusion she felt.

Another of the train cars balanced precariously, looking as if it might topple at any moment. A piece of broken railing fell to the ground, hitting the metal of the track with a crash. The noise jolted Hazel out of her daze, and remembering her friends lying injured inside the train, she spurred herself forward. She hurried between the people, searching for whoever was in charge, but the conductors looked as lost as everyone else. Whom could she ask for help?

She came to the area that appeared the most damaged, where two train cars were completely separated and looked as if they had been blown apart. One of them lay on its side. Between them the track was a giant hole of broken wood and twisted metal. The ground was scorched, and some small fires still burned in the underbrush. The sickening smell of burning skin met Hazel's nose. Had there been an explosion? Would there be another? Pieces of luggage lay all around, their contents strewn over the ground and in the trees. Some of the piles weren't clothes at all, but people. They didn't move. Hazel's insides felt as though they were falling, and she breathed heavily. People had died. Others were moaning in pain.

Seeing two men carrying an injured woman, she followed them, stumbling away from the crater. Once the woman was settled in the shade, Hazel approached the men.

"If you please, por favor, senors, my friends need help. I can pay you; please, senors." She motioned for them to follow, using gestures to explain her friends' injuries and that she would happily compensate the men for their trouble.

They came to the car and climbed inside. The men stood in the compartment doorway as Hazel checked on Captain Bryant. "Nella, I brought help," she said and then made her way through the mess to where her friend rested against the wall. Hazel looked toward the captain. "He still hasn't woken?"

Nella shook her head.

"Should he be moved?"

"I don't know." Nella sighed. "Typically, that is a doctor's decision. But in this case . . ." She glanced around the tilting compartment and at the hanging luggage rack that looked as if it could break free at any moment. "I think it is not safe for us here."

Hazel dug among the glass and broken dishes and found her handbag, offering the men a wad of bills and explaining with signs that her friends needed to be moved from the train.

The men declined the money but still carried Captain Bryant from the compartment.

Hazel crouched down by her friend. "Your ankle is broken, I think, Nella. What should I do?"

Nella shook her head. "For now, there is nothing to do but wait for the swelling to dissipate."

"Have you anything for pain, perhaps in your bag?"

Nella shook her head again and closed her eyes.

Seeing the pain in her friend's face, Hazel did not ask her any more questions. She held Nella's hand instead, settling down among the wreckage to wait.

After a few moments, the men returned and carried Nella from the car.

While her companions were being relocated, Hazel gathered their things. The three of them had only their travel bags and a few hatboxes in the compartment. The larger traveling trunks were in the luggage car.

When she joined them outside, the two men tipped their hats and departed, leaving Hazel, an unconscious Captain Bryant, and Nella on a grassy spot in the shade. Hazel set down their bags and sat on the ground beside them, surrounded by other burned, broken, and bleeding train passengers.

Now that the immediate shock had passed, reality set in, and a surge of terror washed through her, leaving her lightheaded. She and her friends had come close to death. And Captain Bryant was still unconscious. What was she to do? She crossed her arms against the chill that went over her. She did not speak the language, she did not understand what had happened to explode the train track, her two companions were in need of medical care, and she had no way of knowing how to transport them to a hospital or even in which direction one might be found. She didn't know when or how they would return home nor, more immediately, what to do for food and shelter. The entire circumstance felt so helpless that Hazel could only stare at the scene as her mind turned through scenarios and her worry grew. Panic threatened, and she fought to keep herself calm, closing her eyes and breathing in and out steadily.

"Hazel." Nella poked at her arm. "What are you doing?"

"I'm so sorry." Hazel blinked. She turned to adjust the travel bag behind Nella's back. "Are you uncomfortable? What can I do?"

"All of these people"—Nella motioned around to the train passengers—"they need help."

Hazel glanced around her, taking in the wounded people in the clearing. "I don't know—"

"You helped the captain and myself," Nella interrupted before Hazel could voice her hesitance. "You are very capable."

"But I only did what you told me," Hazel said. "I—I'm not a nurse." Embarrassment heated her cheeks. "I haven't completed my training."

"You can do this." Nella squeezed her hand. "They need you."

Hazel opened her mouth to argue but stopped when the steward who had brought their meal stumbled by, holding his arm. Blood dripped from between his fingers.

She glanced at Nella, and the older woman motioned toward the man.

Hazel rose, stopped the steward with a hand on his uninjured arm, and pointed to a rock for him to sit near Nella.

"Examine the wound," Nella instructed.

Hazel helped the man pull off his jacket. She tore his sleeve open, exposing a long cut just beneath his shoulder. "It needs stitches," she muttered.

"For now . . . ," Nella started.

"Apply pressure. Stop the bleeding," Hazel finished. She found a shirt lying on the ground, brushed it off, and held it against the wound. Then she took the steward's hand, showing him where to hold the shirt, and motioned for him to press tightly. She put his coat over him, wanting to keep him warm.

Nella nodded her approval.

A woman with a child cried out, and Hazel hurried over to her. The little girl clasped her arm closely against her chest. Her wrist was purple and swollen. The bone may have been broken. Hazel sat the little girl down near Nella, helping her lean back against a tree.

"You cannot set the bone yourself," Nella said. "So you must immobilize it."

Hazel found an apron from the dispersed clothing and tore it to make a sling, wrapping the wrist. She motioned for the little girl to stay still and not move her arm.

When Hazel returned to Nella, she saw her friend's face was becoming paler. She brushed a curl off the woman's forehead, noticing how cold her skin felt. She remembered learning about shock and thought Nella was exhibiting symptoms. "You need a doctor's care."

Nella leaned back against the tree. "For now, there is nothing to be done." She closed her eyes.

Hazel found a wool coat and a pair of trousers and laid them over Nella to keep her warm.

"Help the sick, Hazel," Nella said in a quiet voice. "That is a nurse's calling."

Hazel recognized Miss Nightingale's words. She'd heard them often enough when the famous nurse addressed the nurse trainees. "But I'm not . . ." Seeing that Nella had fallen asleep, her words trailed off. She looked around the wreckage, feeling useless. Nella knew just what to do, but Hazel felt unsure. What if, in her attempt to help, she made things worse?

A throbbing came from her palm, and Hazel glanced down, surprised at the cut in her hand. She had a vague recollection of slicing it on a piece of glass and saw that the wound had not begun to close. She found a handkerchief in her handbag and wrapped it around her hand, using her teeth to pull the knot tight. The small action gave her a bit of confidence. Surely a little help was better than none. And anything was better than sitting helplessly. She would do what she could.

Over the next hours, she gathered more clothing and a few blankets to cover patients who appeared cold. Then, with the help of the young girl's mother, she bound a slashed thigh. A man with a broken nose she ordered to sit quietly and gave him a wad of cloth to hold against the bleeding as she tied a strip of fabric around it to keep it in place.

Luckily, the train had plenty of water, and she, along with some of the other passengers, distributed it to those who couldn't retrieve it themselves. Some—the burn victims, in particular—were injured far beyond Hazel's abilities to help. She offered water and soft words but had little more to give.

She was pleased to see that the men who had moved Captain Bryant and Nella from their car had recruited more to their cause to move others from the damaged train.

Hazel checked often on Captain Bryant, who still hadn't woken, and Nella, who drifted in and out of sleep. Far from feeling cold now, her friend had developed a fever. Hazel dabbed Nella's face with a cool cloth.

She changed the dressing on Captain Bryant's wound again, seeing that the bleeding had at last stopped. As she retied the scarf around his head, Hazel heard a cheer. She stood, looking around for the cause of the passengers' sudden excitement and saw one wagon with a canvas covering approaching along the road beside the train, followed by another. The drivers and passengers each wore a band around their upper arms, bearing a bright-red cross. An ambulance crew.

Relief made Hazel's knees weak. Help had arrived at last.

CHAPTER 2

Dr. Jim Jackson surveyed the scene as the ambulance wagon approached. Some sort of explosive had opened a wide crater, throwing two cars clear of the track and dislodging the others. The entire locomotive must have crashed to an immediate halt, sending people and objects flying.

"Looks like dynamite." Dr. Laurent craned his neck, trying to get a better view of the damage. The sunlight through the trees made patterns on his bald head and spectacles. "Zhey are lucky it did not explode beneath zhe boiler."

"There will still be plenty of burns from the explosion itself." Jim smelled smoke in the air. He squinted, trying to assess the damage. The hours since the incident had dispersed the initial panic, but that didn't mean hysteria wouldn't arise again. Pain and seeing loved ones suffer could cause people to behave irrationally. Grabbing his medical kit, he jumped out of the wagon before it even came to a stop, directing the drivers toward a flat area where they could more easily load the injured.

The other nurses and orderlies climbed from the wagons, grabbed their kits, and joined him, waiting for his direction.

Jim scanned the scene, noticing that some of the injuries appeared to have been bandaged.

"It appears someone has administered emergency treatment, no?" Dr. Laurent said.

"Appears so," Jim said. He turned to the group of medical personnel. "You know what to do. Prioritize. Some injuries can wait. And some of the wounded cannot be saved. Give your resources and time to those who need it now. They are your priority."

Dr. Laurent repeated in Spanish everything Jim had said, and the head nurse, Lucía, repeated everything once more in Basque. Then the medical team spread out, each of the doctors taking with him a pair of orderlies and a nurse.

They split into teams, and Jim and Dr. Laurent started toward the crater.

"Hola, senors."

Jim turned and saw a young woman hurrying toward him from a shady area beneath the trees. Her hair and skin were fair, her eyes a pale blue-gray. There was blood on her skirts, and one hand was bound with a bloody handkerchief. Her hair had come loose from its pins and hung down in a braid over her shoulder. The dress she wore looked ridiculous for the situation, with its layers of skirts. Ribbons and ruffles weren't practical in the least trying circumstances, but here, they could only be an impediment.

"Are you doctors?" She spoke slowly, pointing to the band on his arm and looking between him and Dr. Laurent. Everything about the young lady was soft—her voice, her mannerisms, her coloring. Jim was surprised to hear her speaking English.

"Yes, ma'am. I am Dr. Jim Jackson, and this is Dr. Claude Laurent."

Relief shone on her face as Dr. Laurent inclined his head. "Oh, you speak English. Thank goodness." She started toward the trees, the hem of her dress dragging through the dirt. "My friends are hurt. Captain Bryant still hasn't woken, and Nella's ankle may be broken. They both need medical care right away."

Perhaps it was the surprise of finding a young British lady among the wreckage of a Spanish Civil War bombing, or perhaps it was just because she'd assumed they would accompany her, but regardless of the reasoning, Jim and Dr. Laurent followed.

As soon as they came near the tree line, people rushed toward them or cried out, each competing for the doctors' attention. The orderlies and nurses settled the crowd, and Dr. Laurent reassured the patients in a loud voice that they'd all be tended to, but Jim gave little notice. His entire attention was directed at the young uniformed soldier lying on the ground.

The scene around them faded. Jim stood again on the Gettysburg battlefield with the smell of cannon smoke still thick in the air. Dying horses screamed. Around him soldiers moaned and called out in pain. Most were unnaturally still. Many were his friends. But there was only one he searched for. And when he at last found him, it was too late.

"The bleeding's stopped, but he still hasn't woken." The young woman's voice pulled Jim from his memory.

He glanced at her and knelt beside the soldier, feeling his neck for a pulse. The beat against his fingertips was weak but steady. A scarf was bound around the man's head, holding in place folded napkins soaked with blood. Jim lifted the makeshift bandage. The wound was deep, but the soldier's skull didn't appear to have suffered any damage. Bruising had started around the laceration, however.

He pulled back an eyelid and the pupil constricted in the sunlight. A good sign. The man's brain still functioned.

"He has been unconscious for how long?"

"Hours," the young woman said. "But I don't know exactly what time . . ." She glanced toward the train.

Three hours at least, Jim thought, based on how long it had taken for a message to reach the hospital and the time it had taken the medical team to travel to the scene. For the soldier to be unconscious for so long . . . it was worrying. Brain damage was very likely. Jim motioned for the orderlies to take the soldier to the ambulance wagon.

Dr. Laurent knelt beside a middle-aged woman, inspecting her ankle.

The young lady joined him, adjusting her skirts so she could kneel on the woman's other side and take her hand. "I believe it's fractured," she said.

Apparently, the young woman is a doctor. Jim frowned, but Dr. Laurent nodded to the young lady. "Correct." He motioned for a couple of orderlies. "She may need surgery. And her fever . . . zhis is very troubling."

Jim turned away, examining a slash on a man's shoulder.

Once a nurse cleaned the man's wound, Jim threaded his needle and started stitching. He watched Dr. Laurent and the young lady from the corner of his eye, wondering if she intended to insert herself into the examination of every patient. The assistance of an untrained person would only slow down tasks that were already hours behind.

Jim gazed around the wreckage. The nurses were already sorting patients, and a steady stream was going to the hospital wagons.

The orderlies helped the woman with the fractured ankle onto a stretcher and lifted it slowly. One of the men hitched up his side, trying to get a better grip. The motion jostled the woman, and she let out a word that was best unused in polite circles, especially by a lady.

Dr. Laurent raised his brows.

The young woman gasped at the expletive.

"*Cuidado,*" Jim told the orderlies, stifling a smirk.

The young woman took the elder's hand, walking alongside the stretcher and speaking softly. She brushed a curl from the woman's forehead, and Jim wondered at the relationship. Was the injured woman her relative? And aunt, perhaps? But he tossed away the question. He had dozens of injured to attend to, and personal details made no difference in the patient's treatment.

Once the injured woman had been taken away, the young lady returned. She looked hesitant, as if unsure whether to speak. "There are quite a few who need stitches," she said in her soft voice. "And some with broken bones."

Obviously, Jim thought, but he did not speak aloud. There was far too much to do, and this young woman, pretty though she was, was not helping things with her observations. He dug into his medical bag, and finding a roll of bandages, he set to work splinting a young girl's wrist.

"Zhey have been treated?" Dr. Laurent pointed to the bandages wrapped around various appendages. He was speaking to the young woman again.

Someone had been creative. Bandages were torn from clothing or table linens, and in at least a few cases, luggage was being used to elevate injuries.

"I only tried to stop the bleeding," the young woman said quietly. "And keep the wounds clean."

Jim looked up. "*You* did this?"

"I—yes, well, I did what I could."

Jim frowned, irritated. "You could have easily made their injuries worse. Have you any training for this sort of thing?"

"I—" she began, looking flustered. She clasped her hands and stared at them. "In a manner of speaking, you see—"

"And what is your name, mademoiselle?" Dr. Laurent asked in a kind voice, saving her from embarrassment. Dr. Laurent was much more of a gentleman than Jim would ever be.

The young woman turned fully toward the Frenchman. "I beg your pardon. I didn't introduce myself. I'm Hazel Thornton." She curtsied.

"*Enchantée*, Mademoiselle Thornton." Dr. Laurent took Miss Thornton's hand, kissing the air above it.

"Oh." Her cheeks turned the palest shade of pink. "Yes, thank you."

"Anyone left on the train?" Jim asked, returning to the business at hand. They had no time for the Frenchman's flirting.

"Those men there can tell you if there are others," Miss Thornton said. She pointed to a group of men helping the orderlies with the stretchers. "But they speak only Spanish. Have you someone to translate?"

"I have *moi*, mademoiselle." Dr. Laurent flashed a smile and gave a flourishing bow, then left to speak to the men.

"You don't speak Spanish?" Jim asked when he and Miss Thornton were left alone. "How did you communicate with them?" Jim glanced toward the men and then turned back to continue suturing the man's shoulder wound.

"We used hand motions. Or, occasionally, one of us would understand a word the other said. It was not very effective."

"Got the job done," Jim admitted. Finished with the man's shoulder, he stood and motioned to Miss Thornton's injured hand. She offered it, and he untied the knot and pulled away the wrapping.

Miss Thornton sucked in a breath through her teeth.

Jim looked closer at the laceration. It was deep but not alarmingly so. "This should be sutured," he said. Their eyes met, and Jim felt a pull of attraction. The unexpected response caught him off guard. "To close the wound and minimize blood loss and chance for infection." He kept speaking as he reined in his emotions, irritated with himself. There were people dying around him.

She pulled away and took the handkerchief, wrapping it back around her hand. "It can wait." She motioned to the nurses and their rows of patients waiting for treatment.

Jim agreed. It could indeed. He motioned for his team to follow, tipped his hat, and left the young lady, making his way to the crater, where some form of explosive had obliterated the track, knowing from experience that the most critically injured patients would be there, in the heart of the attack. The nurses were already tending to burn victims there. He smelled the burning flesh from yards away, and his stomach sank as he calculated how many doses of morphine the hospital had on hand. It was never enough.

Jim worked steadily for an hour, assessing injuries, sending patients to the ambulance wagon, and binding wounds. If only he'd arrived sooner. For some, too much time had passed for treatment to be effective. He found himself grinding his teeth, frustrated at the wasted hours.

As he and the other medical staff moved among the wounded, Jim noticed occasionally that Miss Thornton still followed Dr. Laurent as he examined and treated patients. The older man even gave her assignments along with the other nurses. The Frenchman, apparently, couldn't resist the company of the pretty young woman.

The sound of another train drew everyone's attention. It seemed the railway had at last sent its representatives to sort out the mess.

Jim kept at his task, tending the injured, glad he didn't have to worry about the paperwork and lost luggage and interrupted travel schedules. There would surely be legal action taken, and certainly the military would investigate, but none of it was his concern. He stopped and talked to the other medical personnel as they worked, offering advice when asked. The orderlies and nurses from the International Red Cross Hospital had less experience than Jim and Dr. Laurent—none on a battlefield—but they'd risen to the occasion splendidly. They'd had to, with the number of attacks by the Carlists these past weeks and the Spanish Army's retaliation.

There were a few more wounds to sew, a few more bones to set, but for the most part, Jim's work here was done. He needed to get the more seriously injured patients to the hospital, where Dr. Ruiz would be waiting. Some patients required surgery, and in that, time was essential. Dr. Laurent would make certain the others followed soon. Jim climbed into the first ambulance wagon and gave the order to depart.

Behind, in the covered part of the wagon, he could hear groans as the wooden wheels bumped over rocks, and the sounds of nurses and orderlies as they tried to speak comforting words to the patients.

The wagon traveled slowly over the miles to the hospital, climbing up rocky hills and rattling along uneven mountain roads. When they reached the former monastery that served as the Red Cross Hospital, the hour was well after dark. Jim went to his quarters. He washed his hands and splashed water onto his face and then changed into a clean white coat, knowing that, for him, the night was just beginning.

It was nearly dawn when the last burn was treated and the few surgeries had been performed. Luckily there were no amputations, for which Jim was grateful. The procedure reminded him too much of the Virginian battlefields, and those were memories best left alone.

The other ambulance had arrived just an hour after the first, and the hospital wards were so full that some beds were made up in the passageways. He thought it ridiculous that an entire chapel stood empty when the space could be put to better use, but padre de Leon, the priest assigned to the hospital, would not hear of it.

Throughout the night, Jim had kept an eye on the soldier with the head injury, but the man still hadn't woken. At least his wound hadn't become infected. Jim suspected there may be swelling in the brain, but he would reassess in a few hours.

The first rays of morning shone through the hospital windows as Jim made his final rounds. He'd sent most of the medical staff to bed hours earlier, but he was sure Dr. Laurent would still be attending to patients. Even though, at fifty, he was over twenty years Jim's senior, the man seemed to possess endless energy, and his dedication to helping the sick was unmatched.

Jim left the West ward, closing the wooden door quietly behind him, and strode along a well-worn path across the grass of the cloister to the other ward. The early-morning breeze stirred the sheets, clothing, and bandages that hung in tidy rows on their lines at one end of the courtyard. When the Red Cross had sent Jim and Dr. Laurent to Navarre in search of a location for the hospital, the monastery's garden was a primary factor in the decision. Of course, the proximity to the Carlist state and besieged cities with their endless fighting were the main considerations, as well as the large dormitories that could easily convert to hospital wards. But the open cloister, where patients could take in fresh air, safe from the bullets and cannon fire was priceless. The monastery was built like a square fortress surrounding the garden cloister. The rectangular chapel comprised one entire end of the building; long dormitories ran along each side; and kitchens, offices, and other necessary rooms took up the other end.

Jim took in one last breath of fresh air before entering the other ward. Once he was inside, he was struck with the familiar smells of sickness, blood, and medicine as he stepped along the rows of beds, reading charts and making examinations.

As he predicted, Dr. Laurent was at the far end, doing the same. When Jim reached him, he was speaking to the female patient with the fractured ankle.

A woman poured a glass of water and gave it to the patient. When she turned, Jim scowled as irritation tightened his muscles. It was the young lady from the train, Miss Thornton. It was a testament to how tired he was that he hadn't recognized her dress immediately. It stood out in the hospital like a peacock among a flock of chickens.

"What are you doing here?" Jim's voice came out sharper than he'd intended, probably due both to the fact that he hadn't slept for more than twenty-four hours and to his being caught off guard once again.

Miss Thornton blinked. She looked down at the woman in the bed. "This is my traveling companion, Miss Westbrook, and I—"

"No visitors in the ward." Jim pointed toward the door.

"But I am not visiting," she said. "Miss Westbrook and I are traveling together, and so—"

"This is not a hotel, miss," he said, cutting off her words. "We don't offer accommodations for our patients' *traveling companions*."

"I don't expect you to, Dr. Jackson," she said, her eyes tightening at the sarcasm in his voice. "I intend to earn my keep."

"And how will you do that?" Jim folded his arms across his chest. The young woman didn't look as if she'd done a day's labor in her life. She certainly had no concept of the work required to keep a hospital running during an armed conflict. Perhaps she thought she would offer fashion advice to the wounded or plan a delightful picnic in the cloister.

"I thought I would tend to patients." Miss Thornton looked at him and then down at her hands.

"Mademoiselle was very helpful at zhe scene of zhe attack," Dr. Laurent offered. "And ever since, she has been assisting in zhe care of zhe wounded."

"I appreciate that," Jim said, finding it hard to infuse patience into his tone. "But in this hospital, 'helpful' simply isn't enough."

"She is a nurse." The woman on the bed spoke up for the first time. Her words slurred with the pain medicine she'd taken. "Trained at the Florence Nightingale School in London."

Jim turned to Miss Thornton. "A fully trained nurse? Why did you not mention this earlier?"

Miss Thornton glanced at the patient, then Dr. Laurent, then back to Jim before lowering her eyes. "I am partially trained," she said, her cheeks taking on color. "I haven't entirely completed the courses."

That explained it. Jim shook his head. "It's not going to work. I don't have the time or the resources to train you. If you haven't noticed, Miss Thornton, we're in the middle of a war."

"I know that, and—"

"The answer is no." Jim was exhausted, and the last thing he wanted to do was argue with a person who thought this was all a delightful adventure. He'd seen the spectators at Bull Run, bringing their picnic blankets and luncheon to enjoy the battle. None of them had had the slightest idea what an actual war entailed, what price it would exact from their lives, their families, and their very souls. And this young lady was no different.

"But, Doctor—" she began.

Jim held up a hand to stop her words. "This isn't a fancy city infirmary fully supplied with medicines and equipment and pretty curtained windows, where gentlemen come for a cough remedy. It's an active military hospital in a warzone. The patients brought through those doors have suffered injuries so barbarous that sometimes all we can do is put the pieces back together and call the priest."

Miss Thornton held herself straight, and something flickered in her eyes—a flash of something familiar. Jim knew that look from the eyes of soldiers who had seen more than a person should have to witness. "You do not know my history, Dr. Jackson." She spoke softly. "I am not a stranger to the horrors of war." Her lip quivered the slightest bit, but instead of making her look afraid, the movement only added to her air of surety. "I have had training, and I will not be a burden to you or to the hospital." Her voice did not get louder, but it was somehow stronger.

"We can always use more hands," Dr. Laurent said. "One more nurse would be most valuable. If she's willing to work and she is trained, however partially, she would be an asset."

His words were true. The small staff was always overwhelmed. One more nurse would make a substantial difference. But was Miss Thornton capable? Jim doubted it. "Very well," he said, too tired to argue further. He picked up a chart from the foot of another bed, looked it over, and set it back into its holder on the iron footboard. "Just remember I warned you." He looked between the three of them, then nodded to Dr. Laurent and left the ward, ready to sleep and certain he'd just made an enormous mistake.

CHAPTER 3

An hour later, carrying her hatboxes and handbag, Hazel followed Lucía, whom she understood to be the head nurse, along the covered passageway that surrounded the garden. Lucía was short and sturdily built with thick dark hair pulled back tightly and hidden beneath a starched white nursing cap. Based upon the frown lines around her mouth and her disapproving scowl, she was a person who had no tolerance for nonsense.

Dr. Laurent had introduced the women. He'd had a brief conversation in Spanish with the head nurse and then explained to Hazel that he'd placed her into Lucía's charge and she'd be shown to her sleeping quarters. She could begin her work once she'd rested. Hazel had thanked Dr. Laurent, seeing by the dark circles beneath his eyes that he needed rest as well, and bid him farewell. She was pleased that she'd found a champion in the kind bald-headed man. He had spoken to the train personnel on her behalf, arranging luggage and sending messages to Uncle Archibald in London and her father on the Gold Coast. He'd washed and stitched up the cut in her palm. And he'd brought Hazel to the hospital, confident that she would be a valuable addition to the staff—even if it was only in a temporary capacity.

If she'd not been permitted to remain at the hospital . . . She frowned, remembering Dr. Jackson's resistance to the idea. What had he expected her to do? The small town they had passed on the way to the hospital was surely too small for an inn. Did he think she could somehow find her way back to England alone? With no mode of transport and no understanding of the language? She wasn't even sure where exactly they were. Somewhere in the Basque country, she assumed. If only she'd studied a map before she'd come. As it was, she'd taken only a quick glance of the train routes and the major cities. Her focus had been upon the final destination, not the regions along the way.

At least for now, she had somewhere to stay while she figured out how to get herself and her two companions home safely to England. Hazel's and the head nurse's footsteps on stone echoed in the quiet of early morning. Seeing that Lucía was moving quickly, Hazel hurried her step, glancing at the laundry hanging in neat rows at the end of the garden. She shivered at the chill in the mountain air.

Reaching the far end of the passageway, Lucía entered another wing of the hospital and continued on without glancing behind to see whether Hazel was keeping pace.

Hazel pushed through the door, her arms full of her things from the train compartment, into a windowless passageway lit only with candle lamps set at intervals in niches in the stone walls. It felt very old-fashioned to be in a place lit solely by candlelight rather than gas lamps, and the effect, with the tall Gothic arches, was a bit eerie.

As she passed the various rooms, Hazel took quick glances, trying to get her bearings in this new place. Most of the doors were closed, but the kitchen was easily recognizable by the noises of food being chopped and the smell of . . . something that involved sausage. A cook must be preparing breakfast. Hazel's stomach rumbled, reminding her she'd not eaten since luncheon on the train the day before.

From another doorway came the smell of soap and steam. Lucía entered, crossing to an open wardrobe. A pair of nurses folded a pile of sheets. They greeted Lucía and stared curiously at Hazel.

Aside from a small nod, Lucía paid the women little notice. She took a light-blue cotton dress from the wardrobe and held it up in front of Hazel, as if to judge the size. She handed the dress to Hazel. From one shelf Lucía took a white apron, from another a starched white cap, and finally, an armband with a red cross.

"Gracias." Hazel accepted the clothing, juggling hatboxes and bags to balance it all.

Lucía gave another nod and left the room, and Hazel waved to the other nurses and followed her as she turned down a different passageway.

Halfway down, Lucía stopped in front of a door, took a lamp from a wall niche, and held it out. Hazel set down her load and took it. Lucía motioned to the door, and Hazel opened it, pushing the heavy wooden panel and entering a small windowless cupboard of a room. She held up the lamp, but it took only a quick glance to see the entire contents of the bedchamber: a wooden cot with a folded blanket, a straight-backed chair, a small table with a worn copy of the Bible, and on the wall a carved wooden cross.

Lucía said something, and seeing that Hazel didn't understand, she pointed to the key in the lock.

"Gracias, Lucía," Hazel said, making a note to learn more Spanish words.

Lucía gave another one of her sharp nods and left.

Hazel brought her things into the room, pulling the door closed behind her. She turned the key. The room seemed even smaller once the door was shut. She set the lamp on the table and laid the clothing over the back of the chair.

For a moment, the room's size made her worry she would panic, but she waited, breathing, and felt surprisingly calm. She sat on the bed, realizing there was no mattress or sheets. And she had no nightclothes. The barren room was the furthest thing from cozy, but at least it was a room. According to Dr. Laurent and the railway officials, the luggage of those who had come to the hospital should be delivered within a few days, once the mess was sorted. She shifted on the cot, feeling sorry for the monks who had lived such a spartan life. Hadn't they at least wished for a pillow?

But exhaustion quickly supplanted any complaints of discomfort, and Hazel laid her head on the folded woolen blanket and slept.

When Hazel opened her eyes, the world was entirely dark. She felt a stab of fear, but it lasted only an instant, and she remembered where she was. The candle must have gone out. Was it night? Or was the small room too far hidden for any sunlight to find it? Either way, she was sure there was plenty of work to do. Patients didn't stop hurting just because the hour grew late.

Her thoughts turned to Nella and Captain Bryant. Had their condition improved? Dr. Laurent had worried about Nella's fever. And the captain . . . had he awoken?

She sat up and stretched, her body aching from the hard bed and, she suspected, from the train accident. Sleeping in a corset hadn't done her any favors either. She waited for her eyes to adjust but gave up after a moment when the room remained every bit as dark as it had been when she woke. She'd have to remember to conserve her candle in the future, and perhaps she could locate some striking matches.

Blasts sounded in the distance, startling her. Was it the sound of gunfire? Surely it couldn't be. The stone walls were thick, and from what she'd seen, the hospital was fairly secluded. Perhaps she was just hearing the usual noises made by an old building and embellishing them with her imagination.

She fumbled with her buttons, feeling her way to removing her traveling dress, underskirts, and tournure and realized her shoulder ached more than yesterday. Her palm stung beneath the bandage Dr. Laurent had applied. She breathed a sigh when she removed the tight corset. Blindly, she pulled the blue nurse's dress over her head and put her arms into the sleeves. The cotton felt worn and soft. She fastened the buttons. Then, feeling as if she were decent enough should someone walk past, she unlocked and opened the door.

A candle lamp in the passageway gave a paltry bit of light, but Hazel was grateful for it. She put on the apron and, having no hairbrush, finger-combed her hair, pulling it back into a knot and fastening it with pins. She put the nurse's cap on her head and buttoned the armband above her elbow. A thrill went through her as she smoothed out her uniform. It had always been her dearest wish to be a nurse. And even though the turn of events that had brought her to this point were unusual, to say the least, here she was. And she could not help but be pleased.

Having nowhere to hang her traveling clothes, she laid them carefully over the chair and left the room, closing the door behind her and pocketing the key. In the passageway, she hesitated, glancing in both directions. She hadn't noticed a water closet when she'd come with Lucía earlier. And surely there must be somewhere to wash her face. Instead of going back toward the kitchens, she turned and walked in the other direction.

She found the privy soon enough—a stone room at the end of the corridor. Unsurprisingly, the monks hadn't installed water pipes, counting on the running water of a mountain stream to carry away their waste. But Hazel was not a stranger to simple amenities after her years in India and did not balk at the hygiene conditions. A pump dispensing frigid water into a basin was in the washroom next door and, beside it, a thick bar of lye soap. She gasped when the cold water touched her face, and performed her morning ablutions quickly, then hurried toward the kitchen, feeling at least slightly more presentable. She still hadn't seen another person since she'd woken. She supposed the other medical staff were either sleeping or tending to patients.

As she neared, the smells of roasting meat woke her stomach, and the rumbles echoed in the stone passageway. She stepped into the kitchen and found a woman with a round middle chopping carrots with a long knife.

The woman looked up, and seeing Hazel, she rattled off a string of words that were entirely indecipherable, waving the knife around as she spoke. She had a motherly look, short with plump cheeks and kind eyes that looked as if nothing would please her more than to ensure that all within her care were comfortable and well-fed.

"Hola," Hazel said. "I'm sorry, I can't understand you. I was hoping I might trouble you for some breakfast?" She motioned to the pot of stew boiling on the iron stove.

The woman's smile didn't falter. She set down the knife and continued speaking as she ladled stew into a bowl and set it on a wooden table. She motioned for Hazel to bring a stool and sit, and cut a slice of bread to go with the stew.

"Gracias," Hazel said, taking a seat. "It smells delicious." She took an exaggerated sniff, closing her eyes to show how much she enjoyed the aroma. "My name is Hazel Thornton," she said, putting a hand to her chest. She lifted her palm toward the woman. "What is yours?"

"Alona," the woman said.

"Pleased to meet you." Hazel knew the woman couldn't understand her words. But hopefully, she would perceive their meaning. She was beginning to see that there was quite a lot of communication that did not require words.

The woman gestured again for Hazel to eat and returned to chopping.

Although she reminded herself that she was a well-bred young lady who had been taught manners by her governess, Hazel could not help but gobble up the stew. She could not remember the last time she'd been so hungry. The bread was thick and hearty, and she used it to sop up the last drops in her bowl.

"Delicious," Hazel said, her cheeks warming as she realized how her poor etiquette must have appeared to Alona.

Alona looked pleased, not appearing in the least disappointed in Hazel's table manners. She took the bowl to the stove as if to fill it again, but Hazel stopped her. "No, thank you. Gracias. That was quite enough." She patted her belly to show that it was filled. "It was very good."

Alona put the bowl in a washbasin instead, and Hazel contemplated what to do next. She supposed she should find Lucía and report for duty. But she would need Dr. Laurent to translate. Both were likely in one of the wards with the patients.

She thanked Alona again and excused herself, starting back toward the hospital ward to check on her friends. But before she had taken more than a few steps, she heard yelling from the other direction. The voices sounded frantic.

Hazel spun and rushed back past the kitchen, past the passageway leading to her bedchamber, and toward where she believed—if the sides of the hospital all joined together—was the entrance where she'd arrived the day before.

When she got to the entry hall, it was filled with people and noise. It took a moment for her to fully make sense of the disarray.

Men carried stretchers upon which others lay, their bodies in various states of damage. Women and some children were in the entry as well, some weeping, others calling out or comforting one of the wounded. Some injured men stumbled in, assisted by a companion. All bore wounds. There must have been an attack. Or a battle.

Hazel hesitated, unsure of what to do. She glanced back along the passageway and then scanned the entry. Where was the medical staff? Someone would come any moment and take charge. Until then, she wasn't certain—

"*Enfermera*!" an older man yelled. He rushed toward her. His face was filthy, his lip split and bleeding, and a bruise was growing on his cheek. He grabbed Hazel's arm and pulled her toward one of the stretchers.

Hazel opened her mouth to protest, to explain that she was waiting for orders, but seeing the state of the man lying there, she froze entirely. A shirt was bound around the man's arm just below the elbow, but the makeshift bandage didn't stop the blood saturating it and dripping down onto the canvas. More blood spread from what looked to be a wound in his gut. The man's eyes were open, but they didn't seem able to focus on anything at all. His face was pale with the loss of blood.

The people around all spoke at once, perhaps trying to explain what had happened. Or maybe they were telling her what care the man needed. Hazel's uncertainty was overcome by the need to help. She pressed on the bandage, knowing pressure was necessary to stop the bleeding. Remembering a page from her anatomy book, she felt along the underside of the man's arm and clenched her hand tightly to pinch off the flow of blood from the brachial artery.

More voices came into the entry hall. More rushing footsteps and shouting.

Without releasing her pressure on the man's arm, Hazel looked up, relieved that doctors and nurses had arrived.

Dr. Laurent gave instructions in a loud voice. Nurses moved through the crowd. The chaos turned immediately to order as patients were evaluated and family members calmed.

Dr. Jackson appeared at Hazel's side, and a blush crept up her neck. She'd felt something the day before when he'd held her hand, something that had made her skin tingle and filled her with warmth. The feeling had, of course, been squelched by his irritation at seeing her in the hospital, but she secretly wondered if it might return.

His gaze flitted to hers for an instant, and then he lifted the shirt covering the man's arm.

Hazel started to pull away.

"No, don't move," Dr. Jackson said. His American accent made his words sound clipped. With his chin, he motioned to her hand that was clamped on the man's upper arm. "Don't loosen your hold."

He pulled away the covering to examine the wound, and the muscles around his eyes tightened. "The ligaments are sliced," he muttered. He looked up at the older man, who hovered nearby. "*¿Que hizo esto*?"

"*Una bayoneta*." The man wrung his hands so tightly that his knuckles were white. "*Los británico*s."

Británicos? Even with her limited understanding of the language, Hazel recognized the word. But to her knowledge, the British army wasn't in Spain. Surely she'd have heard about it if they were involved in the fighting. The man must be mistaken.

She looked back at Dr. Jackson, but seeing as he was examining the patient's abdomen, she held her questions for later.

"Keep pressure on the artery." Dr. Jackson spoke without looking up, as if he sensed that Hazel had been distracted by the interchange. He motioned to an orderly and, with help, rolled the patient carefully to look at the man's back.

Hazel kept hold of his arm, leaning forward as the man was moved.

"No exit wound," Dr. Jackson muttered. They rolled him back. "He needs surgery immediately." He called out in Spanish, giving orders.

Hazel realized the wound had been made by a bullet. In spite of herself, her stomach went hard. The idea that the man had been hurt deliberately, that an enemy had inflicted this wound with the intent to kill . . . it unsettled her much more than the injuries caused by a train accident. She pushed the thoughts away and focused on the patient. She could ponder the full implications later.

"Senor," Hazel said to the older man. "Is he your son?"

Seeing his blank look, she tried again, tapping the injured man's chest softly with her free hand. "What is his name?"

"*¿Cuál es su nombre?*" Dr. Jackson said, standing and motioning for orderlies to lift the stretcher.

"Mikel," the older man said.

"*¿Su hijo*?" the doctor asked.

"*Sí*."

"Mikel is his son," Dr. Jackson told Hazel.

She straightened with the stretcher, keeping her grip on Mikel's arm, and gave a smile she hoped was reassuring to the father. The man looked beside himself with worry, and with good reason. Hazel had never seen so much blood.

Dr. Jackson pressed a wad of cloth to the bullet wound, holding it in place as they hurried from the entryway toward the surgery.

The operating chamber was a small room that had likely been used by the monks for storage. Shelves lined the walls, holding bottles, surgery instruments, and bandages, and there was very little space for moving around the surgery table. For just an instant, a pang of worry pinched in Hazel's chest. A small, crowded room . . . but she shook her head. Sometimes one of her spells came on just because she feared it might.

Breathe in. One . . . two . . . three. Breathe out. One . . . two . . . three. She breathed steadily and kept her thoughts on the patient. She slid along the side of the table, reassuring herself that she could get to the door easily if needed, and maintained her hold on Mikel's arm as he was transferred from the stretcher.

A nurse scooted behind her, pressing Hazel against the table as she passed. The nurse's hair was streaked with gray. Her brows were dark and pulled together in a serious expression. She took her place at the head of the table and settled a cone over Mikel's nose and mouth. Pulling the cork out of a bottle, she tipped it, letting a few drops of chloroform fall onto the cone. The patient's eyes closed.

A younger nurse with pink cheeks and bright eyes took the doctor's place, applying pressure to Mikel's abdomen.

Dr. Jackson rolled up his sleeves and began scrubbing his hands and arms with a thick chunk of soap. Hazel was pleased to see he subscribed to Lister's theory of germs. Miss Nightingale was a believer in cleanliness as a means of preventing disease as well. The doctor dipped his hands into a basin of water to rinse and then spoke to the pink-cheeked nurse in Spanish, motioning toward Hazel with his chin.

The nurse came to stand beside Hazel, and she slid her hand into place to hold the artery. She nodded, indicating that her grasp was sure, and Hazel released her grip, understanding that she was being dismissed. She was too embarrassed to look at the others, and started toward the door, her face heating. Of course she would not be permitted to assist. Not when Dr. Jackson believed her to be entirely incompetent.

"Where are you going?" he asked, his voice gruff.

Hazel turned back. "I—"

"I require all in my surgery to wash." With his hands raised to dry, he darted his eyes to the water basin.

Hazel blinked, feeling even more embarrassed at her assumption. She hurried to the basin and scrubbed her hands quickly, washing around the bandage that covered her palm. Once she was finished, she stepped back to the table.

"Keep hold of the brachial artery, Miss Thornton," Dr. Jackson said.

She returned to her place and took hold of Mikel's arm.

The young nurse washed, and when she finished, she brought a tray of instruments.

Dr. Jackson spoke again to the pink-cheeked nurse, who released the pressure on Mikel's abdomen. The wound bled only slightly. The doctor moved to stand beside Hazel.

The younger nurse cut away the patient's shirt, coordinating her movements with Hazel to keep the artery compressed as they pulled off the sleeve. The woman peeled away the cloths that covered his arm and used a sponge to wipe away the blood.

The older nurse held her fingers to Mikel's neck, and after a moment, she surprised Hazel by speaking in French, reporting what Hazel assumed was his pulse rate.

Dr. Jackson set to work, requesting in Spanish the instruments he required. Hazel tried to commit the names to memory. *Pinzas*, she decided meant forceps, and *escalpelo* was the word for scalpel. She mouthed the words silently.

The doctor worked quickly, speaking only when necessary. Hazel watched, fascinated as he reattached ligaments and repaired tendons. He used ligatures of silk thread to tie off the arteries and blood vessels. She leaned closer to get a better view. Though she had read about the muscular system of the human body in her anatomy book, seeing it directly was something new, and it fascinated her.

Dr. Jackson glanced at her. "You may release his arm now, slowly."

Hazel opened her fingers carefully, watching to see if the bleeding returned.

After a moment, Dr. Jackson nodded. "Good. We'll not need to cauterize."

The older nurse reported again on Mikel's pulse.

Dr. Jackson pursed his lips together. He spoke to the younger nurse, and she threaded catgut into a suture needle. His manner was calm, but he wasn't relaxed, and Hazel considered how difficult it must be to manage a surgery where he was required not only to tend to serious wounds but to do so while speaking three different languages.

"Hold the skin together, if you please, Miss Thornton."

Hazel blinked, glancing at him and waiting for him to realize his mistake. The other nurse was surely more experienced. But perhaps he asked Hazel because she was in the best position to perform the task. She reached toward Mikel's arm but hesitated, unsure of how exactly she was meant to follow through on his orders.

"With forceps, like this." Dr. Jackson guided her hands, showing her how to hold the instrument to pinch the edges of the wound closed. "Good."

Standing so near in the small room, the doctor had to lean over Hazel to do his work, his shoulder nearly brushing her face. Her pulse jumped at his closeness. She tilted her head to the side to watch. He made the suture knots impossibly fast, snipping them off and starting on the next. In only a few short moments, he was finished.

"*Vitaux*?" he asked the older nurse.

She reported back.

"Bandage his arm, please," Dr. Jackson said to Hazel. "But not tightly."

She took bandages from the shelf behind her and wrapped Mikel's arm carefully, moving it as little as possible. As she worked, she smelled a sweet odor. She recognized it immediately as carbolic acid and, looking up, saw the nurse adding the liquid to a bowl of water, then using the dilution to clean the instruments.

Dr. Jackson had already turned his attention to the bullet wound.

The young nurse set a small metal bowl on the man's chest and handed the doctor a pair of long forceps at his order.

"The key is to get the bullet out through the same path it went in," he said as he worked. "We want to do the least amount of damage to the tissue."

Hazel realized he was speaking in English. He was speaking to her.

"Is there internal damage, Doctor?"

He pulled out the forceps, dropping the bullet into the tray with a plink, then looked back into the wound. He pressed on the sides, and only a small amount of blood came from the puncture. Then he bent and sniffed. "I don't believe so," he said. "Wound appears clean. Seems to have missed his organs completely."

Sweat beaded on Dr. Jackson's forehead.

Without thinking, Hazel used a swatch of bandage to dab it.

He glanced at her, and Hazel blushed, but the doctor didn't look angry.

The young nurse threaded the suture needle again.

Once he was finished, Dr. Jackson stood straight, bending his neck from side to side and rubbing his lower back. He spoke to the young nurse, and she left the room.

The older nurse removed the anesthetic cone.

Dr. Jackson washed the blood from his hands in the basin. "No signs of infection, but it's early yet." He used a towel to dry. "It's up to him now."

The older nurse left the room and Dr. Jackson started after her. In the doorway, he stopped, then came back. "Miss Thornton, your hand." He took it, removing the bandage.

"Dr. Laurent stitched it yesterday," she said.

He touched the edges around the cut. "It's a clean cut. It should heal well."

"I—yes, thank you." She wasn't sure what else to say, so she stood quietly and let him wrap the bandage back around her hand.

"Good work today, Nurse," Dr. Jackson said. "That was quick thinking, pinching the artery to slow the blood loss." He met her gaze, nodded once, and left.

Hazel remained. She looked between the door and the patient, wondering whether she should follow or remain. It hardly felt right to leave Mikel alone. She washed off her hands and straightened the room. A few moments later, orderlies arrived with a gurney to take Mikel away.

Once she was alone, she let out a heavy breath. The past hour had been intense and terrifying and had left her both mentally and emotionally exhausted. But despite it all, her chest tingled, and she felt pleased. Dr. Jackson had called her Nurse.

CHAPTER 4

Jim checked on the other surgery chambers. Drs. Laurent and Ruiz had both removed bullets and sewn wounds in a short time, their patients having less-serious injuries than Mikel's. In point of fact, Jim could hardly believe the man had survived at all. He very likely wouldn't have, if not for Miss Thornton's quick actions. To say that Jim had been surprised by the woman's anatomical knowledge was an understatement. Based on her fine clothes and high-born manners, he'd assumed immediately that she was simply a bored young lady who'd decided nursing might be an exciting distraction from royal balls and garden parties.

He couldn't have been more wrong. In the surgery, she'd been remarkably steady, and she hadn't flinched away from what was one of the more gruesome wounds that had come through the hospital doors. Jim had underestimated her.

He glanced toward the surgery chamber where he'd left Miss Thornton, wondering briefly where she'd gone once they'd finished tending to Mikel. But the thought lasted only a moment. There was far too much to do. Once he'd taken stock of the new patients, he continued on with his rounds. He lifted a chart from the foot of a patient's bed, reading the man's vitals. If patients continued to arrive at this rate, the Red Cross Hospital ran a legitimate risk of running out of beds—they were already short on supplies—but the attacks were becoming more frequent. He touched his fingers to the patient's head, checking for fever. The man's skin was cool, so he continued on to the next.

He rubbed the back of his neck, feeling frustrated. In Virginia, at least, he'd been in the field. He could only imagine how many more men could be saved if they didn't have to be transported through the mountains to the hospital. If they could be treated sooner.

The patient in the bed before him was the soldier from the train. Jim pursed his lips together when he read the blood-pressure report. The young man had woken during the night, delirious and in such pain that he'd vomited immediately. He had been weak and confused and had only settled when Jim administered a dose of morphine.

Seeing Dr. Laurent, Jim waved for the man to join him.

"Zhe blood pressure is still high," Dr. Laurent said, glancing at the chart. "And his breathing, it is very shallow." He leaned over, pulling up the young man's eyelids and looking closely at his pupils.

"What is your diagnosis?" Jim asked. Although Jim had been the doctor primarily treating this patient, Dr. Laurent was more experienced, especially when dealing with head traumas, and Jim trusted the man not to make rash decisions.

"I would recommend a lumbar puncture to be certain," Dr. Laurent said. He lifted the young man's arm, holding his wrist to measure a pulse. "But I expect, once zhe cerebrospinal fluid is measured, we will discover swelling around his brain."

Jim scratched his cheek, frowning. That was the conclusion he'd come to as well. Intracranial pressure would explain the young man's symptoms, especially with the head injury he'd suffered.

"Shall I have a surgery chamber prepared?" Dr. Laurent asked.

"Yes." Jim put back the chart. "And you'll perform the procedure?" When it came to setting bones and suturing soft tissue, he was entirely confident, but drilling a burr hole required precision and patience, qualities Dr. Laurent possessed in much greater quantities.

"*Bien sûr*. I will if you wish it, my friend."

"I do."

Dr. Laurent nodded. Jim appreciated that the man didn't try to encourage or reassure him that he was indeed capable and turn the circumstance into a teaching opportunity. He knew when to push and when to assist. The two had developed a rapport over the years, and Jim saw the older man as a mentor figure. Dr. Laurent's capability was unmatched, and his balance of empathy and competence was the reason that once the war between the states was finished, Jim had joined the International Red Cross and accompanied his colleague from Virginia to Bohemia to Spain, following revolutions and natural disasters in the name of humanity and relief.

While the surgery chamber was being prepared, Jim continued his rounds quickly. He crossed through the cloister, breathing in the damp mountain air for just a moment before entering the other ward and heading straight for the most critically injured patient, Mikel.

When he arrived, he found Mikel's father seated at his son's bedside. Someone had apparently brought a chair. And Jim assumed that someone was the young lady dabbing with a wet cloth at the crusted blood on the older man's lip. A hint of his earlier annoyance with the young woman returned.

"A visitor?" he asked, knowing his voice sounded irritated. "Miss Thornton, you know the policy." Visitors were not allowed in the hospital wards, especially for the more critical patients.

"He . . ." She winced, and her cheeks colored. "I thought it might reassure him to see his son. And he is injured as well." She indicated the blood on her cloth. "So he is, in a sense, a patient too."

Jim decided to ignore the breach of hospital protocol for the moment. "Has he stirred?" He lifted his chin toward Mikel.

"No."

Jim took the stethophone from his pocket and listened to Mikel's heart. The beat was weak but steady. "Measure his temperature, if you please."

"Yes, Doctor." Miss Thornton hurried toward a medical cart for a thermometer.

Jim continued on and came to the bed of the older woman with the ankle injury.

Her eyes popped open, and she lifted her head but looked disappointed when she saw him. She laid back on the pillow.

"How is your pain today . . ." He glanced at her chart to remind himself of her name. "Miss Westbrook?"

"I won't say it doesn't hurt, because it feels like the devil's fiery poker is stabbing into my flesh, if you'll forgive me for saying so."

Jim raised a brow at the woman's salty language. "I imagine it does." He made a note on the chart. *Pain level: Devil's fiery poker.* Dr. Laurent would get a chuckle out of that one. Jim touched her forehead, noting that she still had a fever. That was worrying. "You're lucky the doctor was able to set your bones as well as he did. The way they were crushed—"

"She's doing well, isn't she?" Miss Westbrook interrupted with a smug expression.

At her words, Jim glanced at Miss Thornton without even thinking, so he couldn't very well look like he didn't know who she was talking about. "Acceptable." He turned a page in the chart.

Miss Westbrook grinned, looking across the ward at her young friend. "I knew it. I knew she would be capable, even with . . ." She looked back at Jim and her voice trailed off. In spite of her pallor, her cheeks reddened.

"With?" he prodded.

Miss Westbrook put a hand to her forehead. "Oh, but I am in such pain. Where is Dr. Laurent? I'd hoped he might have a moment to talk or even play some pinochle. Something to distract me from this blasted ankle."

Jim didn't allow the woman's profanity to distract him. "What were you saying about Miss Thornton?"

"Oh, goodness me." Miss Westbrook gave a distressed whine and started fidgeting. "Where is that bedpan?" She turned her head to the side, and seeing another nurse, she groaned. "Nurse? Would you be so kind?"

Jim dropped the chart back into its holder and left.

As he walked the short distance back to Mikel, he wondered what the woman had meant. Was there some problem? Miss Thornton had appeared healthy, at least from what he'd observed. Did she suffer from some other unnoticeable ailment? Was there a problem that might impede her ability to perform her duty? Or was the older woman's pain causing her to misspeak?

When Jim returned to Mikel's bed, Miss Thornton took the glass tube from beneath his armpit and held it up to read the temperature.

"Good," Jim muttered. He started to note it on the chart but stopped, motioning for Miss Thornton.

She stepped around the bed, and he handed her the chart. "Mark it here."

She did so, writing the numbers neatly with his pencil.

Jim stood behind her, watching over her shoulder as she worked. He tapped on another space. "Here, you record blood pressure. Here, pulse."

"And this is for the time and date," she said, touching the proper spot with the tip of the pencil. She glanced up at him with a questioning look that made her blue-gray eyes large and very pretty.

Jim nodded. She caught on surprisingly quickly. He'd taken much longer to remember the Spanish words.

He slid the chart back into its holder and started to leave, but he turned back and spoke to Mikel's father.

The old man frowned, but he agreed.

"What did you tell him?" Miss Thornton asked.

"I told him he can remain for one hour, and then he will have to return tomorrow. Otherwise, he'll have to deal with Lucía, and that would earn him a bed of his own."

An hour later, Jim held the English captain's head still as Joelle, the French nurse, sedated him, and Dr. Laurent carefully drilled a burr hole into the young man's skull. The results from the lumbar puncture were as they'd predicted. The young man's head was bleeding.

The necessary procedure required precision, and although Jim had seen it performed multiple times—he'd even done it himself—he'd never known a surgeon as skilled as Dr. Laurent and watched, mesmerized. The holes were drilled, the bone between them scraped away, and the extradural blood drained in record time.

"Zhat should ease zhe lad's pain," Dr. Laurent said, patting the unconscious soldier's shoulder.

Joelle reported the patient's pulse rate, and Jim traded places with his colleague. He threaded a suture needle to close the wound.

A blast sounded, followed quickly by another. The explosions were not close, but the noises—and their implications—were worrying. Another attack. Another battle. And soon enough, the wounded would be at their door.

Jim stitched the soldier's scalp, his ears pricking at the sounds of gunshots echoing in the mountains. "How far away?" he asked.

"Miles," Dr. Laurent said. He tilted his head, as if the adjustment might improve his hearing through the stone walls of the monastery.

Jim clenched his jaw, frustrated. Miles meant it would be hours before the wounded were treated—in the best scenario. It could be longer. In a business in which moments meant the difference between life and death, such a wait only decreased the chances that the patients would survive in order to be treated at all.

"A field hospital," he said. "That is what we need. That is how we can save lives."

Dr. Laurent shook his head. "We do not know where zhe attacks will take place. Zhere is no battlefield. Ambushes on rocky mountains or bombings in a town—zhey cannot be predicted. Unless you propose asking zhe armies for an advanced notification of zheir battle plans."

"We could get closer," Jim said. "The majority of the attacks have been in the area around Santa Rosa, haven't they? We could at the very least mount a rescue."

"You are right, of course." Dr. Laurent shrugged.

Jim finished and motioned for Joelle to bandage the soldier's head. If the wound could resist infection, there was a strong probability the young man would survive. His mental state if he did was yet to be determined. Injuries to the brain were unpredictable. Some patients recovered and resumed their lives easily. Others were never the same. At the very least, Jim feared the soldier would suffer recurring headaches and perhaps some memory loss.

The orderlies returned the soldier to his bed in the ward, and Jim and Dr. Laurent headed to their respective sleeping quarters, knowing they had only a few short hours of calm before the storm.

It was, in actuality, three hours later when Jim was called from his bed. He rushed to the hospital's entryway, pulling on his white coat. Though he did not think the garment at all practical for the work he did, the sight of the coat garnered respect from patients and family members alike. It calmed people at the worst moments of their lives, and they would listen and defer to the man wearing it.

He didn't pause in the doorway but strode straight into the chaos, assessing the needs of the various wounded as he moved through them. Some were already deceased. Others had injuries that could wait.

People yelled for help and, in their panic, grabbed on to medical staff, begging assistance for either themselves or their companions. The confusion of noise and movement made it difficult to take measure of the wounded.

Jim yelled above the clamor in a loud voice. "If you are not wounded, you must leave the hospital immediately."

Dr. Laurent repeated the order in Spanish, and Lucía repeated it in Basque.

Orderlies opened the doors and escorted people outside.

At Jim's orders, Lucía directed nurses to clean and bandage wounds. Dr. Laurent was already rushing a patient with a head injury into surgery.

"Doctor," a faint voice said.

Jim spun. Hearing a voice speaking English among all the others was so unexpected. A young soldier in a red coat lay on a blood-stained stretcher. At the sight, a memory flashed through Jim's mind, hitting him with a wave of emotion.

Miss Thornton hurried to the soldier and knelt beside him. "You're English."

"British Legion, ma'am." His voice was quiet and speaking took an effort. He sucked in a pained breath.

"You're in good hands here, Private," Miss Thornton assured him.

Jim crouched on the young man's other side. He lifted the bloody pile of cloth off his abdomen, letting loose a foul odor. The laceration was deep, and it had torn the bowel. Jim's stomach was heavy. Infection had probably already set in. There was no saving this patient.

"Doctor?" Miss Thornton stared at the wound, her eyes wide. She looked up at him, and seeing his expression, her brows drew together.

He gave a small shake of his head.

Miss Thornton blinked, pulling in a quick breath. She swallowed hard.

"Stay with him," Jim said in a quiet voice. "It won't be long."

She stared at him, various expressions flitting across her face, but she nodded. Her face softened. She took the young man's hand. "What is your name?"

"Private Daniel Wilson, ma'am." He shifted and winced at the movement. "It hurts."

She brushed the hair from his forehead. "I'm Hazel."

The young man's eyes fluttered, as if he were struggling to keep them open. "Pretty." He lifted his other hand and then dropped it.

"Where are you from, Daniel?"

"Sussex." The word was little more than a whisper. Daniel closed his eyes.

"Oh, I know Sussex," Miss Thornton said. Her voice was gentle. She put a hand on his cheek. "The downs in spring are the most glorious sight. The bluebells on the green hills and all the lambs frolicking . . ."

Jim rose and moved on to tend to other patients. As he drew away, he could hear her speaking in her soft voice, though he could no longer make out the words.

When he returned half an hour later, Miss Thornton still knelt beside Private Daniel Wilson, holding his hand. The soldier was dead. Jim put a cloth over the young man's face.

Miss Thornton glanced up. Her eyes looked very tired. She set the soldier's hand on his chest, pressed it gently, and then with Jim's help, she stood, swaying on her feet.

Jim grabbed her elbow to steady her. "Miss?"

"I'm sorry. I am well. I need to check on Nella. It's been hours since I saw her." Her voice sounded near to breaking, and her face was noticeably pale.

"When did you last eat?" Jim asked. He kept hold of her arm.

She squinted, blinking as if she were trying to remember. "Earlier—breakfast? I don't know. It may have been supper. I don't even know if it was today." She motioned toward the wall. "There are no windows here."

"It is eight o'clock," Dr. Laurent said. They both looked toward him as he approached from surgery. "In zhe evening. Miss Westbrook is sleeping." He snapped his pocket watch closed and gave Miss Thornton an appraising look. His brow rose. "For how long have you been on duty, mademoiselle?"

"I don't know." She rubbed her forehead. "I woke and . . . Mikel was here." She motioned to the side of the room where the patient had been on a stretcher. "I changed bedsheets with Sofia and now . . ."

They'd found Mikel in the early hours of the morning. Had the young lady been working ever since then? She was surely exhausted.

"Come along," Dr. Laurent took her arm. He bid Jim good evening and led her toward the kitchen. "You must eat. Zhen you must sleep. Zhen in zhe morning, Lucía will assign you more bandages and more patients. And you will be exhausted again tomorrow."

In spite of her weariness, Miss Thornton chuckled.

Jim watched the pair walk from the entry hall, wondering why he felt so unsettled. The day had not been much different from every other in the Red Cross Hospital, but Miss Thornton's presence had changed his perception of it somehow. Perhaps it was the experience of seeing it all through fresh eyes. But he didn't think that was all. He recognized something in her. Something he'd felt himself years ago in the medical tents on the Virginia battlefields.

Miss Thornton genuinely cared. She was compassionate and felt deeply for her patients.

Jim had been like that once. He'd felt the desire to heal, to relieve pain, to alleviate suffering. But that was before. After his brother's death, medicine had become Jim's religion. He was consumed with a sense of urgency. He'd joined the Red Cross, following wars and disasters, foolishly believing each patient he cured would ease the pain in his heart, the guilt for the one he couldn't save.

Jim crouched down, crossing the young soldier's hand over the one already on his chest, and said a prayer for Private Daniel Wilson.

CHAPTER 5

THE NEXT DAY LUCÍA ASSIGNED Hazel to work in the laundry, and when she arrived, she found that the younger nurse from the operating chamber the day earlier—Camila—was to be her partner. Hazel was relieved when Lucía left since she didn't want the head nurse to see that she was unfamiliar with the task. Camila seemed to be much less strict than the older woman, demonstrating the process patiently instead of giving orders. She had a happy smile and a giggle that sounded almost nervous. Hazel liked her very much.

Camila showed her how to rinse blood out with cold water, then boil the linens, stirring them in a large pot with a paddle. They scrubbed and rinsed, and after only a few minutes of washing, Hazel's apron and dress were soaked and the cut on her hand burned from the lye soap. To distract herself, she tried to learn more about her companion.

Though they didn't speak the same language, the women discovered quickly enough that they could somewhat communicate. Hazel had studied with a French tutor, so she understood some of the words Camila spoke in Spanish, as the languages had some similarities. And the two ended up using a very inelegant version of sign language when they couldn't come up with the words they needed. The result produced quite a few laughs.

As they scrubbed sheets and soaked bandages, Hazel learned that Camila was only a year younger than her own age of twenty-one. She had two brothers, one of whom served in the Spanish Army. The other was younger and still in school. Her mother was a midwife, which was the reason Camila had chosen to study nursing and how she'd come to serve in the International Red Cross.

Hazel, in turn, told Camila about her father stationed in Africa and her childhood in India. She'd tried to explain how she'd intended to spend Christmas in the Canary Islands, by making the chugging sound of a train and showing with her hand movements that she had been traveling south but then was turned around. She didn't think she'd communicated the tale effectively until Camila made a booming noise, expanding her hands apart to mimic an explosion.

"Yes, that's right." Hazel spread her arms, palms up in a motion of finality and shrugged. "And here I am."

Camila spoke, pointing from Hazel's head down to her feet, then crossed herself.

Hazel understood her meaning, putting her hands together as if in prayer. "You're right. I am very fortunate." She had come out of the train accident with no more than a few aching muscles and a cut hand. The result could have been so much worse. She shivered and vowed to be more grateful.

The morning passed pleasantly, and once the laundry was cleaned and rinsed, the two women hauled it in large tubs to the cloister to hang it on the lines.

When they stepped out into the courtyard, Hazel tilted her head toward the breeze. The monastery, with its lack of windows, felt stuffy and closed. She was certain Miss Nightingale would not at all approve, being a strong believer in the benefits of clean air.

The day was cool, but they had been working hard, and the mountain chill felt welcome.

The women made quick work of pinning laundry to the clotheslines, and once they were finished, they stood for a moment, admiring the rows of white sheets.

Since no more washing could be done until the first batch dried, their task was finished, for now. Hazel bid farewell to Camila and went into the East ward to visit Nella. She had hardly seen her friend in the past few days, and she was eager to tell her about the surgery she'd assisted with as well as the final moments of the poor British soldier. She also hoped to learn about Captain Bryant's condition.

When she arrived at Nella's bedside, Dr. Laurent was there. He sat on a chair in the space between Nella's bed and the wall, holding a fan of playing cards. Nella held cards as well. When she saw Hazel, her face lit up. "Oh, there you are, dear. You just missed luncheon." She motioned to a tray of dishes that sat on a small table next to her.

Dr. Laurent stood, inclining his head. "Good day, Miss Thornton."

Hazel greeted the doctor and moved to the other side of the bed, taking her friend's outstretched hand. "How are you feeling today, Nella?"

"Much better." Nella released Hazel's hand and waved at her elevated leg. "The pain has become quite bearable." She flicked her gaze to Dr. Laurent, fluttering her eyelashes. "Especially when I have something pleasant to distract me."

The man's cheeks were red.

Hazel blinked, unsure of what she was witnessing. Was Nella flirting? And was Dr. Laurent blushing? She stared for a moment before remembering her manners. "Thank you for taking such good care of her, Doctor."

His cheeks darkened again, as did the top of his bald head. He was definitely blushing. "Of course, mademoiselle. She is a very . . . *amiable* patient." He cocked a brow at Nella.

"Oh, you." Nella swatted at him with her cards.

Hazel was suddenly desperate to leave. Or, at the least, for a change of subject. "I thought to check on Captain Bryant. Do you know, Dr. Laurent, how he fares?"

"Ah, *oui*." The doctor's expression turned serious. "Zhe poor captain, he has still not fully woken, but I believe his pain has lessened. His breathing is deeper, and his blood pressure—"

Explosions sounded in the distance, cutting off his words, and the three glanced toward the wall, though of course they could not see anything. The sounds were not unusual. Hazel had heard them often enough since her arrival two days earlier, but these continued longer than was typical. And some of the blasts, such as the one that had interrupted the doctor, were much louder than any she'd heard before. She wondered if they were closer or if the fighters were using a more powerful explosive.

Dr. Laurent turned back. "As I was saying—"

But he was cut off again when Dr. Jackson rushed into the ward. "The ambulance wagons are loaded. We leave now."

Dr. Laurent set the cards on the bed beside Nella and turned to face Dr. Jackson. "I must stay here." He motioned toward the other patients in the ward. "Zhere are patients who still need care."

"Dr. Ruiz can manage the hospital with a small staff of nurses for a few hours," Dr. Jackson said. "The fighting is close—in Santa Rosa, I believe. If we can reach the wounded even an hour earlier . . ." He pushed back his white coat to rest his hands on his hips and scanned the ward. "I'll take Lucía, of course. Isabel, Sabrina . . ." He motioned to the nurses.

The women left the patients they had been tending and joined the doctors at Nella's bedside. Dr. Jackson spoke Spanish, with Dr. Laurent adding to his orders.

The women looked uncertain, but they put aside the charts, instruments, and linens they'd been using and started away toward the entry hall.

"And Miss Thornton, if you please." Dr. Jackson motioned after the women with a jerk of his head. "Bring a medical kit. We leave immediately." He strode away quickly, not waiting for a reply.

Dr. Laurent rushed off as well.

Hazel felt frozen, her heart racing. The idea of going onto a battlefield was terrifying. But knowing he'd chosen her specifically . . . Could she do this? Or was this just another opportunity that would be ruined by her panic spells? She stared after Dr. Jackson and then looked at Nella. "He can't mean it, can he?"

"Of course he means it, dear." Nella made a shooing motion with her hands. "Go on, then."

Still feeling stunned, Hazel bid Nella farewell and followed the nurses to the hospital wagons waiting outside the monastery. Lucía gave her a medical kit, and they climbed into the back, sitting on the benches beneath the canvas coverings. More nurses, among them Camila and Lucía, and some orderlies joined them, and a few moments later, the wagon lurched and started off.

Having nothing else to hold on to, Hazel gripped the wood of the wagon seat. The benches ran along both sides of the wagon's interior. It was strange to travel sideways and have no view of where they were going. Except for the rear, the wagon was completely covered. And behind, where the other wagon followed, Hazel could see only dust. The day was not hot, but within a few moments, the orderlies were loosening their buttons and the nurses tugging at their bodices, trying to get some airflow in the stuffy space.

Hazel wiped her brow with her sleeve. Although she couldn't understand the conversations happening around her, she could sense the apprehension the hospital staff felt about traveling in the direction of the fighting.

Their reactions surprised her—this was not so different from the rescue at the train site—but as they drew closer, the sounds of gunshots were louder, and with them yelling, and she understood their misgivings right away. The battle was still active, and they were headed directly for it.

An explosion echoed through the mountains, and Hazel instinctively ducked. One of the nurses slid off her seat, kneeling on the floor. Camila pulled her back up to sit on the bench, speaking words of comfort.

After a few more explosions, the gunshots came less frequently, and eventually, they stopped altogether.

The wagon halted. Hazel peeked out, and seeing there was no obvious danger, she climbed down. Carrying her kit, she followed the others to where

Dr. Jackson and Dr. Laurent were already assisting a man with a bleeding head wound.

A woman was with him, speaking rapidly as she pointed toward the town.

Behind them, the town of Santa Rosa had suffered extensive damage in the attack. Smoke and dust hung in the air, and holes were punched through stone walls and tile roofs. Some of the buildings were nothing but a pile of rocks. Others had only a wall to mark where a structure had once stood. Loose rocks and piles of rubble blocked further passage of the wagon into town.

Dr. Jackson called Lucía over, and once she took his place, holding a cloth against the man's head, he and Dr. Laurent came to the rest of the group. "According to this man, the Spanish Army is just over the hill, there." He pointed past the town to a rocky hill. "They have their own medical staff and will probably not require our help, although we will provide it if needed." He waited for Dr. Laurent to finish translating, then continued.

"The Carlist army is that way." He pointed in the other direction. "Dr. Laurent will take his group to help the wounded fighters, and the rest of us will tend to the townspeople."

Hazel gazed around at the destruction, and her limbs felt heavy. The silence following the battle seemed somehow more dreadful than the explosions and gunfire.

"Move with caution," Dr. Jackson said. "There could be unexploded artillery shells. And even though some of them still stand, the integrity of the buildings' structures may be compromised."

He and Dr. Laurent split the group, with Dr. Laurent taking most of the medical staff. Hazel was assigned to Dr. Jackson's smaller group; aside from herself, the doctor, and the head nurse, there were two orderlies and Camila. The two groups set off in different directions, and Dr. Jackson led his down a narrow street, passing between houses built of warm-colored bricks with tile roofs.

Hazel stayed close to Lucía and Camila.

The doctor walked ahead, arms raised, calling out in a loud voice. Hazel didn't understand all of what he said, but she heard the word *médico*.

Lucía called out as well, but the word she used was *medikua*, which Hazel assumed was a Basque translation.

As they picked their way through the town, faces appeared at windows and heads popped up over walls. Some were accompanied by rifles.

Seeing weapons were pointed at them, Hazel grabbed on to Lucía's hand.

Although the woman had not necessarily shown herself to be tender, she squeezed Hazel's hand, speaking in a reassuring voice and giving a kind smile.

That, more than anything, calmed Hazel's worries. A bit.

They came to a wide-open space that appeared to be the town square. A fountain with colorful tiles in its basin sat directly in front of a large church. The church was the largest structure in the town. Carvings of saints decorated the facade around a tall wooden door with layers of arches that drew up to a point in the center beneath a large cross. Two bell towers rose from the front corners. From what Hazel could see, the building was undamaged by the bombings.

The door opened, and a man poked his head through the crack. He stepped out wearing the robes of a priest. Sunlight shone on his bald head, and he looked around him as if he were bewildered.

Lucía released Hazel's hand and approached. She crossed herself and knelt to kiss the priest's hand.

He made a gesture above her head in return, looking as if he were doing so out of habit. His eyes were glazed, stunned.

Lucía spoke to him, waving for Dr. Jackson to join them.

After a moment, the priest's facial expression cleared and his shoulders relaxed. He called out in a loud voice, speaking words Hazel could only assume were reassurances to the townspeople that the Red Cross group were there to assist the injured and were not a band of spies.

A man came from behind a crumbling wall, leading a child. The little girl held her arm tightly against her body. Another man stumbled through a doorway with blood coming from a gash in his head, and another assisted a companion as he limped forward.

Within moments, the town square became a hospital.

At Dr. Jackson's orders, Hazel cleaned wounds, assessing whether stitches were needed, and if not, she wrapped them in bandages. Lucía stitched those that were more serious. Camila helped Dr. Jackson set broken bones, and orderlies carried patients who required more intensive treatment toward the ambulance wagons once their condition had been stabilized enough to move them.

The priest had snapped out of his daze now that he had a purpose. He moved among the injured, speaking in a calming voice. The townspeople seemed reassured by his presence, and Hazel thought he must be a very good clergyman to provide such comfort to his flock.

They all worked quickly, and in spite of the cool mountain air, the hair at the back of Hazel's neck was soon damp.

Dr. Laurent returned, reporting to Dr. Jackson in a grim voice that most of the Carlists had retreated farther into the mountains but that he and his group had treated those they were able to. Those with serious injuries were stabilized and moved to the ambulance wagons for further care.

"Take them back to the hospital," Dr. Jackson said. "We will follow soon." He glanced beyond the church at the more damaged part of the town.

Dr. Laurent departed, taking his larger group with him.

Hazel remained with Dr. Jackson's small team and continued with her duties, wetting a cloth in the fountain and using it to clean dried blood from an old woman's forehead.

Dr. Jackson knelt beside her. He looked into each of the woman's eyes but apparently did not see any reason for alarm. He patted Hazel's shoulder and moved on to talk to the priest.

The touch reassured her, and she felt through the simple gesture that not only was he pleased with her work but he considered her a part of his team.

A few moments later, once the patients in the town square had been tended to, he called the team together and led them up one of the curving roads behind the church.

Hazel looked in the other direction, toward the ambulance wagons. Where was he leading them? Into the mountains? Surely not. Perhaps he was simply turned around. She quickened her pace to walk beside him. "Shouldn't we be returning to the hospital?"

Dr. Jackson glanced at her. "Most of the men in town have either died or fled from the army," he said. "Those remaining are searching among the rubble. Before we leave, I want to ensure we haven't missed anyone; any survivors they locate will need medical care."

And they would need it quickly. Hazel nodded her understanding. Anyone who had still not been found by now would have been buried or trapped for hours.

They came to the part of town where some of the buildings had been completely destroyed, their bricks spilling over the road. Here and there, a piece of furniture lay among the wreckage. Papers fluttered past. Hazel saw a ceramic vase—somehow unbroken—and imagined that it had once sat upon a shelf or table. Clothing, books, tools, toys—treasured possessions were strewn about, and the townspeople picked through them with a hopelessness that made their bodies sag. The air smelled like smoke and dust. A group of elderly men directed a search effort that was made up of mainly women and children. On the flat floor of a house without walls lay a row of bodies covered with blankets. As Hazel looked around at what had once been a lovely street of houses, all she could see was destruction.

"Stay away from the buildings," Dr. Jackson said to the group. "Even those that look stable. The damage may not be outwardly apparent, and they could come down at any time." He repeated the words in Spanish.

The team spread out. Hazel knelt beside a small boy who was sitting on a chair in a front garden. He held a cooking pot. She looked him over. Aside from a covering of dust, he appeared unharmed—physically, at least. "Hola," she said.

The boy looked at her curiously.

Hearing footsteps crunching on gravel, they both turned and saw Camila approach. "*Kaixo*," she said to the boy, crouching beside Hazel.

He replied, and they spoke for a moment. Hazel realized he must not speak Spanish at all, but Basque, and she felt a surge of frustration at her inability to communicate.

Camila stood. She patted the boy's head and nodded to Hazel, indicating that the boy was all right.

The women continued together, stepping around piles of rock and over wooden beams.

It appeared the search for survivors was nearly concluded. The town was small, and most of the people were returning to what appeared to be their homes—or what remained of them. The priest was talking to a small group of women, placing a comforting hand on the shoulder of one who wept. Another woman held a framed photograph to her chest.

Dr. Jackson motioned for the nurses and they started in his direction, but hearing a noise, Hazel paused. It sounded like a cat. She turned, trying to discover from where the sound had come.

Camila paused as well. She pointed toward a dark space beneath where a wall had toppled against a neighboring building and remained, leaning at an odd angle. "*Allí!*" The space was apparently an alleyway between the buildings, but now it was filled with broken chunks of plaster and stone. The late afternoon made the shadows in the alleyway deeper. Hazel and Camila stepped closer and heard the noise again, but it sounded more like a whimper. Something moved among the rubble.

"Dr. Jackson," Hazel called, waving her hands in the air. "Someone is here." She and Camila hurried to the alleyway's opening, crouching down to peer inside. Her eyes adjusted to the gloom, and she saw that a person lay there, trapped beneath pieces of broken wall. She and Camila moved quickly forward and found it to be a woman.

"*Kaixo*," Hazel said, kneeling beside the woman. "You're safe now."

The woman lay on her back and had pushed her shoulders off the ground, but that was as far as she was able to move. Her torso and legs were stuck. "*Eskerrik asko*," she whispered, clinging to Hazel's hand.

"Gracias." Camila translated her words for Hazel.

Hazel swept the dark hair off the woman's face. The kerchief she'd apparently been wearing on her head had fallen to the ground. Sweat and dirt were stuck to her skin. "Rest now. Don't worry anymore. You're safe." Hazel picked up the kerchief, certain the woman wouldn't want it lying in the dirt. She ran her finger along the simple embroidery at the kerchief's edge, then folded it and put it into her pocket.

The woman's eyes rolled back, but she didn't loosen her hold on Hazel's hand. She kept muttering, but Hazel couldn't understand her words. She was certain the woman was in excruciating pain, and she was very likely delirious.

Camila moved out of the alley as the men came in to lift away the rocks, giving them room to work.

Hazel started to get to her feet, ready to move as well, but Dr. Jackson shook his head, motioning with his hand out that she should remain where she was. "Keep her calm," he said.

She turned back to the woman. "We will get you out of here, and Dr. Jackson will know just what to do." Hazel spoke in a comforting voice, knowing the woman couldn't understand her but hoping she would recognize the tone of her voice.

The woman kept muttering, her eyes flying open and then fluttering closed. Worry and pain were etched into her face, making her brow furrow and her breath come in short gasps.

Hazel would never have believed so many people could fit into such a small space. She kept ahold of the woman's hand, speaking softly as Dr. Jackson, the orderlies, and a few of the townspeople pulled away the chunks of debris that trapped her in place. The woman spoke in a whisper, repeating the same words over and over: "*Nire haurra.*"

"Don't move her," Dr. Jackson told the others. "If her spine is damaged, it could make her injuries worse." He glanced at the mouth of the alley as if judging the time that remained until dark. Only a few hours, by Hazel's estimation.

"They are nearly finished," Hazel said to the woman. "Then we will get you out of here."

"Nire haurra," the woman muttered again.

"Yes, of course." Hazel squeezed her hand. She wondered if she was telling them her name. Or perhaps she was explaining what had happened or where she hurt. Perhaps Camila could translate again once they could move the woman out of the alleyway, where the others waited.

Heaving together, the men lifted a large slab of stone from the woman's torso, and she gasped.

They moved the slab away, and then Dr. Jackson crouched to examine her.

Over her blouse she wore a sort of vest made from a thick material that fastened up the front with laces. She had a short apron over her skirt. Her clothes were dirty, but they were not torn. The men brought a stretcher, setting it beside her and sliding her carefully onto it.

One of the woman's shoes was missing.

The woman gasped again, pressing her hand to her abdomen, and Hazel saw worry in Dr. Jackson's expression. Her injuries must be worse than they appeared.

The orderlies took their places at the woman's head and feet, lifting the stretcher.

Hazel set the patient's hand gently at her side. "It will be all right, now." She turned, thinking to find the missing shoe.

With a surprising strength, the woman grabbed Hazel's arm. "Haurra." Her voice was clear and loud in the space. "Nire haurra."

Hazel started, but she gave a smile. "Yes, don't worry anymore." She tried to pull her hand away, but the woman held on.

"Nire haurra." Her voice was softer, but the words were still clear. Her brows drew together, making a deep furrow, and she tugged, pulling Hazel closer and staring hard into her face. "Por favor," she spoke in Spanish. "*Mi bebé.*"

My baby. Hazel sucked in a breath. *There is a baby.*

Dr. Jackson stopped, his eyes widening.

Hazel darted her gaze around the small alleyway, her insides clenched in panic. The space was so small—surely the men would have found a baby when they moved the debris.

She turned back to the woman—the mother—on the stretcher. "Where? Where is the baby?" she said, knowing the mother would understand her meaning even if she couldn't understand the words.

The outburst must have used the remainder of the injured woman's strength. She rolled her head to the side, fluttering her fingers toward the house.

Hazel and Dr. Jackson looked in that direction as the orderlies carried the stretcher from the alley. There was no door on this side of the building, but one part of the wall had buckled where the neighboring building had crashed into it, leaving a narrow opening to its interior.

As if in answer to their query, an infant's cry came from inside.

The sound penetrated Hazel's heart. She turned toward the door but looked up at Dr. Jackson. "A baby," she said, feeling an ache in her throat.

He must have seen the intention in her gaze. His eyes tightened. "No. That building could collapse at any moment."

His words had the opposite effect than the one he'd intended, dispelling any hesitation about her course. She could not leave behind a baby—she wouldn't.

He shook his head. "You cannot—"

Hazel rushed toward the opening. Seeing him reach for her, she pushed herself faster. She was closer to the opening than the doctor, and she trusted the piles of plaster and loose bricks to slow his footing enough that he would not be able to stop her.

CHAPTER 6

"Miss Thornton!" Jim lunged toward the nurse, reaching to stop her, but his hand caught only air.

She didn't glance back before plunging through the narrow gap in the wall.

Jim cursed as an angry wave of heat flushed through him. What was the woman thinking? Her expression—that defiance, the complete confidence in an irrational decision—was exactly how his brother had looked before he bolted off to join Pickett's charge at Gettysburg. The memory made his stomach sick. Teddy hadn't listened either, and an hour later he'd paid for his stubbornness with his life.

Jim clenched his jaw and balled his fists, moving closer to peer through the gap. It was hardly more than a foot wide, and he couldn't get through it even if he'd wished to.

If the building hadn't been in danger of collapse, he would have driven a fist into the wall. How could she be so reckless? Rules and procedures were in place for a reason. To prevent impulsive actions and further loss of life. And watching someone in his charge disregard his orders and rush headlong into danger left him feeling powerless—a state Jim avoided above all others. He was furious.

Camila came back into the alleyway. Her eyes went wide when she realized where Miss Thornton had gone. She remained quiet, standing near the alley's entrance, but her expression was worried as she watched.

Jim wished for a match or a lamp or something to help him see what was happening on the other side of the wall. Through the crack he could see only shadows. It appeared the few windows had been blocked, perhaps by shifting furniture, or maybe there were curtains. He didn't dare lean against the weakened house to get a better look.

The baby's crying had stopped, but the house wasn't silent. As Jim strained his ears, he heard the creaking of floorboards and a sweeping sound that he hoped were Miss Thornton's steps returning to the opening.

Something shifted, and what sounded to be a shower of pebbles fell within the house. The building was not strong, and Jim feared a bump against the wrong doorframe could be all it took for the upper story to collapse.

Jim looked up to discern the strength of the beams overhead, but of course he couldn't see them. His pulse felt hard, blood moving through his veins at a quick rate. He clenched and unclenched his jaw, willing her to hurry.

Something creaked and rattled. He peered into the darkness, still seeing nothing but shadows.

"Dr. Jackson?" Miss Thornton's voice came from within. The sound was high-pitched and shaking. "Where . . . ? I can't find the opening, and the door is jammed."

"This way. Miss Thornton, can you hear me?" Jim called.

"Yes, but it's dark."

"Just follow my voice," Jim said.

"*Estamos aqui*, Hazel," Camila called into the opening.

At last Jim saw movement among the shadows, and eventually he could make her out. "Yes. This way."

Miss Thornton moved slowly, one hand feeling along the wall and her feet sliding carefully over the floor to keep from tripping. Jim could hear her breathing heavily. When she reached the gap, she handed the baby through, maneuvering the infant carefully to avoid the rough bricks.

Jim gave the baby to Camila and reached into the opening, grabbing hold of Miss Thornton's arm and pulling her through. In his anger and his haste to get her safely away, he was not gentle. He kept hold of her arm, and only once they'd stepped from the shadows of the alleyway did he release her. He turned to face the young woman, ready to unleash his fury, but his torrent of outrage stopped when he saw her face.

Miss Thornton was white as a sheet. Her breathing was still labored, and she was shaking. Tears were on her cheeks. She didn't look at him. She didn't look at anyone. She crumpled to sit on the dirt road, resting her elbows on her knees and holding her head.

"Hazel!" Camila gave the baby to Lucía and rushed back to kneel next to Miss Thornton on the ground.

"I'm all right," Miss Thornton said. She sounded as if pushing out the words was difficult. "I'm not hurt. I just . . . need a moment."

Camila looked at Jim.

He translated for her, then gave a shrug, telling her he wasn't certain what the problem was either. He studied Miss Thornton, looking her over to make certain she'd truly not been hurt. He didn't see any sign of injury. The young lady was obviously frightened, but her reaction seemed much greater than the situation called for. She was safe now. The building still stood, and the baby was free from danger.

He sent the orderlies and Lucía with the mother and baby to the ambulance wagon, then scanned the area. The shadows were growing longer.

People moved among the wreckage, salvaging what they could. Some huddled together in groups. The priest sat in front of what had earlier that day been a house, talking to a small boy. Jim had been impressed with the man and trusted he would continue with the relief effort. Santa Rosa was in good hands.

When he returned his attention to Miss Thornton, Camila was helping her to her feet. She was still pale, and she held herself as if she were cold. Her breathing was uneven. Was she suffering from some sort of fit? She had endured a fright, but her reaction seemed out of proportion to what had actually happened.

"Miss?"

"I'm all right." Her tone was sharp. She looked up at him, wincing, and softened her voice. "I'm sorry. But really, I . . . I just need a moment." Her words came between shaking breaths. She shook her head and started in the direction of the ambulance wagons.

Her dismissal was an insult to his status, and his worry quickly reverted to anger. He reached to stop her but then thought better of it. "We'll discuss this later, Miss Thornton."

She glanced back but didn't fully turn to meet his eye.

Once the wagons returned to the hospital, the night was completely dark. Jim spent the next several hours either preparing for surgery, performing surgery, or moving to the next surgery. He still felt angry as he thought of Santa Rosa and the damage that had been done. Why were so many innocents hurt during war? Why had the Carlists chosen to make a stand in the town? Had they believed the Spanish Army wouldn't attack for fear of hurting civilians? How could they put their families at risk in that way? And why had the Spanish Army chosen to attack, knowing full well that there were women and children in the range of their artillery? Did they think the innocents were expendable? Was the cost ever worth it?

His thoughts could not still. He thought of the mountains beyond the town, where the fighting men had gone. Dr. Laurent had thought there were more injured who didn't trust the doctors not to turn them over to the Spanish Army. He tapped a finger against his leg, wishing he knew how to reach them, how to convince them—and everyone—that the International Red Cross was indeed who they claimed to be—an impartial organization dedicated to helping victims of armed conflict and natural disasters. There was no agenda. They worked for no government. But gaining the trust of people whose neighbors and even family members had turned against them was no easy task. A civil war was more complicated than simply choosing a side, something Jim knew far too well.

He shook his head, washing a poor young man's blood off his hands. He'd asked himself the same questions over the years but had never reached a satisfactory answer. The only thing that made sense, in his eyes, was *saving* lives. Following procedures, making difficult decisions, and ensuring as many people as possible survived.

Jim's thoughts flashed to that instant before Miss Thornton had lunged for the opening in the broken wall, to the flash of defiance in her eyes. He ground his teeth, swallowing a bitter taste. The anger and *fear* he'd felt as he'd waited for her had nearly choked him. He breathed for a moment, pushing away the memory so he could focus.

He dried off his hands and turned to survey his next patient. The elderly woman's knee had been crushed beneath falling rocks. He glanced at her face, all but her eyes and forehead hidden beneath the chloroform cone. She slept soundly, unaware of her pain now, as the drug moved through her body, depressing her central nervous system. Jim could feel his own exhaustion, dark at the edges of his mind. But for him, sleep would have to wait.

Once the emergency patients were attended to, Jim continued his rounds. As usual, he was pleased by the progress of some but discouraged at its lack in others. The young man Mikel had regained some use of his hand, but the skin around his bullet wound was still red and hot. Jim worried that his weakened state would leave him unable to fight infection.

Finished with his rounds on this side of the building, he crossed through the cloister into the other ward. When he stopped by the bed of the soldier who had suffered a head injury in the train attack, he was pleased to see a note in the chart that indicated he'd woken and even eaten some broth. Jim touched his fingers to the captain's head, pleased that he had no fever. His bandages had been changed recently, so Jim decided to wait until the morning to examine the burr holes.

He continued along the ward and joined Dr. Laurent at the bedside of the mother who'd been rescued in Santa Rosa. A small group of nurses was at her bedside as well, and among them was Miss Thornton, gently bouncing the brown-eyed baby.

Seeing Jim, she turned away, keeping her attention fully on the child in her arms. She spoke in a soft voice to calm the baby, and hearing it, Jim found it difficult to hold on to his anger.

The other nurses were arranging a basket, where the baby could sleep, on a small table beside its mother.

"What is your assessment?" Jim asked Dr. Laurent. He lifted his chin, motioning to the patient.

"Jakinda complains of pain in her abdomen. At least two ribs are broken, but her lungs, zhey are intact." He glanced at the woman, then back to the chart. "She cannot sit up without becoming dizzy."

"Internal bleeding?" Jim asked.

"I see no outward signs," Dr. Laurent replied. "But it is possible." He turned a page on the chart, tapping his pencil against the paper. "Zhe only way to know for certain is to operate, and I do not know if she is strong enough to survive a surgery."

Jim nodded. It would be foolish to put the woman's body through trauma that could potentially be lethal in order to confirm whether such a surgery was needed in the first place. "A paradox," he said.

"Oui." Dr. Laurent closed the file. "I have instructed zhe nurses to monitor her carefully, and if anything changes, zhey will notify one of us immediately. But, for now, we will keep her comfortable and hope to manage zhe pain."

Jim agreed. It was all they could do.

Jakinda rolled her head to the side and reached her hand toward Miss Thornton, who settled the baby into its mother's arms. Miss Thornton placed a pillow beside the woman so the child wouldn't roll off the bed if its mother's hold became too weak.

Jakinda smiled a thank-you, then looked down at her baby. She seemed to have difficulty keeping her eyes open, most likely because of the morphine.

Miss Thornton smoothed the sheets and picked up a glass of water from where it sat on the bedside table, returning it to the rolling cart in the aisle. When she passed Jim, she kept her gaze from meeting his.

Even though he was exhausted, Jim knew he needed to speak to her tonight. Otherwise, the gentle way she treated patients and her quiet efficiency would make him forget how she'd defied his orders. He could already feel his temperament softening toward her, and if he was to enact the proper discipline, he needed to do it now. It was crucial that she understood the rules and the consequences for breaking them, and it was crucial for him to regain the control he'd lost. He couldn't let her put herself in harm's way again. He needed to know she wouldn't.

"If you please, Miss Thornton, I should like a word with you."

She turned, a hint of worry wrinkling her forehead. It was smoothed out and gone in an instant, and she met his gaze steadily. It was the most confident expression he'd seen on the young lady. "Of course, Dr. Jackson."

He turned and started away, beckoning her to follow with a flick of his wrist.

Miss Thornton's steps echoed softly as they left the ward and walked through the darkened corridors, past the kitchen, to the office shared by the three doctors. Jim took a lamp from an alcove and opened the door, holding it for her.

She stepped to the threshold and hesitated.

Jim glanced into the room beyond her. The office had once been a library, its walls lined with dark wooden shelves, and it contained one of the few windows in the building. Medical instruments and equipment were arranged on the tables and shelves, including vials and tubes and even a microscope. The few books the doctors had brought were stacked on the center table, even though empty shelves surrounded them. They were used so often that it seemed a waste of effort to return them each time. In the daylight, the room was bright and welcoming, but at night, it had an entirely different appearance, bordering on sinister.

Jim reached past her, holding up the lamp so she could enter.

Miss Thornton stepped inside. She stood just inside the doorway as Jim lit the candles around the room, then placed the lamp on the table. The light did little to disperse the shadows—Jim had rarely noticed before—but at least the two could see one another.

He considered sitting at the table but changed his mind and remained standing. He thrust his fists into the pockets of his white coat. "Miss Thornton, as a member of the hospital staff—my staff—you have a responsibility, not only to the patients but to all of us. I must impress on you the seriousness of what you did today." Jim knew his voice could be intimidating, and he felt a pang of guilt for using it, especially toward a gentlewoman in a semidarkened room.

Miss Thornton flinched—the slightest tightening of her eyes—but she did not look away.

"You disobeyed a direct order, putting yourself and the life of a patient in danger. That house could have come down with no warning." The anger he'd felt earlier returned, as did the memory of her face as she'd defied him. Just like his brother. "What do you have to say for yourself?" His words were sharp.

"There was a baby. A *baby*." Her voice was soft, but it was strong. "I couldn't leave her alone to die in that—" She shivered, visibly upset by the memory. "In there." She shivered again but appeared to gather herself tightly, as if she refused to think of it. "I'm not sorry that I went in after her, but I am sorry that you, as a doctor committed to saving lives, would just leave her." Her chin trembled and she crossed her arms, but her gaze never wavered.

Jim had expected emotion, but he'd thought she would display guilt or anguish. This—she was afraid. But he didn't believe it was directed at him. She'd been terrified in that house. What had happened to cause her reaction? Had it been the darkness? The fear that the roof would collapse? He thought back to her panicked reaction and tried to hold on to the last bits of anger, but they slipped out of his grasp. He sighed, feeling suddenly exhausted. "I need to trust the people I work with, Miss Thornton." He leaned back against the table, crossing his ankles. "I need to know that you will follow through when I give an order. Lives depend on it. Including yours."

"I understand, Doctor Jackson." She looked down, for the first time showing a hint of remorse. "I am sorry that I disobeyed your directions. But I cannot say that I wouldn't do it again." Her voice was soft.

Jim waited for her to look up, but she kept her gaze firmly on the ground.

"I will speak to Lucía concerning your discipline," he said. "She will likely assign you to laundry or bedpan duty."

She gave a slight nod.

"And you will not be invited to the next rescue mission."

"Is that all, Doctor?"

"Yes. You are dismissed."

She started toward the door.

"Miss Thornton," Jim called after her. "I would not have left the baby behind," he said. "We would have found a way—a safe way—to get her."

She didn't turn, but Jim could see by the tilt of her head that she was listening.

"I wanted to make sure you understood that," he said.

Miss Thornton gave another nod and left.

Jim hooked his foot around the leg of a chair, pushing it out from beneath the table, and sat heavily. He stared at the empty doorway as an uncertainty itched at him. He let his memory return to that moment, the instant right before Miss Thornton had rushed into the gap. To the look in her eyes that was so like his brother's. Was he really angry that he'd been defied? Or was it something different altogether? His emotions, the shaking of his limbs, and the hard rock in his belly couldn't be attributed completely to anger. Or to fear. He was hurt that the two of them had so easily gone against what he'd told them. That they hadn't trusted him. His own brother and now this woman, whose conception of him mattered more than it should.

He rubbed his eyes, resting his elbows on his knees. Miss Thornton had considered him a monster willing to leave an innocent baby to be crushed when a building inevitably collapsed. And what she thought mattered to him. That was the real surprise. For the first time in years, he cared about someone's good opinion. And that scared him.

CHAPTER 7

Hazel left Dr. Jackson's office and hurried down the shadowy passageway toward her bedchamber. Or, rather, she stormed down the passageway. Or perhaps she retreated down the passageway. It was difficult to tell. Her emotions ran the gamut. Anger, embarrassment, hurt. Here was another man telling her what she could and couldn't do. That moment in the alley—it had simply been too much.

Echoes of her panic in the dark house made her breathing come in bursts and her skin tighten. The building had been, for the most part, undamaged, but the bombings must have shaken it, spilling the contents of cupboards and toppling furniture. Dust had hung in the air, making the rooms appear dark, even in the afternoon light. A curtain rod had broken on one side, and it hung at a strange angle, with the curtains crumpled in a heap at the bottom. Hazel had moved carefully, stepping around pieces of dishes.

She'd found the baby easily enough. The cries had led Hazel into the back bedroom, to a wooden cradle at the foot of a bed with turned posts stained a dark umber color. There had been a moment, right after she picked up the baby, when she became completely turned around and couldn't tell which direction led to the gap where she'd entered. Even before her mind had fully realized what was happening, Hazel could sense it. Her lungs compressed and her skin flashed from hot to cold as the feeling of being trapped made the room spin.

Just the memory made her stomach turn.

And worse than the panic was the worry that Dr. Jackson had seen it. She already feared disappointing him, and now she'd done it, and more efficiently than she would have believed possible. Her cheeks burned at the memory of their conversation a few moments earlier. He had already been hesitant about allowing Hazel's presence on the hospital staff. If he knew she fell apart with such regularity, he'd banish her from the hospital for certain, and then where would she be? The nearest town was in pieces. She had no idea if the train tracks had been mended, and of course she couldn't leave without Nella and Captain Bryant.

She grabbed a candle lamp from an alcove, irritated with herself that she still hadn't located any striking matches to use in the morning. She held the lamp aloft, letting it illuminate her path. When she arrived at the door to her bedchamber, she reached into her pocket for the key. But before drawing it out, she stopped, and all other thoughts went from her mind when she saw that the door was ajar. Had she been robbed?

She stepped back and counted the doors in the passageway to make certain she was at the right room. An uncomfortable feeling tingled her nerves. But perhaps she was being silly. Was she certain she'd pulled the door completely closed when she left earlier? Straining her ears, she pushed the door with her fingertips. It opened just over halfway and stopped, bumping into something hard. Hazel hesitated. But hearing no movement, she took a step inside and raised the lamp.

A dark shape occupied most of the room. When the light fell on it, Hazel's worries disappeared. Her traveling trunk had arrived. And so, she saw, had Nella's, along with Captain Bryant's portmanteau.

Hazel closed the door, noting that the chair had been removed. There wasn't room for it with all the luggage. Her trunk sat on the floor beneath Nella's, their travel bags, and the hatboxes. The portmanteau was between the trunks and the wall.

She scooted along the narrow space between the cot and the trunks and set the lamp on the table, glad that at least that one bit of furniture remained, and she considered the puzzle of how to access her trunk. There was not sufficient space on the floor for both trunks to sit side by side—unless she took away the cot. And she wasn't sure she could lift the trunk back up if she did manage to push it off onto the floor anyway. In the end, she put the lamp on the trunks, lifted the little table onto the wooden cot, along with the hatboxes, and pushed and pulled until the cot was flush against the trunks. Then she put the table and hatboxes in the small space between the cot and the wall and pulled Nella's trunk onto the cot.

Hazel's earlier exhaustion was gone, and her senses hummed with the thrill of using her hairbrush and toothpowder.

She squeezed into the space beside her trunk and lifted the lid. Inside, the contents looked as if they'd been tossed around. Her clothing was in disarray, and lavender water had leaked all over everything. Remembering the clothing and damaged luggage around the wreckage of the train, she was grateful that her things were at least accounted for, even if they were not all in first-rate condition.

She lifted out her clothing, assessing which needed laundering, and found the bag of grooming items near the bottom of the trunk. When she reached for it, her fingers brushed a wrapped parcel. A smile tugged at her lips as she remembered her final night in London.

Digging among her stockings, shoes, and underclothing, she found the rest of the parcels, lining them up on Nella's trunk, and a rush of homesickness hit her, making her eyes sting. She again dug in the trunk and brought out a handkerchief, then closed her trunk and sat on it, looking at the row of gifts. They were all small, of course, meant to take up a minimum of space in her luggage, but right now, those four parcels seemed nothing short of magnificent.

She pulled her feet up so that she leaned back against the stone wall, resting her elbows on her knees, and her tears began to fall.

She wondered what her friends would think if they could see her now—wearing a blood-stained apron, with hair that hadn't been combed properly in days, sitting on a chest in a little stone room that was so crowded that she had to climb over the furniture to get to the door.

A noise that began as a sob turned into a laugh as she imagined the four women opening the sleeping-chamber door and staring. Dahlia would be horrified at the accommodations but would somehow make the room welcoming and comfortable with a few well-placed decorations and lovely linens. Vivian would set about figuring out a scientific way to provide light and heat to the room. Sophie would bring a basket filled with meat pies, tarts, and sweet cakes. Elizabeth would, of course, have plenty to say about the inequality between the men's and women's positions in the hospital.

Hazel picked up one of the gifts, holding it against her chest and imagining she could feel the affection of her friends radiating through the paper. She weighed the package in her hand, considering. She'd been told not to open it until Christmas. But nobody could have predicted that she'd find herself in such a circumstance. And besides, for all she knew, it was Christmas already—she'd quite lost track of the date. She thought there were a few days yet, and even here, Christmas wouldn't simply pass without anyone taking notice, would it? Well, she wasn't going to take the chance. She set the parcel back down with the others, climbed back over the cot, and slipped through the small opening of the doorway, returning a moment later with two more lamps. The effect of the extra light in the room made the chamber surprisingly pleasant, and she decided that she would light three lamps before bed every night—even if it was for only a few moments.

Hazel returned to her place, sitting atop her traveling trunk. She chose a gift. The package was a small rectangular shape, wrapped in striped tissue paper, and tied smartly with a string. She tore off the paper to reveal two books and a card.

> *A journal to record all of your adventures—I do hope there are many and that they are at least scandalous enough to make them worth the ink.*
>
> *And a Spanish-to-English dictionary to make certain you are able to fend for yourself among strangers.*
>
> *With love,*
> *Elizabeth*

Hazel studied the cover of the pocket dictionary. *Standard Spanish-English and English-Spanish Dictionary*. She opened it, figuring out quickly how to find the words she was looking for. Whether she was in need of a word to explain or one to understand, the book would be immensely helpful in communicating with patients and her fellow nurses. And it was small enough to fit in her apron pocket.

The next package was wrapped in gorgeous floral paper with an enormous silk ribbon that had been smashed a bit in the trunk. Of course it was from Dahlia. Hazel opened one end and pulled out a very soft and, knowing Dahlia, very expensive silk shawl. The color was a lovely blue with flowers embroidered along the edge.

> *For cool nights and lonely days or anytime at all that you need a bit of comfort. Envelope yourself within and imagine you are in the embrace of those who miss you.*
>
> *All my love,*
> *Dahlia*

Hazel draped the shawl around her shoulders, holding it tightly and closed her eyes, trying to imagine the feel of her friends' embrace.

The next gift was the largest. A box containing an assortment of mechanical parts. When Hazel unfolded the paper that was enclosed, she found illustrated directions for assembly.

In December, the temperature in the Canary Islands is said to be pleasant, but the atmospheric moisture content in a tropical climate tends to be high, and while this mechanism will not dissipate the water vapor in the air, it might make it more bearable.

Love,
Vivian

P.S. Benedict has enclosed a gift as well. I put it in the motor housing for safekeeping. He says to tell you it is a moonstone, meant to provide protection for travelers. If one is to believe potassium feldspar possesses such capabilities.

Hazel didn't know what a motor housing was, but after a moment of searching in the box, she found a small velvet pouch inside a box of gears.

When she tipped it, a necklace with a white-stone pendant fell into her palm. The stone was cloudy, but it shimmered in the candlelight with an opalescence that took her breath away. "Beautiful," she whispered.

She studied the schematics and understood that once assembled, the parts Vivian had so carefully created and packed into the box would make an upright fan with a motor that was powered by a windup key in its base. Practical and thoughtful—just like Vivian.

The final gift was a box wrapped with colorful paper. Inside she found a pretty box of stationery with a jar of ink and a quill. There was also a paper sack filled with peppermints. The sweets, Hazel knew, were from Sophie's fiancé, Inspector Jonathan Graham. Peppermints were a favorite indulgence of his. She removed the smaller box and sack and saw another wrapped parcel in the bottom of the first box. The parcel was small, only slightly larger than her palm.

When she removed the tissue paper, Hazel gasped. Inside the carved frame was a painting of herself. On this small canvas, Sophie had recreated every curl, the curve of her brow, and even her fine eyelashes with such detail that Hazel could only stare. She recognized the dress and the setting immediately. She was sitting on a bench in the garden of Uncle Archibald's London house, looking over her shoulder at the artist. Sophie had captured her expression just as her face was transitioning between surprise and delight.

Hazel remembered the day well. Her panic spells had been happening more often, and worried that the crowds would cause her to experience another, she'd remained at home while her friends had attended an air-balloon ascension. Hazel had been feeling sorry for herself, watching the balloon soar through the sky over the garden and imagining how her friends must be enjoying themselves, when the members of the Blue Orchid Society arrived with a picnic and souvenirs from the park. Hazel had kept the painted silk fan with the image of a floating balloon on the mantel in her bedchamber in her uncle's house.

She smiled at the memory. Her friends had always known when she needed them, and it seemed their concern did not disperse with distance.

At the bottom of this box was another card.

Hazel,

I hope you enjoy your holiday with your father and that you do not forget to write often. It is not the same as sharing confidences while we secret ourselves away in a library during a ball, but we make do with what we have, do we not? I have grown quite accustomed to talking with you nearly every day and fear I will miss you dreadfully. I do not know what I shall do if I have no word from you for months.

When I considered what to give you, I thought you would wish for something you could also give. It is always in your nature to do for others. I believe your father would be fond of this painting. And I hope it will bring joy to the holiday. I cannot wait to hear about all of your adventures, but more especially, I cannot wait to see you again, my dear friend.

Love,
Sophie

Hazel sat awhile longer on the trunk, letting the warm feeling of her friends' love enfold her. She could not imagine a person more fortunate in their association than herself, and even if tomorrow held nothing but bedpans, laundry, and Dr. Jim Jackson's disapproval, knowing that her friends were thinking of her was enough to give her the strength to shove the trunk back and move the cot before she fell asleep wrapped in a gorgeous silk shawl.

CHAPTER 8

Jim walked through the West ward, making his morning rounds. Two days had passed since the rescue mission to Santa Rosa, and the number of occupied beds had decreased, either by patients recovering sufficiently to leave the hospital or, in unfortunate cases, the reverse. But Jim was certain the hospital team's quick response had been effective. The majority of critical patients would not have survived if they'd not been treated when they were.

Seeing a nurse from the corner of his eye, he glanced toward her, feeling a small burst of disappointment when he saw it wasn't Miss Thornton. He'd hoped for an opportunity to speak with the young lady—not about anything in particular, but he wanted her to understand that he bore no resentment toward her. He was not the type of man to hold a grudge, and before the incident in town, he had thought they were developing a comfortable working relationship. He considered her to be a very promising nurse. She was a quick learner, and her instincts were sharp. Teaching her and watching her learn had been . . . satisfying. And he didn't want their relationship to be strained.

He glanced in the other direction, wondering if she might be removing linens from some of the empty beds, but he was disappointed again. Over the past days, he'd caught only quick glimpses of Miss Thornton as she carried bedpans or loads of laundry. Lucía had made certain to keep her busy. A few times, Jim had seen the young nurse carrying the baby or speaking with Jakinda or Miss Westbrook, but he'd not been able to think of a reason to interrupt.

About halfway down the ward, something strange caught his attention. A small table had been set up with what appeared to be some sort of motorized fan blowing toward the beds on one side. He watched it for a moment, and when the fan's motor stopped, Dr. Ruiz hurried over. He twisted a key in its base to restart the motor and turned the fan to face the patients in the other direction.

"What is this?" Jim asked him while staring at the device.

"*Un ventilador*," Dr. Ruiz said. "A . . . fan."

Jim turned toward Dr. Ruiz, who was near his own age, small in build and stature, and extremely competent. The quiet man was a native to Spain, which was helpful when it came to communicating with patients, but it also made some of them nervous, as they wondered which side he supported in the war.

"I can see that it's a fan, Doctor," Jim said. "Where did it come from? And what is it doing here?"

"The English nurse," Dr. Ruiz said, motioning vaguely in the direction of the laundry. "She brought it to move the stagnant air."

Of course she did. Jim had read some of Miss Nightingale's publications. The woman was obsessed with proper ventilation in the sickroom. It made sense that one of her students would be as well.

"I thought there was no harm in it," Dr. Ruiz continued. "But if you wish for it to be removed . . ." He reached toward the fan.

"No, it's all right," Jim said, stopping him with a wave of his hand. "I don't believe it will hurt anything either, and it does get warm in here." Without opening windows in the wards, "warm" was an understatement. In the summer, they had propped open the doors to the cloister, but the mountain air was chilly this time of year, and with the doors closed, the rooms were stuffy. Moving air did seem healthier. "I'll have a nurse transfer it to the other ward tomorrow."

Dr. Ruiz nodded.

In the distance, they heard a blast. Both men tensed and looked in the direction of the sound, waiting, but it was not followed by more.

"I hear from some patients that the Spanish troops and the British Legion are moving closer to the Carlist strongholds," Dr. Ruiz said, crossing his arms and leaning a hip against the little table. "Bilbao and San Sebastián are still occupied by the rebels, but they will not be safe for long. Another attack will happen soon, if rumors are to be believed."

"We should be out there too," Jim said. "The little good we are able to do here is nothing compared . . ." He rubbed his eyes, frustrated. If only he knew where the attacks were going to happen and when.

Jim checked the charts and vitals of the patients, enjoying the breeze from the fan as he did so. After a few moments, the fan's motor stopped, and he turned the key to wind it. He studied the contraption. The parts were made of a variety of materials that seemed to have been repurposed from other things. Had Miss Thornton made this?

It appeared he had something to talk to her about.

Jim found her a few moments later in the cloister. She sat with her traveling companion Miss Westbrook on one of the benches, their heads bent close together as they studied something the older woman was holding. A chair was pulled close so Miss Westbrook could keep her ankle elevated, and a pair of crutches lay on the ground at their feet.

"A perfect likeness, isn't it?" Miss Westbrook was saying as Jim came toward them. "What talent."

"I was very surprised," Miss Thornton said. "He will be pleased, don't you think?"

"Undoubtedly."

Miss Thornton glanced up, and seeing Jim, she stood. "Good afternoon, Dr. Jackson."

"Good afternoon," he said to the pair of them. "How are you feeling, Miss Westbrook?"

She set the object down on the bench next to her. "Tired of being a patient, truth be told. Not that I've not been quite well taken care of. But I'm ready to be finished with this." She motioned to her ankle with a sweep of her hand.

"I understand that," Jim said. "How is your level of pain?"

"Manageable," she said. "Though, it does throb, especially at night."

Miss Thornton patted her friend's arm in consolation.

Jim nodded. It was expected, but keeping her limb elevated would reduce the swelling, and in time, the throbbing would disperse. "And your fever?"

"Gone, and good riddance to it, I say," Miss Westbrook said.

"Glad to hear it." She really did look better. Her skin had regained a healthy color, its pallor gone, and he saw none of the strain around her eyes that he'd noticed before. "The lingering fever was worrying but not unexpected with the inflammation in your ankle. Your body suffered a great trauma, miss."

"Don't I know it." She sighed and held a hand to her breastbone.

Miss Thornton's lips pulled as she suppressed amusement at the woman's dramatic response. Her eyes caught Jim's, and the two looked away quickly, not wanting the older woman to see that they were sharing a smile at her expense.

"But I am telling you things you no doubt already know, aren't I, Nurse Westbrook?" Jim continued, wishing he had a chart to write on. He felt as though he should be doing something with his hands, so he thrust them into his coat pockets.

"Yes," she said. "But it is very different to be the patient. I do hope the experience gives me a bit more tolerance in the future for those poor patients under my care."

"Oh, don't be silly, Nella," Miss Thornton said. "You are nothing if not compassionate."

"Perhaps," Miss Westbrook said. "It is easy enough to appear compassionate. But patience is another thing entirely."

Miss Thornton shook her head and raised her brows at her friend in a way that indicated she didn't believe the woman's assessment of herself to be the least bit true.

Lucía came into the courtyard. "*Ven*, Miss Westbrook," she said. "*Es hora de descansar.*"

Jim opened his mouth to translate, but he didn't have the chance.

"She said it is time for you to rest," Miss Thornton said first. She lifted the crutches, handing them to Miss Westbrook.

Lucía gave Miss Thornton a nod of thanks for her assistance in communicating with the patient.

Jim was surprised that Miss Thornton had understood. And rather impressed with how quickly the young lady was assimilating to her new circumstance. He'd not have imagined she would adapt so quickly.

She and Lucía helped the older woman stand and situate herself with the crutches.

Lucía then walked beside Miss Westbrook, watching her carefully as they moved slowly to the walkway.

"Gracias, Lucía," Miss Thornton said, watching them. She glanced at Jim and gave a quick curtsey. "Excuse me, Doctor. I need to tend to the laundry."

"One moment," he said.

She raised her brows, fair-colored arches over soft blue eyes. The expression made her eyes wide as she looked up at him. It was entrancing.

Jim stared for a moment, noticing how her forehead wrinkled in delicate lines. He had entirely forgotten what he'd come to speak to her about. Certainly he'd had a question in mind when he'd come to find her, but the topic was gone.

"Yes, Doctor Jackson?"

He cleared his throat, searching for something to say. "You're learning Spanish." It was the only thing that came to mind, and once he said it, he realized how foolish it sounded.

"Yes." She took a small book from her apron pocket. When she turned the cover, he saw it was a Spanish-to-English dictionary.

"May I?" Jim asked.

She handed him the book, and he glanced through. A sheet of paper was tucked between the pages, and he saw that she'd made notes of particular words, their translations, and their pronunciation.

"Very useful," he said, giving the book back.

She put it back in her pocket. "It is."

The conversation was becoming more uncomfortable by the moment when he at last recalled his original purpose for seeking her out. "I noticed a windup fan in the West ward," he said, pleased that he'd remembered a topic that could lead to a normal discussion.

"Does a fan violate hospital rules?" Her brows were no longer lifted, and her forehead was smooth. She tipped her head to the side, her expression defensive.

"No, of course not," Jim said quickly. "I was simply curious about it. The item is very unique. Did you make it?"

"It was a gift."

"I see."

"If that is all, Doctor, I should return to my duties." Her expression was polite, but there was no warmth in it. She apparently still felt the sting from his reprimand.

Having nothing else to say, Jim nodded and watched as she started toward the lines of sheets drying on the other side of the cloister.

Camila came through the door then, and seeing him, she hurried over. "Dr. Jackson!" She started an explanation, motioning toward the ward behind her and speaking so quickly that he had difficulty understanding.

"*Despacio*," Jim said, motioning for her to speak more slowly. Though his mastery of the language had improved immensely over the past months, he still had difficulty when people spoke too fast.

She started again, sounding excited but managing to speak at a more understandable rate. This time Jim understood. "Dr. Laurent sent me to fetch you. The soldier Captain Bryant is awake."

"Captain Bryant?" Miss Thornton turned abruptly and hurried back. She darted her gaze between the two of them, her expression looking anxious. "Camila, what has happened? Dr. Jackson, what did she say?"

"The captain has awoken," Jim said.

"At last!" Miss Thornton clasped her hands together and ran off to the ward without another word.

"Gracias, Camila," Jim said, smiling at Miss Thornton's reaction. Seeing the brightness in her eyes was a pleasure, especially after the cool way she'd treated him lately. He started toward the doorway Miss Thornton had just gone through, but seeing something from the corner of his eye, he paused. Miss Westbrook had left something on the bench. He lifted it. It was a small frame, and within . . . Jim stared, and his stomach did a slow roll. The subject of the painting was Miss Thornton, who seemed to have been caught in a moment of surprise. The image was bewitching. The artist had captured the young lady's likeness expertly. And not just her appearance. The small portrait seemed to contain her very essence.

Jim blinked, remembering what the women had been saying when he'd approached them in the garden. The picture was intended for someone. He put it in his pocket and started toward the West ward. But as he walked, an uncomfortable feeling nagged at him, like an itch he couldn't reach or a rock in his shoe. Was this picture meant for Captain Bryant?

Jim felt foolish that he hadn't realized it before. Why else would the pair be traveling together with a chaperone if they were not . . . together? A burning sensation grew in his chest, and Jim was irritated at the discomfort.

He stepped through the doorway and came to Captain Bryant's bedside as Miss Thornton pulled back from embracing the man and kissed his cheek.

The burning sensation returned.

"Miss Thornton?" Captain Bryant's voice was hoarse. He cleared his throat and glanced at the others. "Where . . . ?"

Camila handed him a glass of water and helped him drink.

Dr. Laurent gave Jim a pleased smile. The patient's vital signs must be favorable.

"You're in the International Red Cross Hospital in Santa Rosa," Miss Thornton said, arranging the pillows behind him.

Captain Bryant leaned back. "I don't remember . . ." He lifted his hand to touch the bandages on his head.

"Careful." Miss Thornton caught his hand. "You are injured." She sat on the edge of the bed beside him, still holding his hand. "There was an accident on the train. We've been so worried about you, Captain."

Jim pulled his gaze from the pair's joined hands. "Dr. Jim Jackson," he said, introducing himself. "And you've already met Dr. Laurent?"

"Yes, I . . . just now." The captain turned his gaze to Jim, then to Dr. Laurent with eyes that seemed slightly unfocused.

"This man saved your life," Jim said, motioning with his chin to Dr. Laurent.

Captain Bryant looked at the older man. "I am very thankful to you, Doctor." His words were sincere and accompanied by a genuinely grateful smile.

Miss Thornton beamed.

"It was not I alone," Dr. Laurent said, his cheeks and bald head reddening. "My associate, he treated you as well."

"Thank you, Dr. Jackson," Captain Bryant said.

"How do you feel?" Jim asked, embarrassed by the attention. He bent close, pulling up one eyelid and then the other to look closely at the patient's pupils.

The captain blinked, his eyes focusing. "My head hurts," he said. "Especially here." He moved his hand to point at his forehead but did not touch it.

"That is where you suffered a laceration," Jim said. He accepted the offered chart from Dr. Laurent. "Any pain in this area?" He pointed with his pencil to his own head to illustrate where the drainage hole had been made in the captain's.

"Yes," Captain Bryant said. He moved his head, then closed his eyes. "I beg your pardon; my head is swimming."

Miss Thornton squeezed his hand. "It's all right." She spoke in a soothing voice that made Jim's jaw clench.

To distract himself, he looked over the newly recorded numbers. Temperature and heart rate were both within the normal range. If the captain continued along this trajectory, he was set to make a complete physical recovery. Jim could not make the same assurance about the man's mental state. His mind may never fully heal. The Red Cross Hospital was not equipped for that type of care anyway. Once the man was recovered enough to travel, he would likely need to convalesce in London.

"Has the patient eaten?" Jim asked Camila in Spanish.

"Just a bit of broth."

"When he is ready, he should eat something more substantial," Jim said, "but he should eat slowly." Solid food would give the captain strength and speed his recovery.

"Yes, Doctor," Camila said.

Miss Thornton looked between them. She seemed to be concentrating on their words, but from her confused expression, she hadn't fully understood.

Jim didn't take time to explain. His mouth tasted bitter, and he was irritated with his unexpected reaction to something that was very much none of his business. There was nothing he wanted more than to be far away from this situation. He gave the chart back to Dr. Laurent. "The patient should rest," he said.

"I'll come visit soon," Miss Thornton said. She smoothed the bedsheets. "I'm so glad you're awake, Captain." She kissed his cheek again.

Jim promptly left. The bitter taste in his throat had moved down to churn in his stomach. He felt foolish at his reaction. Was he actually jealous? Was he so simple that a pair of gentle eyes were all it took to make him resent a patient?

He closed the ward door behind him and continued on toward his bedchamber, walking at a quick pace, as if he might be able to outrun his feelings. Of course, he couldn't. Once he was inside his room, he lit a lamp and sat hard on his bed. An object in his pocket bumped against his leg. Jim sighed and took out the painting. Although his good sense told him to put it away, somehow, his reason seemed to have fled. Maybe he simply wished to torture himself.

He held the painting up close to the lamp, studying it. He'd thought when he'd first met Miss Hazel Thornton that the perfect word to describe her was *soft*. But now he knew that was a simplification of a woman who was intelligent and determined and could, at times, be stubborn. And who, Jim realized, had unlocked something inside him that he'd avoided for years. He saved lives—cured people who were ill or hurt—but by letting Miss Thornton into his heart, he feared he couldn't save himself from the inevitable pain it would cost.

CHAPTER 9

Hazel cupped water in her hand and let it run over the baby's soft head, laughing as Nerea kicked and splashed water out of the basin. Droplets sprayed over Hazel. Her skirt was already soaked. "My goodness, Nerea! This is your bath, not mine." She wiped her sleeve over her face.

The baby grabbed Hazel's necklace in her fist. She kicked again, grinning with her toothless smile, and Hazel couldn't help but grin back at the delight in the child's face. She carefully pried the necklace from Nerea's grip and tucked it back under her collar. "You love your bath, don't you, dearest?" Once she was certain the soap was completely rinsed away, she wrapped Nerea in a clean towel, holding her close to keep her warm. "You're all clean now. Won't your mother be pleased to see you?" She bounced the baby as she walked her over to the folding table, speaking in a singsong voice. "Look at this beautiful baby. Nerea, you're a beautiful baby."

The laundry room was quiet today, as was the rest of the hospital. Most of the staff had gone with Dr. Jackson and Dr. Laurent on a rescue mission earlier that morning when they'd heard the sounds of fighting in the hills.

Hazel had remained behind with Dr. Ruiz and two other nurses. The three women had already prepared the empty beds with clean sheets and stocked operating rooms with bandages and surgical supplies in anticipation of the new patients, and having no pressing duties beyond regular checks of the patients, they had little to do now but wait.

Hazel swaddled the baby in clean linens, singing a lullaby she remembered from her ayah. Nerea was wide awake, her shining brown eyes watchful as Hazel carried her through the hospital, walking slowly in hopes that the baby would grow tired. The nurses had discovered over the past few nights that she would fall asleep only if she was being held. Perhaps the hospital basket was uncomfortable, or maybe this was how Jakinda had lulled her to sleep before they'd come to the hospital. Nerea was especially fitful at nighttime, so the nurses had taken turns walking her up and down the wards and passageways for hours, hoping to calm her.

Hazel didn't mind the walking at all. She enjoyed her time with the baby, especially when Nerea's head finally laid down on her shoulder and her breathing deepened. That was the moment Hazel loved. She didn't imagine anything was quite as restorative to the soul as holding a sleeping infant.

She hummed softly as she walked into the West ward and stopped at Captain Bryant's bed. He had been awake for a few hours earlier that morning and had seemed even stronger than the day before. Hazel was disappointed that he was asleep now.

She walked away quietly, remembering Dr. Jackson's bad temper when he'd examined Captain Bryant. She carried no delusions that the doctor had any pleasant feelings toward her, and his dislike was further apparent in the way he'd ignored her in the cloister the day before, speaking only to Nella until he'd been forced to speak to Hazel after Nella had been escorted back to the ward. Perhaps he was irritated with Captain Bryant's slow recovery because it meant she wasn't leaving soon enough for his liking.

The sensation of knowing a person so strongly disapproved of her was uncomfortable, to say the least. And in Dr. Jackson's case, Hazel felt it especially, because there were times—such as during Mikel's surgery or when he'd shown her how to mark the patient's charts—when she'd thought there'd been a connection. She'd believed Dr. Jackson had seen her as someone who was capable of learning, that he'd been pleased by her hard work. But she'd ruined any hopes of remaining in his good graces when she'd disregarded his orders and rushed into the house after Nerea.

Hazel gazed down at the child in her arms. "I would disobey a hundred doctors for you, little one," she whispered.

Before returning Nerea to the East ward, she stopped at her bedchamber to fetch her writing paper, ink, and quill. She retrieved her hairbrush as well, slipping them all into a bag, and by the time she came to Jakinda's bed, the baby slept.

Jakinda looked pleased when she saw Hazel. She lifted her hand, but the movement was weak. Hazel brought Nerea close so her mother could see her face. Jakinda kissed her, and Hazel tucked the baby into the basket.

She put the ink and paper on the small table and took Jakinda's cleaned scarf from her pocket. It was a bit damp from Nerea's bath. She sat on the bed and gently teased the tangles from Jakinda's hair with the brush. Hazel thought the hospital's combs much too stiff, and in Jakinda's state, she believed a soft hairbrush would feel much better.

Jakinda closed her eyes as Hazel brushed her hair. Once the brush moved smoothly without tugging on Jakinda's scalp, Hazel used the firmer comb and divided the strands to weave them into braids. She tied the scarf around Jakinda's head in the style she'd seen on the other women in Santa Rosa and stepped back to survey her handiwork. "There you are. *Que hermosa*," she said, using words she'd looked up earlier and making her voice cheerful.

Jakinda smiled, but it was hardly more than a slight movement of her mouth.

Hazel had hoped having her hair arranged would make her feel at least a little better. But, in truth, Jakinda looked worse than she had in the days since the men dug her out from under the broken wall. Her skin was pale and clammy, and her pulse was weak. Hazel checked her abdomen every few hours, just as Dr. Laurent had ordered, and though the bruises there were not growing, Hazel's instinct told her something was wrong. Jakinda wasn't improving.

"*¿Tienes hambre?*" she asked, hoping Jakinda's appetite had returned.

"No." The reply was a whisper.

Hazel helped her sit up and take a sip of water, and then she assisted with the bedpan.

Jakinda winced at the movement and sucked in a breath, pressing a hand to her belly.

Hazel worried at the pain in the woman's grimace. She held a hand gently against her back.

Jakinda's head swayed, and she lay back on the pillow, wincing again at the pain.

"I brought paper," Hazel said. She showed Jakinda the blank pages, then looked through her dictionary for the right word. "For *una carta*," she said. "For Ramiro."

Jakinda's eyes focused for just a minute as she understood. She moved her head the slightest bit in a nod. She had spoken about her husband, and Camila had translated when she'd been near. From her, Hazel had learned that Ramiro had fled with the other Carlists when the Spanish Army came to Santa Rosa. He must have thought that, with the rebels gone, the army would leave the city alone. Hazel prayed that he was alive somewhere. She had no confidence in her ability to write the letter in Basque, but with the dictionary and Jakinda's help, she thought they could at least communicate in Spanish. She hoped Ramiro would understand what she wrote, at least enough to learn where his wife and baby were.

Hazel brought a chair and sat beside the bed. "Ramiro," she said, writing the name and turning it for Jakinda to see.

Jakinda closed her eyes and spoke words Hazel couldn't understand. Hazel repeated them and consulted her dictionary often, making certain they were correct before she wrote them on the paper. Her eyes prickled when she wrote the words for *love* and *frightened*. The short letter took over an hour to complete, and before Hazel had even finished signing Jakinda's name, the poor woman had fallen asleep.

Hazel tucked the sheets over her and cleaned up the space. She put the letter in her pocket and the ink, quill, hairbrush, and paper back in her bag. She poured a fresh glass of water, leaving it on the bedside table, and took the bedpan to empty.

On her way from the ward, Hazel stopped at Nella's bed. While she and Jakinda had worked on the letter, she had seen her friend moving about on her crutches with the assistance of a nurse, and now Nella was back in her bed with her knitting in her lap. She grinned when she saw Hazel, but her nose wrinkled when she saw the bedpan in her hands. "Don't miss that duty, you can be sure of that."

"Do you need . . . ?" Hazel motioned toward the pot beneath Nella's bed.

"Heavens, no!" Nella dropped the knitting and put her hands on her hips. "I'll use the privy, thank you very much, even if it takes me an hour to get there."

"You do seem to be proficient with the crutches," Hazel said.

Nella shrugged. "It's not so difficult, with a bit of practice." She picked up the needles and counted the stitches to where she'd left off. "I'm coming to realize I'm very lucky," she said. "Poor Captain Bryant. Dr. Laurent is afraid his mind will never be the same. He'll certainly suffer with headaches."

"But he's recovering," Hazel said defensively. She didn't like the idea that her friend might not fully mend. "He'll heal much more quickly in London; I'm certain of it. I imagine he'll be well enough to leave within a few days. Then we'll all be able to return to England and leave this place behind." Saying the words aloud brought a surprising sadness.

"Of course. You're right, dear." Nella kept her gaze on her knitting. Her tone was strange, as if she were only agreeing in order to end the conversation. Perhaps she was sad as well.

"I'll leave you to rest." Hazel excused herself and made her way to the privy. Her conversation with Nella left her feeling uneasy, but why exactly she couldn't say. She didn't like the way Nella had avoided answering her directly, but what was her reasoning? Was she just trying to placate Hazel's worries about Captain Bryant? Or was there something else? Something about what Nella said didn't feel quite right. Was the captain's condition worse than the doctors were telling Hazel?

She set aside her uncertain feelings for the moment and considered how to get Jakinda's letter to Ramiro. Perhaps Mikel's father would have a way of finding the men hiding in the mountains. Or he might at least know someone who could.

Her mind was still occupied as she performed the less than pleasant task of emptying the bedpan. But her thoughts stilled and her hands froze as she poured out the contents. Jakinda's urine was colored with blood.

CHAPTER 10

The ambulance wagon bumped along the mountain road, seeming to hit every rock on the way. Jim thought it high time the International Red Cross invested in some modern conveyances. The springs were old and hardly functioned properly, and if the seats had once borne some sort of padding, it had long since worn away. His lower back ached and his legs were tired from bracing.

This rescue mission had been the shortest yet. The fighting had taken place on a rocky hillside away from any town, and the most difficult part had been hauling the wounded over the rough terrain to the road. Luckily, there had been no town damaged and no civilians hurt.

Dr. Laurent shifted beside him, searching for a comfortable position. The patients in the wagon were unusually quiet, which Jim hoped was a good sign. Or perhaps it was an indication of their training. Most of the wounded men they were transporting belonged to the British Legion.

As the wagons drew near the hospital, Jim saw a nurse waiting in front of the large arched doors of the hospital entrance.

"It is Hazel," Dr. Laurent said needlessly. "She appears to be distressed."

Jim squinted, sitting up on the seat for a better view. He assumed, at first, that she must have been waiting in order to assist with the new patients, but from the agitated way she held herself, shoulders high, hands clasped, he could tell something was wrong.

Before the wagon stopped, she hurried toward them, walking alongside as they drew to a stop. "Dr. Jackson, you must come at once. You must help Jakinda."

"Has something happened?"

"Blood. She has blood in her urine and her tears."

Dr. Laurent's breath came out in a hiss.

Miss Thornton twisted her fingers together. "Dr. Ruiz says nothing can be done, but there must be something. Please, you must come."

"Dr. Ruiz can be trusted to evaluate the patient accurately." Jim climbed out of the wagon and started toward the rear, where orderlies were already unloading the wounded. "I'm sorry. But if he says there is nothing . . ." He motioned for Lucía to help one of the men attempting to climb down from the wagon.

"Dr. Jackson, please." Miss Thornton touched his arm.

The tremor in her voice pierced him. He turned and saw her eyes were red and wet with unspilled tears. Her hand was shaking on his arm.

He glanced to where Dr. Laurent and Lucía were giving directions, sorting the patients either for surgery or to the ward to wait. The other nurses and Dr. Ruiz had joined them. He looked back at Miss Thornton, acquiescing. He supposed he could spare a moment.

She rushed through the doors ahead of him.

Jim followed, hurrying to keep up as they walked quickly through the stone passageways to the West ward.

"I discovered the blood hours ago," she said, speaking quickly. "Just after lunch. Since then she has developed a fever."

"Has her pain worsened?"

"Yes. She seemed to be in much more pain today. She could hardly sit up for a drink of water."

Miss Thornton spoke with assurance, and Jim couldn't help but notice how her confidence had grown in the short time since she'd arrived.

When they reached Jakinda's bedside, Jim saw a cooling rag had been placed on her head. He touched her cheek. Her skin was hot and her breathing shallow. "Has her temperature been taken recently?" He felt her wrist for a pulse. It came fast but very weak.

"About half an hour ago." Miss Thornton handed him the chart.

He glanced at the numbers. Blood pressure was low—severely so. And her temperature had risen significantly.

Orderlies hurried by, pushing a gurney into an operating room. Dr. Ruiz hurried after, rolling up his sleeves.

Jim looked back at the chart, seeing Dr. Ruiz had given Jakinda a higher dose of morphine. He nodded. It was exactly what he would have done. He saw a bit of blood on her lips and in the corners of her eyes.

"She needs surgery," Miss Thornton said. "You can stop the bleeding inside."

Jim set the chart on the bed and turned to the nurse. Her eyes were wide, and she looked nearly frantic. "Miss Thornton, her organs are failing. Surgery won't . . . it won't restore them."

"Perhaps there is still time. You could try." Miss Thornton's voice was getting higher.

"I'm sorry. At this point, surgery would do more harm than good."

Her gaze darted back and forth between Jim and the patient, and she blinked rapidly, looking as though she were searching for an alternative. "Will she . . . ?" She breathed heavily. "Is there a chance that . . . ?"

Jim didn't answer. He only shook his head.

Miss Thornton pressed her lips together and wrapped her arms around herself.

"She's not in pain any longer," he said. "We will keep administering the morphine regularly until . . ."

She turned away, swiping at her cheeks as she moved around to the other side of the bed. Taking the damp rag from Jakinda's forehead, she dipped it into a basin, wrung it out, and replaced it gently.

The baby stirred in her sleep, and Miss Thornton rubbed her back until she calmed.

Although she kept her face turned away, he saw her tears. "Come," Jim said. "She is resting now. You can check in on her soon. But, for now, there is plenty to be done." Work would be a welcome distraction for Miss Thornton.

She raised her gaze to his, her chin quivering. "What would you have me do, then, Dr. Jackson?" Her voice was resigned.

"The patients who've just arrived are, for the most part, English."

Miss Thornton blinked, looking surprised.

"They will have difficulty speaking with the majority of the medical staff, as you can imagine. But between you, Dr. Laurent, and myself, we should be able to facilitate communication."

"Yes, of course."

"Lucía will be grateful for your assistance." He motioned for her to join him, and they started from the ward to the entry hall, which was acting in its new role as a patient reception area.

At the doorway, Miss Thornton glanced back, but she straightened her shoulders and continued on.

They found Lucía exactly where Jim had expected her to be, in the entryway, directing the other nurses.

A young soldier with thick straw-colored hair and a sunburned face was holding a wad of rags against his arm. "I need to find my commander, Nurse. Captain Wilmington. Do you know where he is?"

Lucía directed him to wait until his arm could be stitched, but of course he couldn't understand. He continued to ask about his commanding officer.

Miss Thornton crossed the room. "My name is Hazel Thornton, Private. Come, sit here. Lucía will repair the damage to your arm, and I will make inquiries about Captain Wilmington."

Relief relaxed the young man's face. "You speak English." He sat on the floor where she directed him.

"This is Lucía," Miss Thornton said, moving a lamp closer for the head nurse to see the injury better. "And what is your name?"

"Jenkins," the young man said. "You'll find Captain Wilmington?"

"I'll do my best, Private Jenkins."

Jim remained for a moment, taking a quick assessment of the patients before he started toward the surgery. When he left, he could hear Miss Thornton speaking to Lucía in her broken Spanish and then translating as well as she was able for the soldiers.

As he walked, he analyzed the strange combination of emotions that had taken over his mind and heart. He was extremely pleased with Miss Thornton's progress as a nurse—proud of her. She worked extremely hard and cared deeply for her patients. But with the caring came the inevitable pain. Seeing it and being unable to fix it frustrated him. He ached, seeing her hurt. And it would only get worse. Jakinda wouldn't last long.

But knowing that in her desperation, Miss Thornton had come to *him* . . . his insides warmed pleasantly at the thought.

That evening, Jim was passing through the East ward on his way to the kitchen when he heard raised voices. He changed direction, hurrying past the other beds until he reached the far end, where the nurses were gathered. Mikel's father and Camila were arguing in Basque. The man's face was red. He spoke loudly as the nurse tried to placate him.

Miss Thornton stood between Mikel's bed and the one next to it, holding a pitcher of water and a glass as if she'd been interrupted in the act of pouring. She had backed as close to the wall as possible.

Lucía was next to her. Or, rather, in *front* of her, as if she were protecting the young lady from the angry man.

Hazel's face was pale. She breathed deeply, as if trying to calm herself.

"What is the meaning of this?" Jim said in Spanish. "Explain yourself, sir."

"I will not allow this nurse to treat my son." He jabbed his finger toward Miss Thornton.

"And why is that?" Jim asked.

"I heard her speaking with the soldier." He pointed with his chin toward the patient in the bed beside Mikel's. It was Private Jenkins. "She is working with the enemy." Mikel's father glared at Miss Thornton. "*Británica!* You stay away from my son."

Lucía stepped further in front of Miss Thornton, and Camila moved so she blocked the young woman as well. Lucía spoke again in Basque, and although Jim couldn't understand her words, by her tone, he knew she wasn't complimenting the man's red beret.

Mikel's father argued back, pointing to the British soldier and back to Miss Thornton as he did.

"Enough," Jim said. "This is a hospital, sir, and the only reason you have been allowed to remain here with your son is because of this nurse's wishes."

Mikel's father started to argue again, but Jim cut him off. "*¡Alto!*" His voice echoed through the high ceilings of the stone hall. "Check on the baby, if you please, Miss Thornton," he said in English.

She edged between the beds, keeping her distance from the angry man. When she passed Jim, their gazes met, and he smiled, hoping to reassure her.

The corners of her mouth moved very slightly, but he recognized the gratitude in the expression. She set the cup and pitcher on the table and hurried away.

Once she'd left, Jim sent Lucía for the orderlies and rounded on Mikel's father. "If you wish for your son to remain in the care of this hospital, you will both respect this staff."

"This staff?" Mikel's father's face reddened further. "A British nurse, an American doctor, and Spanish nurses . . ." He snorted. "How can I trust my only son to your care?"

Although he acted aggressive, there was fear in the man's eyes.

Jim reined in his own anger, calming his voice. "I promise you your son is safe here. The International Red Cross chooses no sides. We assist without discrimination. Within these walls is only neutrality."

The man's eyes narrowed. "And what happens when he leaves? The *liberales* lie in wait to take us prisoner when we return to the hills."

Jim hadn't known that. But it made sense that the Spanish Army would intercept the returning soldiers. Part of him wished to say that what happened outside of the hospital was not his problem, while another part wanted to reassure the man that he would find a way to return them safely to their camps. Neither one felt right. "Mikel is safe here," he repeated. And for now, that was all he could promise. "But the other patients as well as the medical staff must feel safe as well." Seeing the orderlies from the corner of his eye, he motioned the men forward. "And for this reason, I will not allow any more visitors."

The men escorted Mikel's father from the ward.

Luckily, aside from some colorful insults, he didn't put up a fight.

Jim wondered briefly where the man was living if he could not return to the Carlist camps, but he did not let himself think about it for long. The hospital was his primary concern.

He turned to Mikel, noticing the young man's pallor compared to his flushed father. "If you wish to remain under my care, you will treat the staff and the other patients with respect. Do you understand?"

Mikel nodded.

"I have your word?"

"Sí."

Jim studied the man's expression but saw no sign of defiance. He actually looked too exhausted to argue.

"Good." Jim glanced briefly over the young man's chart. He was healing, but his pain level was still high. Hardly surprising. He considered the limited supply of morphine locked in the apothecary cabinet and wondered when it might be replenished. He tapped his pencil on the chart as he made calculations. They would surely run out within the next few weeks. A shipment could come at any time. But if it didn't . . . He blew out a breath and made a note in the young man's chart to increase his dosage. It was just another decision that felt like a gamble.

Lucía returned, and Jim gave her the chart.

Her brows raised when she saw the change, but she didn't comment.

"The patients need to be separated," Jim said. "The Carlists have a difficult time trusting, and with good reason. Have the English and Spanish soldiers moved into the West ward." He glanced along the row of patients and saw Dr. Laurent speaking with Miss Westbrook. "And English civilians as well." He didn't want a repeat of the anger that had been shown to Miss Thornton directed at her older friend. Searching for the young nurse, Jim looked toward Jakinda's bed, but Miss Thornton wasn't there.

He found her, finally, in the cloister. The night was brisk, but she wore a shawl. She sat on the bench, where he'd found her before with Miss Westbrook. Moonlight glowed off the rows of white sheets that rippled in the breeze, and off Miss Thornton's apron and nursing cap, turning them a silver-blue color. Overhead, the stars were bright. Jim stepped lightly on the path, not wanting to make a noise that would disturb the serenity of the setting.

Seeing him, Miss Thornton shifted, moving as if she would stand.

"Don't rise." Jim stretched out his hand.

She stilled, watching as he drew closer.

A shadow fell across her face, but her eyes reflected the moonlight.

"May I?" He motioned to the spot next to her on the bench.

"Of course, Dr. Jackson."

Her tone was even, not betraying her feelings, which he imagined must be anything but peaceful. She slid a bit to the side.

Jim sat. He stretched his legs in front of him and leaned his head back to look at the stars. He pondered how to begin, not wanting to dislodge any emotions she might be holding in check. After a moment, he decided upon a safe course.

"I found this and assumed it belonged to you." He took the picture from his pocket, feeling a stab of regret as he handed it to her. His bedside table would be sadly lacking without it.

"Oh, thank you." She took it, holding it with both hands in her lap. "I must have left it behind when I brought it to show Nella—Miss Westbrook." She tipped the picture so the moon lit the image within the frame. "It is for my father. A Christmas gift."

Her father. The wave of relief that crashed over him rendered him speechless.

She glanced at him, sliding the picture into her apron pocket.

"You were traveling to London to see your father?" Jim had never asked the reason for Miss Thornton's journey, nor had he inquired about the destination. In fact, he didn't know where she was traveling from either. Why had he not thought to ask before now?

"It is a rather complicated story," she said. "I left London at the beginning of December to join my father in the Canary Islands for Christmas. The officers have a private villa there, you see, for such familial visits." She folded her hands together. "When Nella and I arrived in Cádiz, Captain Bryant met us at the station. Apparently there was an emergency in the Gold Coast—that is where Father is stationed—and he was not able to meet us after all. He couldn't be spared."

Although she tried to hide it, Jim could hear the disappointment in her voice.

"The captain was traveling home to Northumberland on leave, and he accompanied us on our return journey."

She had traveled nearly fifteen hundred miles, only to have to turn around and go home? Jim was indignant on her behalf. How could a man expect his daughter to travel through a war zone, not bother to meet her when she arrived, and send her back with a stranger to accompany her? The entire journey would have taken weeks. His initial assessment of Miss Thornton in her fancy gown felt cruel now. She was just a young lady hoping to spend a holiday with her father. Her plans had been disrupted long before the dynamite. "That must have been a disappointment."

"It was."

Jim waited, unsure of what to say next. He wished she would continue her sentence, tell him that while it was initially a disappointment, the unexpected destination and their resulting acquaintance had more than made up for it. But she didn't say that.

"I sent Mikel's father away," he said.

"That wasn't necessary," she replied. "The poor man is only angry because he worries about his son. It must have been frightening to see the same soldiers who nearly killed Mikel in the very hospital where he was being treated, and then for his caregiver to speak to his enemies in their own language . . . I understand why he acted how he did."

Jim was again impressed by the depth of her compassion, even for a person who had, not an hour earlier, screamed obscenities and threats. "The hospital must be a safe place," he said. "For everyone."

She nodded her understanding.

After a moment of silence, Miss Thornton turned toward him, her knees nearly bumping into his as she did. "Dr. Jackson, before, the way I spoke to you in your office . . . I shouldn't have said what I did. I should have known you wouldn't just leave a baby behind. I was just impatient, I suppose. And stubborn. I apologize—for all of it. But especially for how I spoke to you."

Jim was surprised. Had this been weighing on her mind all this time? He considered her words. "Impatient?" He raised his brows in an exaggerated tease. "Is that your justification for racing alone into a building that could have at any moment fallen down your head?"

She smiled the slightest bit. "I did confess to being stubborn as well."

"One might say *reckless* is a more appropriate description."

She tipped her head, studying him, and seeing that he wasn't reprimanding her, the smile remained. "Perhaps we could compromise . . . *dedicated*?"

Jim laughed. "I can agree to that." He held out a hand to shake.

Miss Thornton took it. Her hands were small with delicate bones, and her skin was soft. She gave a shake, bowing her head as she did so, as if to seal the deal, and returned her hand to her lap.

Jim wasn't certain what to do with his own hand now. What had he been doing with it before? What appeared natural? He put it on his leg but thought it might look strange, so he wove his fingers together, resting them between his knees. That felt strange as well. Where did he usually put his hands?

"Why don't you call me Hazel?"

Her question caught him off guard, and he looked up, forgetting about his awkward hands that didn't seem to belong anywhere. "I beg your pardon?"

"You call all the other nurses by their Christian names, but still I am Miss Thornton. Is it because you do not consider me qualified for this position?"

"Of course not."

"Or . . . is it because . . . ?" Her voice trailed off, and she looked back down at her folded hands.

Even in the moonlight Jim could see that her cheeks were pink.

"Is it because . . . what?" he said, prompting her to continue.

"I apologize, Doctor. I shouldn't have said anything."

Her voice was strained. She sounded distressed—or perhaps embarrassed. Jim wasn't about to let this go. "I disagree. Clear communication is essential for people who work closely together. If there is an issue, we should resolve it."

"Because you do not like me?" Her words came out in a rush, and she didn't raise her head to see his reaction.

"I . . ." Jim didn't know what to say. He stared as his mind fumbled with words.

"I know it sounds childish," she said. Apparently, now that she'd said it, she was going to finish what she'd begun. "But it's been apparent ever since I arrived that you disapprove of me."

"Miss Thornton—"

"I know I'm not entirely trained as a nurse, but I am learning. I borrowed an anatomy book from Camila, and I study every night with the Spanish-to-English dictionary."

"Miss Thornton—"

"And it bothers you that I keep doing things wrong. I allowed Mikel's father to stay even though you specifically said that visitors aren't allowed."

"Miss Thornton—"

"But I work hard, and I am getting faster at laundry and at replacing bandages and—"

"Hazel."

The sound of her Christian name stopped her words midsentence. She paused, her mouth still open.

"If I gave you that impression," Jim said, "it is because I am not a man who communicates emotions well." He swallowed. "And because I feel completely the opposite."

She closed her mouth, tipping her head to the side and looking confused as she tried to make sense of what he'd said.

"It is extremely inappropriate, given our particular situation, and of course unprofessional," Jim continued, feeling both brave and terrified, which should by all reasoning be impossible. "But I am afraid I cannot control it." His wayward hand reached out and took hers. "I like you very much." His voice lowered as he leaned closer.

"You do?"

She didn't pull away her hand, which he took to be a good sign. "I think you are an exceptional nurse, and I am sorry I caused you to doubt it."

Her lips pinched together in a shy expression. "Shall we agree to dispense with the apologies, Doctor? Between the two of us, we have apologized for everything beneath the heavens this evening." She glanced down at their joined hands and then looked back at him. "I am fond of you as well." She leaned the slightest bit toward him.

In the moonlight, Jim could see each of her pale lashes. They glowed, surrounding her blue eyes like rays. Small freckles were on her fair cheeks. He brushed back a strand of hair that had come loose from her cap, his fingers skimming her jaw. He came closer, his pulse pounding as he watched for her reaction.

Hazel moved the slightest bit to rest her cheek against his hand, her eyes closing.

Jim hesitated for only an instant before he kissed her, the soft press of their lips sending a jolt through him like an electric shock. His skin went hot where they touched, his chest expanded, and his thoughts evaporated. All his concerns about the hospital, his doubts, his pain, his loss, all of it faded, and there was nothing but the two of them.

The kiss lasted only a short moment, but it was different from anything he'd felt before. It was nothing like a schoolboy's stolen kiss or a young man's lighthearted flirtation. This kiss changed everything. It changed him, deepening the emotions he already feared had grown beyond his capacity to manage. And his immediate instinct was to put up walls against this fresh vulnerability, especially against the glimmer of hope that had forced its way inside his heart. Because any plan for a future with Hazel was nothing more than a wish. She wouldn't stay here once her friends were well enough to leave. Her home was in London. And he could imagine her there, caring for patients in a hospital that was not under constant threat and was lacking basic medical necessities. He sighed. Hazel deserved better than this. Wishes were for fools.

CHAPTER 11

Hazel remained on the bench in the cloister after Dr. Jackson left. She touched her lips, feeling as if they must be buzzing. An evening breeze blew over her, but it didn't cool the heat that spread inside of her. She leaned back, watching the moon and trying to make sense of what had happened. And, even more, trying to understand her reaction to it.

Dr. Jackson's declaration had come as a surprise. She had been certain he held no pleasant feelings toward her. But this . . . A delicious shiver moved through her at the memory of his touch. Even more surprising than his words—than his kiss, even—was her reaction to them. It was as if his admission had awoken something inside her. But that something didn't seem to be new. It had been there all along, and she'd simply not recognized it. What was it? Attraction? Tenderness? When she tried to give it a name, none felt fully correct. Her sentiment was a combination of emotions, some completely new and others familiar but, in this case, shaped differently.

As she considered, another emotion entered the mix. A feeling of uncertainty made a cold emptiness where there had been a pleasant warmth. Their situation was temporary. As soon as Captain Bryant and Nella were able to resume travel, Hazel would leave. Dr. Jackson must know that. He must know there was no future for them together. Did he hope for a short-lived . . . tryst? Her cheeks went hot at the thought. She didn't think he was the type of man for such a thing. And his affection had felt genuine. But what did she know of men? Aside from her father and uncle—and now Captain Bryant—she'd hardly spent time with any man. Perhaps this was exactly how a tryst happened. And while the idea of a secret romance in a foreign land was exciting, the idea didn't sit easy with her.

The emotions awoken with Dr. Jackson's kiss were too real—too strong to simply be played around with and tossed aside when the time came. His feelings must not be the same as hers.

She left the cloister, feeling naive, embarrassed, and extremely foolish.

Seeing Dr. Laurent in the passageway, she called out, "Doctor, if you have a moment . . ."

He turned, and his round face lit up. "Good evening, mademoiselle. I always have a moment for you." When she got closer, his brows rose, and he looked closely at her. "You look flushed, *ma chérie*. Are you unwell?"

"Just tired, I imagine," she said, waving her hand in a lighthearted manner.

"Ah, oui. Zhat must be it." But he continued to study her.

She didn't think he believed her attempt to appear carefree, but she continued on. "Doctor, I helped Jakinda write a letter. It is for her husband, but I don't know how to send it to him. I'd hoped Mikel's father might take it, but with her condition . . . declining"—Hazel swallowed at the tightness in her throat—"I thought he should have it as soon as possible." Her voice was unsteady as she took the envelope from her apron pocket.

"Oui." Dr. Laurent pursed his lips as if he were considering her words. "Zhe priest, padre de Leon, he should be able to travel undisturbed to Santa Rosa."

The idea hadn't even occurred to Hazel. It was perfect. Nobody—from either army—would bother a churchman. It would be the most natural thing in the world for him to visit a fellow man of the cloth whose town was recovering from an attack. "Do you think he'd be willing?" she asked.

"I believe he would," Dr. Laurent said. His face had softened, and the sympathy in it made her throat tighten again. "I will speak to him if you would like."

"Thank you," Hazel said, relieved that she didn't need to attempt the communication. She was so tired, and the idea of explaining the letter, the baby, and Jakinda's condition in a language she had only the most tenuous grasp on . . . it was more than she was capable of tonight.

"You are so very compassionate." Dr. Laurent put a hand on her shoulder. "But zhere is another side of zhe coin, no? With zhe caring, your heart, it is open to hurting."

A tear slipped down Hazel's cheek. "I shouldn't have allowed myself to grow so close to her—to either of them. It was a mistake, wasn't it?" A real nurse would never have developed such an attachment to a patient and her child.

"It was not a mistake at all," Dr. Laurent said. "Once you lose this"—he tapped his chest—"once you stop seeing each patient as an individual, once you stop loving, you lose your empathy. And you must never lose zhat. Zhe way you care for your patients, your soft heart, it makes you special."

"Thank you," Hazel whispered, taking his offered handkerchief and wiping her eyes. Once she had control of her voice again, she smiled. "I am very grateful to you, both for your kind words and for seeing to the letter."

"Of course, mademoiselle. It is my great pleasure."

Dr. Laurent's encouragement and wisdom touched her deeply, and Hazel felt a strong desire to embrace him. But she had already kissed one doctor this evening, she reminded herself. If she was going to preserve her reputation, she needed to remember to act professionally. She folded the handkerchief and returned it to him, bidding her friend good night.

As she continued along the passageway, Hazel met Camila, who was carrying Nerea on the baby's nightly constitutional. The nurse had a way of walking with a gentle bounce that soothed the infant. Hazel whispered a greeting and peeked at the sleeping baby before she continued on. Before retiring, she would visit her traveling companions and Jakinda to bid them good night, as was her custom.

She lit a lamp and walked through the West ward, stopping at Captain Bryant's bedside.

He smiled when he saw her, but his lamp was dark, and he squinted at the light hers gave.

"How does your head feel, Captain?" She set down the lamp on a table away from his bed, coming closer in the dim light.

"Aches a bit," he said. "But getting better every day."

"I'm glad to hear it." Hazel tried to keep her voice cheerful, but his headaches were worrying. The day before, Captain Bryant had requested something to read, but she saw that the books and newspapers she'd brought hadn't been moved from the chair next to his bed. Reading must be painful. "Rest now, and I'll visit tomorrow."

"I look forward to it," Captain Bryant said. His eyes were already closed. She smoothed the sheets over him, patted his hand, and bid him good night.

Hazel continued on, discovering that Nella had been transferred to the West ward. In fact, it seemed quite a few patients had been moved around. Nella sat in a chair, her bound foot resting on her bed as she knitted. "There you are," she said when she saw Hazel. "I was starting to worry I wouldn't see you tonight."

Hazel sat on the bed.

"How are you feeling?" Nella asked.

"That's what I was about to ask you," Hazel said.

"Yes, I know. But . . ." She squinted, setting her knitting in her lap. "But your well-being is important too. You look . . . different, I suppose. Has something happened?"

The blush returned to Hazel's cheeks, and she considered telling her friend about the kiss, but just as soon as the thought came into her head, she decided against it. Part of her wanted to keep the moment to herself, and another part was embarrassed. Besides, she had seen Nella with Dr. Laurent often enough, and if he were to learn about it, he would surely be disappointed at her lack of decorum. And Dr. Laurent's opinion was important to her.

"It's Jakinda," she said. "Her condition is worsening."

"I'm sorry, dear." Nella squeezed Hazel's hand. "I know it must be difficult for you."

"How do you like the West ward?" Hazel changed the subject before her tears returned. "I imagine a change of scenery is welcome."

"It is indeed," Nella said. She swept her arm around as if giving a tour of her deluxe accommodations. "Dr. Laurent assures me this is the most desirable bed, right here near the door, where I can catch an occasional breeze. Can you imagine building a structure of this size with so few opening windows?" She shook her head and used a book to fan herself. "Apparently the monks didn't intend for middle-aged women to be taking up residence here." She made a face.

Hazel laughed, happy to see Nella's humor had returned. "I imagine they didn't."

They chatted for a few moments longer, and then Hazel helped Nella with the crutches, and the pair walked down to the privy and back. The short trip was enough to tire the older woman, and instead of returning to her knitting, she lay down in the bed.

Hazel pulled up her sheets, gave her a drink of water, and made sure her pillows were comfortable.

"I don't know what I'll do when I don't have you to spoil me," Nella said. "A person can get very used to being pampered."

"Don't worry," Hazel said, turning down the lamp on the bedside table. "I'm not going anywhere. And when the time does come that you're able to travel, we're going together."

Nella opened her mouth to reply and hesitated for a moment. An instant later, she closed her eyes. "You're right, dear."

Hazel bid Nella good night. She cut through the cloister and went into the East ward. Her stomach felt tense as she worried she might encounter Dr. Jackson. What would happen when they inevitably did meet? What would she say? Should she act as if nothing had taken place in the cloister? What if he acted as if nothing had occurred? Would they continue on as they had before?

She reached Jakinda's bedside and saw the woman was sleeping. Her fever had not gone away, and her breathing was still shallow, but at least she appeared not to be in any pain. Nerea slept beside her in the little basket.

"Good night," Hazel whispered and started away, grateful that she would at last be able to sleep. She must indeed be tired when the hard cot in her bedchamber sounded so inviting. After only a few steps, she paused, feeling a pull to return.

She came back, pulling the chair closer, and sat beside Jakinda. There was something about her breathing that sounded different, and Hazel knew she couldn't leave. "I hope you are sleeping," she said in a soft voice. "But if you can somehow hear me, just know I am right beside you. You are not alone."

She took Jakinda's hand, feeling the heat of the fever on her palm. A lullaby came to her mind, something her ayah used to sing. Hazel hummed the melody, careful to keep the sound soft in the ward of sleeping patients—especially for the baby. She thought she felt Jakinda squeeze her hand, but perhaps it was only her imagination. But just in case the squeeze was real and an indication that Jakinda enjoyed the sound, Hazel continued.

"Hazel, wake up." The voice was deep, and there was something familiar in it. The feeling of a hand on her back broke into her consciousness. "Hazel."

Realizing she'd fallen asleep, she blinked herself awake. She had slumped forward sometime during the night, and her head lay on her arm. Her hand still held Jakinda's.

Dr. Jackson's voice came again. "Come, now. She is gone." He pulled her hand away and brought her to her feet.

Hazel was still blinking, feeling as if her thoughts were moving too slowly.

Dr. Jackson had one arm around her waist, helping her stand. She looked at him and then at the priest on the other side of the bed.

The man was muttering, holding a rosary in one hand and making the sign of the cross with the other. When he finished, he pulled the sheet up to cover Jakinda's face.

She was dead.

Hazel's heart was heavy. She laid her head on Dr. Jackson's chest, and he embraced her. She felt numb.

"There's nothing more to be done," Dr. Jackson said, voice rumbling beneath her ear. "Lucía will see to the body, and—"

Hazel pulled away. "Her scarf." She moved to the other side of the bed, where the scarf sat on the table. Someone must have removed it as they'd tried to cool her fever. She pulled the sheet down and wrapped the scarf carefully back around Jakinda's head, tying it at the nape of her neck. She studied the woman's face in the lamplight. The tightness around her eyes was gone, and her lips were slack. She looked peaceful.

Hazel peeked into the basket, but the baby wasn't there. She was most likely being walked through the halls or fed.

She returned the sheet to cover Jakinda's face and glanced at the folded clothes on the shelf beneath the table. They were cleaned and mended, and she'd imagined Jakinda would have been pleased to see they were taken care of when she dressed to return home.

The sight of Jakinda's one shoe struck something inside Hazel, cracking it and allowing all her sorrow to pour out. She pressed a hand against her mouth, closing her eyes tight against the rush of tears. The idea that Jakinda wouldn't be buried with a proper pair of shoes felt like more than she could bear.

Dr. Jackson took her away, guiding her from the ward and through the passageway toward her bedchamber. "You need to rest," he said.

"We left her shoe." She choked out the words. "It is still buried in the rocks by her house."

"Nothing can be done about it tonight." Dr. Jackson didn't pause but continued to lead her along the darkened passageway. "Let your mind be at ease." Lamplight cast shadows over the high arches of the stone ceilings. He tightened his arm around her.

When they reached the right door, she stopped. "It is here." She took the key from her pocket but stopped. She couldn't bring herself to open it. "I don't want . . ." She glanced at him, but she was too tired for embarrassment. "Please, I don't want to be alone." The thought of Jakinda in the cold chamber beneath the hospital sent a chill over her. She swallowed at the ache as she imagined the empty bed with the little basket beside it.

"Are you hungry?" A shadow covered his face, concealing his expression, but his voice was gentle.

Hazel shook her head. "Might we walk? Just for a few moments, until I feel calm?"

"As long as you need." He took her hand, waiting for her to choose the direction they would take.

Hazel turned back toward the main area of the hospital. She walked slowly, letting her thoughts wind down. This must be how Nerea felt in the evenings. Anxious and simply in need of a reassuring stroll around the passageways to soothe her.

"I spoke to Dr. Laurent," Dr. Jackson said. "He told me padre de Leon plans to go to Santa Rosa at first light with the letter you wrote."

A sting of disappointment bit into Hazel's heart. "I'd hoped the letter would reach Ramiro sooner—to give him an opportunity to come to the hospital before . . ."

"I know."

She sighed at the reminder that the letter would arrive just a day too late. "What will happen now with Nerea?"

"A relative will raise her, I imagine," Dr. Jackson said. "If her father is away fighting."

Hazel wondered if the relative would know to warm the milk just until it was skin temperature. And would they have the patience to walk the baby for hours every night?

Dr. Jackson stopped in the entryway, turning toward her. The lamps beside the large oak doors flickered, giving just enough light to illuminate a small space while it cast dark shadows around the edges of the chamber. "You've done all you can, Hazel," he said. "Death is the natural end of things." He took her other hand so he held them both, keeping her facing him.

"I know you're right." She searched her thoughts, trying to put them into words, trying to understand what it was that upset her so badly. "I just wanted it to be different." She felt silly at the simple words. But Dr. Jackson remained silent, listening, so she continued. "When I heard her cry out and found her there, buried beneath the rocks, I felt as though I was meant to save her. I thought I'd been led to her by . . . by something greater than myself." She looked away. "I thought God had intended for me to find her." She hadn't meant to share that thought with anyone. And now that she'd said it aloud, she feared she sounded like a zealot. She glanced at him, wondering what he thought. But he simply listened. "But I didn't save her. So I either failed or wasn't led to her after all."

"Perhaps you were meant to save her baby," Dr. Jackson said. "You gave a dying mother a few additional days with her daughter as well as the assurance that her child would be cared for when she was gone. You even gave her an opportunity to send a final letter to her husband." His hands tightened, as if he were stressing the importance of his words. "I believe if you were able to ask Jakinda, she would tell you there is nothing more meaningful to her than what you did."

"I'd not thought of that."

"You did a good thing, Hazel. And you should rest easy knowing the comfort you gave a dying woman."

Hazel's eyes burned, and she didn't trust her voice, so she didn't answer. She turned and continued to walk through the hospital passageways, holding on to Dr. Jackson's hand. His words gave her a bit of peace. She walked closer to him and rested her head on his shoulder as they continued down the passageway.

"Thank you." She led them back toward her bedchamber. "I feel much better now." She drew out the key and turned it in the lock.

"And you will feel even better after you sleep."

Hazel released Dr. Jackson's hand, but instead of entering her bedchamber, she embraced him.

His arms tightened around her, and they remained together for a long moment before she pulled away and bid him good night. The feel of his embrace lingered, giving her comfort as she laid on the cot and went to sleep.

CHAPTER 12

The next day, Jim passed Hazel occasionally as they went about their hospital duties, but the two never found a moment alone. When he did see her, she seemed more pale than usual and had dark smudges beneath her eyes. He wondered if she'd managed to sleep at all.

In the East ward, he paused at the now-empty bed where Jakinda had died, and considered what Hazel had said the night before. Jim understood her words all too well. He'd experienced the same feelings with patients he'd believed without a doubt he was meant to heal. There were times he'd felt guided by something larger than himself in the surgery, certain his movements were being choreographed by a divine being. And when the patients hadn't survived, he'd wondered if it had all been an elaborate work of his imagination. Or possibly he had only his own pride to blame for his frustration. It was extremely arrogant to believe himself a performer of miracles.

In the end, it was Dr. Laurent's advice that had eased his conscience when he'd come upon Jim after a particularly tragic loss—a young boy who'd gotten caught in the crossfire at Custoza. When the lad was brought to the Red Cross Hospital, Jim had rushed to help him, removing shrapnel from his hip and closing the lacerations in record time. The wounds had been clean, the instruments sterile, but somehow, over the next hours, infection and fever had developed. The boy had died from sepsis within twelve hours.

Jim had stood by the boy's bedside, searching through the chart, trying to discover where he'd gone wrong, when Dr. Laurent joined him.

"I can't understand it." Jim heard the crack in his own voice. "I followed the procedures exactly. I know I did." He rubbed his eyes.

"Zhen, you can set your mind at ease." Dr. Laurent took the chart from Jim's hand and set it on the bed.

"But he should have lived," Jim said. "I should have been able to save him." His throat ached with the shame of failure.

"We must allow God to make zhat decision," Dr. Laurent said. "Or, if you prefer something less spiritual, you may call it fate or providence. We do not control zhese things. A doctor can do no more zhan give his very best effort to the patients in his care. After zhat . . ." He raised his eyes to the heavens. "It is out of our hands."

Jim could see the wisdom in his friend's words even then, but it had taken him years to arrive at the point of believing them. For so long, he'd felt that if he'd only worked faster or arrived earlier or noticed a symptom sooner, he could have saved another life. And each life he'd lost weighed on him.

Gunshots interrupted his thoughts then, sounding in the hills, followed by some blasts, but they didn't continue into the sounds of a battle. The noises had become regular over the past days, as if the Carlists and the Spanish Army were restless in their camps. Jim could sense a battle brewing.

In the afternoon, padre de Leon returned from his trip into town, accompanied by the priest from Santa Rosa, padre Cavallero. The men had traveled by donkey, and when Jim came to the entry hall to greet them, he could see they were both weary from the journey.

Lucía and some of the other nurses had arrived in the hall before him. The head nurse knelt, kissing each of the men's hands and receiving a blessing in return.

Jim greeted the men as well, shaking hands with padre Cavallero. "It is good to see you again, padre. I hope Santa Rosa is somewhat recovered."

"The people of the village are resilient," he said. "We are very grateful for your help, Doctor."

"You must be hungry and tired," Lucía said. "Please, follow me to the kitchen, or if you prefer, I will have supper delivered to you after you rest."

"It can wait," padre Cavallero said, waving his hand as if he couldn't be bothered with such matters as his immediate comfort. "Where is the baby?"

Lucía looked at the other nurses, raising her thick brows in a question.

"I believe she is with Hazel," Camila said.

"Will you bring the baby to me?" the priest asked. "And once I have seen her, I hope you will spare me a few moments, Doctor."

Jim inclined his head in agreement.

Lucía flicked her fingers toward the passageways, and Camila and Sofia hurried off down different passageways in search of Nerea.

While the women were gone, Jim brought chairs from the doctors' office and convinced the priests to sit.

Padre de Leon was particularly grateful. He was not as young as his companion, and the journey had been taxing to his body. He sat with a wince and a groan, rubbing his lower back and muttering that he would prefer to walk next time.

A few moments later, the other nurses returned with Hazel. Her apron was damp and the baby's hair wet. She must have been giving Nerea a bath.

Padre Cavallero rose when he saw them, holding out his hands. "Ah, there she is." When Hazel came close, he cupped the baby's face, kissed the top of her head, then took her in his arms, grinning.

Hazel watched his movements closely, looking very protective, as if she didn't fully trust the man to hold the baby without dropping her.

Nerea clasped the beads that hung from the priest's neck, holding them tightly in her fist.

"You look very well, my child," the priest said, hefting her as if to judge her weight. "Healthy." He lifted his gaze to Hazel. "You have cared well for her."

"Not only myself," Hazel said in her broken Spanish. "We all"—she looked around the chamber at the others—"everyone tends to her."

"I am very grateful for it," padre Cavallero said. He turned back to the baby, adjusting his hold so he could see her face. "This, the youngest member of my flock, is a beacon of hope to the village. A sign of God's love."

The baby put the beads in her mouth, and the priest laughed, carefully prying them from her grip.

"Who will care for Nerea now?" Hazel asked.

Padre Cavallero put the beads over his shoulder, out of the baby's reach. "Her aunt, Jakinda's sister, is very anxious for the baby to be returned home."

Seeing Hazel's unconvinced expression, the priest gave her a reassuring smile. "The aunt—Iraxte Royo is her name—is very kind. She is a widow with grown children and is rather lonely, I believe. This arrangement will be good—for both of them. She will treat this little one with patience and love, as did her sister." The priest's voice became solemn as he spoke the last words. He gave the baby back to Hazel.

Hazel's expression looked worried. Perhaps a bit confused. She held Nerea closely, swaying back and forth and speaking to her in a soft voice.

Jim wondered how much of the man's words Hazel had understood. When he found a moment to speak with her, he'd make certain she knew Nerea would be well-loved.

"You will take Nerea home with you tomorrow, I assume?" Jim asked, stepping up to stand beside Hazel.

"That is what I hoped to speak with you about, Doctor." Padre Cavallero pulled his beads back around so the wooden cross rested again on his chest. He folded his hands. "I would ask a favor."

Jim frowned. He liked the man, but he couldn't let his regard impede the hospital's ability to care for the sick and wounded. "Padre Cavallero," he said, keeping a calm tone, "with respect, the hospital is not equipped to care for a baby on a long-term basis. She requires constant attention, and I cannot spare a nurse indefinitely to tend to her. Not when we could at any time have an influx of wounded who need every available hand to save their lives."

Padre Cavallero bowed his head. "Yes, God bless all those who have been taken, both by the fighting and by the cause." He crossed himself, and padre de Leon followed suit, as did Lucía and a few of the other nurses. "Our little village has lost so many." He sighed, looking utterly devastated by what the people of Santa Rosa had endured. "And now I come to the favor." He glanced at the nurses gathered in the hall and then at padre de Leon.

The other priest nodded encouragingly.

"We, myself and the people of my village, wish to bury our dead in the churchyard of Santa Rosa. I believe there are three who have passed here in the hospital since the attack five days ago."

Jim and padre de Leon confirmed. Jakinda had been the third.

"No men remain in our village to drive a wagon to the hospital to fetch them, I'm afraid." Padre Cavallero looked directly at Jim. "We hope, God willing, that you will bring our people home where they belong."

Jim dismissed the idea immediately. "They will be interred on holy ground," he said. "In the hospital's cemetery. If you would like to perform the burial rites, I'm certain padre de Leon would be happy—"

"So they are as yet not laid to rest," padre Cavallero interrupted.

"I don't believe so," Jim admitted. Bodies were kept in a cold room beneath the hospital until the orderlies and hired men from a local town could dig their graves, but with the shortage of help, he knew the more recently deceased were still not buried.

"Surely it is not too much to ask for you to bring them home to be buried with their families and those who love them," padre Cavallero pressed.

Jim opened his mouth to tell the priest that the ambulance wagons were not hearses, but he glanced at Hazel and his argument dissolved in his mouth.

She was bouncing the baby gently, smiling as she pulled her necklace from the baby's fist and tucked it inside her collar. He didn't believe she understood the conversation, but if she did, what would she say? Jim knew the answer all too well. Seeing Jakinda returned home and buried with her family would be comforting for Hazel, and while they were at it, she could deliver the baby to its relatives. Seeing that Nerea would be well tended to would go a long way to ease the young woman's worries too.

"Very well, padre," Jim said. He scratched his chin, considering his words. "I know it is often the custom for a vigil and a procession to precede a funeral, but these people have been dead for days. They should be buried as quickly as possible."

"Yes, of course," the priest responded without hesitation.

Jim was glad he didn't have to explain about the odors carried by bodies in advanced stages of decomposition. If the bodies were buried right when they arrived at the town, the funeral would follow directly, and he believed Hazel would be appreciative of the opportunity to attend.

"There are some preparations to be made, of course," Jim said. "We'll leave at first light."

"Thank you." Padre Cavallero bowed his head.

From the corner of his gaze, Jim saw the other nurses glance at one another. They had obviously not anticipated that Jim he would agree to the priest's request. He glanced at Hazel and saw that she was still occupied with keeping the baby quiet.

"Lucía will see that you are fed and shown to a room," he told padre Cavallero. "You know where the chapel is, I believe."

"Yes, thank you." Padre Cavallero kissed Nerea once more before Lucía led him away.

Padre de Leon looked pleased that they were at last finished with the conversation and he would be able to rest. He bowed his head in farewell and left, heading toward his bedchamber.

The nurses went in various directions, returning to their duties.

Seeing the others depart, Hazel started back toward the wards, but Jim stopped her. "Hazel, might I have a word?"

"Certainly, Doctor." When Hazel paused, Nerea squirmed in her arms and started to whimper. Hazel bounced the baby a bit more vigorously. "She is ready for her milk."

"I'll walk with you," Jim said. He fell into step with her, and they started in the direction of the kitchen. "I don't know what of that conversation you understood."

"Not much," Hazel admitted. "But I believe whatever you said pleased the priest."

"Padre Cavallero asked if we might deliver Jakinda and the others—the other deceased from their village—back to Santa Rosa for burial."

"And what did you tell him?"

"I told him we would bring them tomorrow."

"Oh." Hazel blinked. "That was very considerate of you. Does the hospital often perform such a service?"

"Not typically." Jim shrugged, cramming his hands into his coat pockets.

She looked at him thoughtfully but didn't say anything more.

When they came to the kitchen, Alona looked up from the dough she was kneading and smiled. "Hola, Hazel. Hola, *mi amor*." She said the last sentence in a high singsong voice, leaving no doubt that she was speaking to Nerea.

Hazel brought the baby close so Alona could make faces at her, speaking words Jim couldn't translate, but by her tone and the lilt of her voice, he understood perfectly. Baby speak was a universal language.

"The milk is warmed," Alona said to Hazel.

Seeing Alona's hands were covered in dough, Hazel gave the baby to Jim and went to where a pan of milk sat on the preparation table beside a baby bottle.

Jim tried to mimic her bouncing motion, but he must have bounced either too softly or too hard. Nerea started to wail.

Alona gave Jim a disappointed look, then started talking to the baby again, babbling in her high baby voice.

Nerea's crying stopped, and she settled, grabbing the lapel of Jim's coat with her fist and putting it into her mouth.

Hazel dipped a spoon into the milk, dabbing a drop onto the inside of her wrist. She must have approved of the temperature, because she poured the milk into the bottle and attached a rubber feeding nipple. But instead of taking the baby, Hazel thanked Alona, bid her farewell, and motioned for Jim to follow her from the kitchen.

In the laundry, Hazel spread a flannel blanket over a folding table. She took the baby from Jim, and with expert movements, she wrapped Nerea up inside until only her head was uncovered. Last, Hazel gave her the bottle, swaying a bit from side to side as the baby drank. She cooed softly, holding her tightly.

As Jim watched the tender moment, he felt a pang. Telling her the next part would be difficult.

"Perhaps you heard padre Cavallero speak of Nerea's aunt, Jakinda's sister."

She glanced up at him and returned her gaze to the baby. "I didn't fully understand what he said." She looked nervous and swallowed.

"She is a widow, her children grown. The priest assured us she is very kind." He touched the small of her back. "Nerea will be well cared for. She will be loved."

Hazel didn't look up. "And we take Nerea to her aunt tomorrow?"

"Yes."

She nodded, still keeping her face turned downward.

"Hazel?" he asked. "Are you all right?"

"Of course." She looked up at him and forced a smile.

Jim could see the tension in her eyes. He knew she cared for the baby, and he feared bidding Nerea farewell would be difficult for her.

Hazel excused herself to put the baby to sleep. She held Nerea close, humming a lullaby and walking slowly down the passageway.

As Jim watched her leave, he hoped he'd made the right decision, that visiting Santa Rosa, attending Jakinda's funeral, and meeting Nerea's aunt would soothe the hurt he saw in Hazel's eyes instead of add to her grief. He realized there was nothing he wouldn't do if it might take away her pain.

CHAPTER 13

Hazel braced her feet against the toeboard and held tightly to Nerea as they rode toward Santa Rosa the next morning. She sat between Dr. Jackson and padre Cavallero on the wagon's bench. The other ambulance wagon, bearing the bodies, was driven by the hospital orderlies and followed behind. The morning air was frigid, especially as they passed beneath shadows on the mountain road, and Hazel thought she might prefer to ride in the wagon's bed beneath the canvas bonnet with Camila and Lucía, but feeling the steady warmth of Dr. Jackson beside her, she discounted that thought immediately. She glanced up at him, receiving a warm smile that turned her insides to jelly.

Nerea was fascinated by the sights around them. She wriggled around, wanting to see everything. She stared up at the towering mountains with snow on their peaks and in their shadows, and with delight she took in the trees and fluffy clouds in the bright-blue sky. Hazel turned the baby around on her lap, giving her a better view, and watched as her deep brown eyes moved from sight to sight. After nearly an hour of travel, Nerea's eyes closed, and Hazel shifted her around into a more comfortable position, wrapping the blanket more tightly around her against the cold. She adjusted the little hat Nella had knitted, making sure it completely covered the baby's ears.

The journey was quiet, partly because it was so early in the morning, but Hazel thought it was also out of respect for the dead they transported. She was content to sit in silence, enjoying the view and allowing herself to ponder.

How much had changed since she'd gotten on the train in London weeks earlier. The circumstances around her were so extraordinary, so different from anything she'd known or imagined she would be involved in. But most surprising of all was how much Hazel herself had changed. She felt confident and capable, more so than she'd ever felt in her life. She was given difficult tasks and managed to complete them. She had become faster in her duties and more knowledgeable in her understanding of the human body and its treatment. The responsibility of caring for a wounded or ill person, for managing their symptoms and care, had seemed so daunting at first, but she'd come to trust her learning, her experience, and her colleagues.

The work had been exhausting and challenging, both physically and emotionally. She felt a heavy aching when she saw her patients' pain and fear. And Jakinda . . . Hazel's heart squeezed as she thought of the woman. She looked down at the baby in her arms, memorizing her face, her round cheeks, the way her lashes curled, her pouty lips. She would not have believed she could come to care for a child the way she cared for Nerea.

The ache inside her grew, and Hazel's eyes burned. She blinked away her tears and lifted her gaze to watch the road, realizing they'd not passed one other person on their journey. Perhaps it was typical for the road to be deserted this early in the morning. Or maybe it was because so many of the men were away fighting.

Just as she had the thought, shots rang out, echoing through the mountains. Hazel wondered if the person shooting the weapon was from Santa Rosa. Could it be a patient they'd treated? What if it were Ramiro?

More shots sounded and Nerea woke, grabbing on to Hazel's necklace. Instead of prying it from her hand, Hazel allowed the baby to hold it. She rocked her softly, speaking soft words meant to calm. Nerea gave a toothless grin that tugged at her heart. Hazel checked that the baby's ears were covered and realized that she had, without knowing it, leaned against Dr. Jackson at the sound of the gunshots. She started to sit up but glanced at him, and seeing his comforting expression, she remained where she was, glad at the reminder that he was near and she was safe. Hopefully the priest didn't notice.

They passed through a meadow crossed with hedgerows that shone with frost. Ahead, Hazel could see trails of smoke rising beyond the trees. When they rounded a bend, Santa Rosa was before them, nestled against the mountain. The towers of the church stood firm in the center of the village, the stone looking solid and timeless. Houses with black slate roofs were trimmed with red or green paint. The town was so charming in its appearance, it was hard to believe they'd suffered such devastation only a few days earlier.

As they drew near, she could see people gathered on the road at the edge of the village. Women in brightly colored peasant dresses and scarves mingled with boys and old men wearing loose trousers and berets. At a word from the priest, Dr. Jackson stopped the wagon, and they climbed out. The crowd came toward them, a child in the robe of an altar boy holding a pole topped by a gold cross.

The priest took the cross, and once the ambulance wagon carrying the deceased arrived, he motioned for it to follow, striding ahead of it in a procession. Two women walked before the priest. They wore black cloths over their hair, and each carried a basket with what appeared to be loaves of bread. Hazel was curious but didn't ask about it, not wanting to break the reverent silence with her question.

Many of the villagers greeted Nerea with quiet whispers and gentle smiles. When the ambulance wagon passed, they bowed their heads.

Hazel held Nerea close, studying the villagers and wondering which was Iraxte Royo. She felt a mixture of emotions toward this woman she'd never met, both resenting her and at the same time praying she was as wonderful and kind as the priest had told Dr. Jackson she was.

A group of women following directly behind the wagon wailed, crying out in mournful laments that made Hazel's eyes fill with tears. They pulled at their faces and clothes, and their cries echoed through the rocky peaks.

Once the mourning women passed by, the remainder of the crowd followed, walking with slow steps, their heads still bowed. Hazel and the other hospital staff joined the villagers in the procession, winding through the town.

Dr. Jackson walked beside Hazel. Once when she stumbled on the uneven road, he caught her arm and offered to carry Nerea, but Hazel just shook her head. Even though her arms were tired, she wanted every last moment with the baby. He remained close.

The path the procession took to the church was not the most direct, Hazel realized after turning down another road in the village, but the route must have some significance. Perhaps they were passing the home of each of the deceased. Footsteps clacked off the cobblestones, and by their sound, she thought many of the shoes must be made of wood.

The roads were cleared of debris. She could see the people had been hard at work, mending their village as well as they were able with the men away. Some of the homes had been repaired, while others remained as she'd seen them before, missing walls and roofs.

When they reached the churchyard, they found the graves were only partially dug. Young boys and older men with thick white hair gratefully gave their shovels to Dr. Jackson and the orderlies, who set to digging in the villagers' place.

Hazel moved to the far side of the churchyard and sat on a stone wall. She took a feeding bottle from her satchel and gave it to Nerea. Her position gave an excellent view, and she was glad to be close enough to watch the activity while remaining far enough not to intrude.

The baby fussed, not at all happy that the milk was cool, but eventually, Hazel persuaded her to drink.

Hazel looked toward the graves, searching for Dr. Jackson, but it appeared he'd gone. She wondered if he was inside the church or if someone had needed his assistance elsewhere.

Women came to the ambulance wagon then, sprinkling the dead with holy water, wrapping what appeared to be candles in the hands of the deceased and adjusting their clothing and shrouds. With the assistance of Lucía and Camila, they moved the bodies into the waiting coffins.

A quick movement from a side street drew Hazel's attention. It was Dr. Jackson. He walked to the coffins at a hurried pace, and when he arrived, he handed something to Camila. A shoe. Hazel warmed inside, and her heart expanded. He must have unearthed it in the little alleyway beside Jakinda's house. She swallowed. When he glanced toward her, she smiled her gratitude.

He gave a small wave and returned to digging. The graves were finished within a few moments.

Camila spoke to the other women, and one, a tall woman wearing a black headscarf, crouched down, putting the shoe on Jakinda's foot.

The coffins were then closed and lowered into the graves.

Hazel came to stand with the others, feeling as if Nerea should be near when her mother was buried, and Dr. Jackson joined her. "You found her shoe," Hazel said in a quiet voice.

He nodded. "It was right where you said it would be."

A rush of gratitude filled her chest and pushed up into her throat and eyes. She was overwhelmed by the emotions that accompanied her attending a funeral and parting with Nerea but also by Dr. Jackson's thoughtfulness. The action was small, and it had taken him mere minutes to perform, but to her, at this moment, it meant everything. "Thank you," she whispered.

His expression was gentle. He stood close, their bodies not quite touching, but she felt him there, and she could not think of another person she'd rather have at her side.

The priest spoke and prayed and read from the Bible. He sprinkled holy water onto the coffins and let the smoke of holy incense cover them. Other members of the village spoke as well, and there was singing.

Hazel bounced the baby softly throughout. She didn't understand a word of the ceremony, but she was moved by the beauty of the music and the expressions of the people around her. The love she felt, the sense of community and their shared sorrow, filled her with a profound sadness. She thought of the friends she'd left behind in London, of her father away in Africa, of the people she'd known in India, of her mother, of Jakinda, and tears coursed down her cheeks.

Dr. Jackson offered her a handkerchief, but Hazel shook her head. She couldn't spare a hand to wipe her eyes just yet, and besides, she wanted to weep, to wail like the mourning women, to sob until her eyes ached and she was out of breath. All her disappointment and fear and pain—it felt cleansing, cathartic to release it, so Hazel hugged Nerea close and let her tears flow.

Dr. Jackson put an arm around her, and Hazel did not care one bit if anyone saw.

As she wept, her grief changed into something else. She felt the love of the village, how they honored their dead, how they took care of one another. Glancing down at Nerea, she realized what a wonderful life the baby would have here, among such good people. She glanced up at the mountains beyond the village, seeing the pine trees and the leafless trees that waited for spring to bloom. Her gaze traveled to the churchyard and the village around it, and she thought of how Nerea would grow here and play as a young girl, her brown eyes shining as she skipped down the cobblestone roads. A wave of warmth comforted her.

When the priest was finished, Dr. Jackson studied her face, offering his handkerchief again.

She must look a sight. Hazel took it then, adjusting her hold on Nerea so she could wipe her eyes and nose. Dr. Jackson didn't say anything, and she was glad for it, not wanting to put her feelings into words.

After a moment, he glanced toward the graves. "I should help, but if you'd prefer, I will stay."

Hazel shook her head. "I am better now." And she was. Though she still felt sadness, it was as if a pressure valve had been released and she could breathe easily. She was at peace.

When Dr. Jackson was gone, Hazel walked back toward the low wall but stopped when Lucía called her name.

She turned to find Lucía and the tall woman with the black headscarf walking toward her. Her stomach got heavy. The moment had come. But she was ready now. She held Nerea close, the baby's forehead resting on her neck.

"This is the child's aunt," Lucía said.

"You are Iraxte Royo." Hazel smiled at the woman.

Iraxte placed a gentle hand on Nerea's back. Her eyes were kind, and though she was taller and older than her sister, Hazel could see the resemblance to Jakinda.

Iraxte spoke—whether to Hazel or to the baby was uncertain. Hazel couldn't understand her words, but she realized there was no need to.

She kissed Nerea. "You be a good girl for your aunt," shc whispered. She leaned the baby back, looking at her round face, and kissed her one more time. She pulled the hat down once more to cover Nerea's ears and handed her to her aunt.

Iraxte took her, nestling the baby against her. She spoke to Lucía.

"She says thank you for returning her family safely."

Hazel nodded, watching Nerea. The baby grinned at her aunt, and the woman smiled back, a warm and loving expression that set Hazel's worries at ease. "Will you tell her that Nerea likes to be walked at night? It is the only way she will sleep." She held out the rucksack, putting it over Iraxte's shoulder. Inside the bag was another blanket that had been cut down to a baby's size, extra bottles, a few hats, and some socks knitted by Nella. "And she prefers to be wrapped tightly in her blanket. It calms her."

Lucía spoke to Iraxte for a moment.

Iraxte replied, her gaze taking in both women. She glanced back toward the churchyard and spoke again.

"The village is to have a funeral dinner. She invited us to attend."

Hazel gave a small curtsy, not knowing how else to communicate her gratitude for the invitation. "Thank you."

Iraxte bid the other two women farewell and started back toward the churchyard, carrying Nerea away. Hazel felt a pang, but that was all.

Another thought came to her, and she hurried after Iraxte. "Wait one moment, please." She unclasped her moonstone necklace and pressed it into the woman's hand. "For Nerea," she said, "when she is grown." She hoped the stone would be worth enough for a dowry or, if Nerea chose, for an education.

Iraxte looked at the necklace and nodded her understanding. She put it into her apron pocket and turned Nerea around to face Hazel. The baby gave an enormous smile, her brown eyes bright. Hazel cupped Nerea's cheek, said goodbye once more, and left, returning to Lucía.

The dinner took place in the courtyard in front of the church. Hazel stood to one side of the space in a sunny spot, watching the preparations. The noonday sun was warm, glowing pleasantly on the tan-colored stone of the church. Tables were filled with delicious-smelling food and drink. There was singing, conversation, and pleasant laughter. She couldn't help but compare the scene again to the same location only a week earlier in the aftermath of the attack, when bricks, wood splinters, and glass fragments were strewn across the ground, mingled with the blood of the injured. It was such a contrast that she stared for a long moment, marveling at the resilience of human beings.

Footsteps sounded on the cobblestones beside her.

She glanced up as Dr. Jackson joined her. His coat was gone and his shirt-sleeves were rolled up, exposing his forearms. Although he'd been shoveling dirt, he must have found somewhere to wash. She studied him—his dark eyes that could be intense and brooding but also kind, the wrinkles at the corners that showed when he smiled or squinted. His hair was longer than was fashionable, curling over his ears and collar.

"That is the aunt?" he asked, lifting his chin toward where Iraxte was holding Nerea and speaking with some other women.

"Yes." Hazel blushed, realizing she was staring. She looked toward the women. "She seems to be a very kindhearted person."

"You are relieved."

"I am."

He studied her face. "You seem much calmer—serene, even."

"I do feel more at peace." She blushed at the intensity of his gaze.

Dr. Jackson clasped his hands behind his back. "And hungry?"

"Hungry?" she said, confused by the change of subject.

"I am, yes. And I don't believe you've eaten today either." He offered his arm. "Shall we?"

Hazel slipped her hand beneath his elbow, and following the beckoning of the villagers, they were seated at a table surrounded by strangers who filled their plates and cups and communicated with exaggerated gestures and facial expressions. Hazel couldn't help but feel warm at their hospitality. She spoke with a few of the women, hardly getting further than her name, but the villagers seemed just as happy as if they'd engaged in a very enjoyable conversation. Dr. Jackson seemed to have an easier time, knowing a few words of Basque.

The hosts offered Hazel more food, filled her cup whenever the level dipped, and treated her and Dr. Jackson and the others as if they were the most valued guests ever to grace the streets of Santa Rosa.

Hazel ate soup that warmed her through, thick hearty bread, and a delicious omelet filled with earthy-tasting mushrooms. When a woman moved to put a slice of meat on her plate, she finally waved her hand and patted her belly to show that she was filled.

A child came to the table then, reaching past Hazel to pinch a piece out of a cake. He crammed it into his mouth just as a woman rushed up, reprimanding him and taking him away.

Hazel laughed with Dr. Jackson, who looked at the cake with the hand-sized chunk missing. He sat back in his chair, taking his cup of wine in hand. "This work, this profession, it's a strange one, don't you think?" His voice had turned pensive.

"How do you mean?" Hazel asked.

"Some of the time, it's utterly miserable, seeing people sick or injured or dying, watching their families mourn, and feeling completely helpless. Other times are the complete opposite. Joyful, even. Seeing a body heal and a family reunited, knowing a patient will have a chance at a healthy life." He sipped his drink. "And sometimes each scenario happens so close together that it's impossible to feel everything at once."

Hazel knew exactly what he meant. "As if your emotions can't keep pace with your circumstances."

"Precisely." He raised his glass in acknowledgment.

"Why did you become a doctor?" Hazel asked. Dr. Jackson seemed to be in a talkative mood, and there was so much about him that she wanted to know.

He took a long drink and let out a heavy breath through his nose. "It was a choice I made during the American War." His eyes looked as if they were seeing something far away. He set the drink on the table and scooted his chair back so he could rest his ankle on his other knee.

"I was enlisted as a medic. Not by choice, but apparently, assisting my father in his veterinary practice was all the qualification the army needed to deem me suitable for the duty." He shrugged as if armies made strange assumptions all the time. "My brother, Theodore—Teddy—he was two years younger than me. He served in the infantry." Dr. Jackson took another drink, and a trace of a smile moved over his mouth. "Teddy excelled in the army. He was obsessed with everything about it: the uniforms, the ceremony, the fighting. He was brash and daring—a bit of a hothead, really—but everyone loved that about him." He raised his brows in an expression of good-natured exasperation.

"You loved him very much," Hazel said. The affection was evident in his eyes. She liked this side of Dr. Jackson, the side that laughed at a little boy's antics and shook his head at thoughts of his eccentric brother. "What happened?"

He looked into his cup, swirling the wine around like a gentle whirlpool. "Of course, you've heard of Gettysburg." His face seemed to darken.

"Your brother fought there?" Hazel winced, and a chill went over her. She knew both armies had suffered immense losses during the famous battle.

Dr. Jackson nodded, still watching the wine move around and around. "From the first shot, the medical tents were overrun. We could hardly keep up with the influx of wounded. So many were injured, and so fast." He set the drink down on the table, clasping his hands together and closing his eyes.

"Teddy wasn't even a part of Pickett's infantry, but General Lee had a way of motivating men, rallying them to his cause."

Hazel watched him, afraid of what he would say.

"I begged him not to join the charge, told him it was a suicide mission. From the medical tents on the hill, I had seen clearly that the Union soldiers were in a stronger position. They were protected behind a stone wall. The assault was doomed before Lieutenant General Longstreet even mounted his horse."

"Your brother joined anyway?"

"He did." Dr. Jackson took another deep drink. "'At least I'm making a difference.' Those were his last words to me." He looked up from his hands. "So, Hazel Thornton, in answer to your question, that is why I became a doctor."

"In honor of your brother."

"In spite of him."

"I'm sorry," Hazel said.

Dr. Jackson's mouth pulled into a semblance of a smile, and his gaze focused on her. "What of yourself? What made you choose to be a nurse?"

Hazel inhaled as the memories flooded through her mind. "Lucknow," she said. "The siege." She saw understanding on his face and was grateful she didn't have to explain about the sepoy uprising or what had transpired. "We—the women and children—crowded into a small room beneath the residency whenever there was fighting. We cowered there, frightened, hearing the blasts of the cannons and the shots of the rifles. Sometimes we could even hear screams. My father was out there somewhere, and I worried that he wouldn't get to us, that we would never be rescued." She realized she'd strayed from the point of her story, and she stopped, brushing her hands over her apron as she considered her words. "Many of the people became ill. Dysentery and cholera, I later learned, and other sicknesses, I suspect. My mother tended to them. When men were brought in, wounded from the fighting, she bound their wounds.

"I was very young, but I followed her, carrying a bucket of water or cloths or bandages—whatever she needed."

"How old were you?" Dr. Jackson asked.

"Four." Hazel glanced at the hole in the cake, imagining the boy who made it must be very close to that age.

"My mother was very gentle, very compassionate. I remember her voice; it was soft, musical. She spoke to people who looked frightened or hurt, and by the time she was finished, their fears had turned to calm. I admired that, admired her." She brushed crumbs off the table. "She died shortly after. Cholera."

"She would be proud of you." Dr. Jackson took her hand, holding it under the table.

His touch felt different than it had before, as if by sharing their stories, they'd broken through a barrier, made their interactions more intimate and their physical contact more significant. Hazel's shiver had nothing to do with the cool mountain air. She moved her hand so her palm pressed more tightly against his and glanced at Dr. Jackson from the corner of her eye. Did he feel it too? The thought that their paths would inevitably separate made her ache. But of course she couldn't remain. Her father would never permit it. And if Dr. Jackson found out about her panic spells, he'd surely not trust her to care for patients. Hazel sighed. She'd thought the deepest desire of her heart had been to be a nurse, but that was before she'd met Dr. Jim Jackson, and she feared her heart would never recover.

CHAPTER 14

Once they'd returned from Santa Rosa, Jim made his hospital rounds. There hadn't been an attack for days, and for what seemed like the first time in months, none of the patients required more than routine care.

He stopped in the West ward to speak with Captain Bryant. The bandages had been removed from the young man's head, and his incision appeared to be healing nicely.

"How is your pain?" Jim asked.

"Constant," Captain Bryant said. He looked discouraged. "But I don't want any more medicine."

Jim lifted the captain's eyelids, looking close at the pupils. "Is the pain localized, or does your head just generally ache?"

"It aches all over," he answered.

"And is it worse when you read?"

"Yes. And light increases the pain as well."

Jim nodded. "I'm afraid your symptoms are all to be expected." He sat on a chair beside the bed. "You suffered a serious brain injury, Captain. You need time to recover."

"How much time?"

Jim held up his hands. This type of healing was impossible to predict. "Weeks. Months. In some cases, it could take years."

Captain Bryant closed his eyes. "There must be some way to speed up the process."

"I'm afraid there isn't," Jim said. He understood the man's frustration. Constant pain and the inability to do anything other than lay in a dark room was nearly impossible to imagine. "Like with a strained muscle, the best thing you can do for your brain is rest it. Too much activity—reading or even speaking too much—could overexert it, slow down the healing, and make your headaches worse. You should sleep often and rest your eyes, and in the meantime, there is no shame in easing your pain with medicine."

"I don't want to develop a dependence," Captain Bryant said. He balled his fists. "It's all so blasted frustrating, to feel so completely helpless." He motioned to the stack of books on the night table. "How am I to live a useful life if I can't even read a book?" His voice caught, and he turned his face away.

Jim wrote in Captain Bryant's chart, noting that he no longer wanted the pain medication but to administer it if he asked. He put the chart into the holder at the foot of the bed with unhurried movements, taking his time to give the man a moment to get control of himself. "If I'd been asked when I first saw you on the ground outside the train," Jim said, "I would have given you less than a twenty percent chance of survival, let alone of waking with a complete memory and full capacity of mind. The fever and the swelling inside your skull made your chances even more bleak." Captain Bryant didn't turn back toward him, but he was still, and Jim could tell he was listening. "But somehow, possibly through sheer will, you have surpassed both my expectations and Dr. Laurent's, and I have no reason to believe that you will not continue to do so." He patted the captain's shoulder. "I have known you only a short while, Captain, but I am convinced you will find a way to make a life that is more than useful."

He left the poor man's bedside, hoping his words had provided a measure of reassurance. Discouragement was expected, but melancholy would not help the healing process.

As he passed Miss Westbrook's bedside, he greeted both the patient and Dr. Laurent, seeing the doctor was helping her rise and take up her crutches.

When he continued on, crossed the cloister, and came into the East ward, he was surprised to see the nurses taking patients from their beds. Camila brought a wheeled chair to the bedside of a man with a fractured leg, and some of the others were assisting Mikel to stand. One patient leaned on a companion as they walked toward the chapel.

Hazel came from the direction of the laundry, pushing a cart that held a basin of water and a pile of towels.

"What is happening?" she asked Camila. "*¿Qué está pasando?*" She left the cart in the aisle and held the wheeled chair steady as Camila helped the patient into it.

"*Es para navidad,*" Camila said.

"Navidad?" Hazel took her Spanish-to-English dictionary from her apron pocket.

"Christmas," Jim translated for her, aware now that he'd lost track of the date. It was already the twenty-fourth of December.

"It is Christmas?" Hazel's face lit up. "I didn't realize."

"Tomorrow," Jim clarified. "Padre de Leon will hold mass tonight for all who can attend."

"Navidad." Hazel spoke the word as if she were getting used to the sound. She assisted another patient out of his bed, steadying him as he stood.

Jim took the man's arm and led him toward the chapel. Hazel followed, taking the arm of another young man who was limping toward the chapel.

"I cannot believe it's already Christmas," she said. "Tell me, how do people celebrate the holiday here?"

Jim glanced over his shoulder at her. "Christmas or not, it is still a hospital, and most of the patients don't feel like celebrating."

"Nonsense." The excited expression on her face hadn't faltered a bit, in spite of his gruff words. "Everyone enjoys Christmas." They helped their patients step across the threshold and sit in a pew in the candlelit chapel. "We will find a way to make the holiday special," Hazel said.

Jim groaned. "Can't we be content in keeping the patients healthy and the hospital running smoothly?"

"Don't tell me you're a Christmas curmudgeon, Dr. Jackson." She wagged a finger at him, shook her head in exaggerated disappointment, and started back to the ward.

Jim followed, trying to maintain a surly expression. He enjoyed a regular schedule, and most of the patients were close to being released. The workload was reduced, and he actually had time to do regular things such as sleep or eat a meal without rushing. But Hazel's good cheer had rubbed off on him, and a small thrill moved through him, a shadow of the anticipation for the holiday he'd felt as a boy. For the first time in years, he found himself looking forward to Christmas Day.

The next morning, Jim slept late, as did the entire hospital. By the time mass was finished and everyone had returned to their beds, the hour was well into early morning. He ate a quick breakfast and went to the West ward to begin his rounds. When he came inside, he stopped, noticing right away the pine boughs that hung over the arched windows. Paper flowers were tucked among the garlands, and when he looked closer, he saw they were cut from old medical charts. Bows had been tied from strips of bandages. There were extra candles on the windowsills, giving a festive glow, their flames sparkling in the glass.

"Happy Christmas, Dr. Jackson." Hazel jumped up from where she sat beside one of the English patients. She excused herself and set down the papers she'd been writing on and came to join him.

"Happy Christmas, Hazel." He motioned around to the decorations. "I imagine this is your doing?"

"The other nurses participated as well." She fished out something from her apron pocket, offering it to him.

He held out his hand, and she dropped it into his palm. It was a peppermint. Jim hadn't eaten a sweet since . . . he couldn't even remember how long it had been. He put it in his mouth and realized he was smiling. "Thank you."

"You are very welcome."

He noticed Dr. Laurent sat at a patient's bedside, writing on a stack of papers just as Hazel had been, as did Miss Westbrook. "What are you all doing?"

"Writing letters for the patients who are, for one reason or another, unable to do so themselves," Hazel said as if the answer were obvious. "For those who can write, we've provided stationery and envelopes," she explained. "Lucía, Camila, and the others are doing the same in the East ward."

"Very considerate," Jim said, impressed with the thoughtfulness of the gift. It would certainly be meaningful to the patients who must be desperate to communicate with their loved ones. But there was a reason the hospital hadn't provided the service before. The postage system in this remote part of the Pyrenees Mountains was nearly nonexistent and was made even worse by the war. Jim had a difficult enough time communicating with Red Cross headquarters, and that was usually done by messenger. "How do you propose to send the letters once they are written?" he asked.

Her gaze slid to the side. "I will take them with me when I leave." She glanced up at him and then away. "Dr. Laurent believes we can send some to the mountain towns with the priest and others with the man who delivers produce." She still didn't look at Jim, but returned to her patient's bedside, lifting the papers back into her lap. "If you have time, we would appreciate your assistance." She motioned toward the other beds in the ward. "There is plenty to be done."

Jim had scarcely heard what she said after "when I leave." Although they'd been spoken in a soft voice, the words had struck like bullets. He watched as she spoke to the patient, returning to writing as the man dictated, but Jim couldn't hear what they were saying. He couldn't hear anything at all besides a dull humming. He continued through the ward, not stopping at any of the bedsides but going straight to the door leading into the cloister. The chilly air was welcome. He sat on the bench, hearing Hazel's voice repeating the phrase in his mind.

Of course she would leave the hospital. It was never a question. The train company would no doubt have contacted both her father in Africa and her relatives in London, and it was only a matter of time before her companions were able to leave as well. But to hear it said aloud . . . He realized he'd not permitted himself to plan for when it inevitably happened. Jim took in a deep breath, the taste of peppermint strong in his mouth and tingling in his nose. She would leave, and everything would return to how it was before.

But would it? Hazel coming to the hospital had not only changed the management of hospital duties; it had changed Jim himself, and in a way that he didn't believe could be reversed.

That evening, Alona prepared a special Christmas meal. Heaven knew where she'd found the ingredients. The patients and staff dined on grilled lamb, potatoes, and delicious bread. For dessert, Alona had made a golden cake with cream filling served with a piece of peppermint.

The hospital was normally quiet, sterile, and orderly, but today, a hopefulness filled the air.

Jim had noticed each of the nurses wore a new hair ribbon beneath their cap that he imagined must have come from Hazel's traveling trunks. Patients who were usually scared, lonely, and discouraged chatted, laughed, and even sang together. He was amazed by what a few handmade decorations and some sweets could do for morale. He stood in the doorway of the West ward, watching as patients left their beds and gathered around Miss Westbrook's bed, where Hazel led them in a Christmas carol. Dr. Laurent was there as well, sitting next to the bed and singing in a strong tenor voice. Even Captain Bryant was smiling, though he leaned his head back and kept his eyes closed.

When the song finished, Jim approached. "Hazel, might I speak with you for a moment?"

"Of course, Dr. Jackson."

One of the English soldiers whistled, as if giving her a warning.

Another, a man with a Scottish accent, grinned. "Yer in trouble now, lass. The doctor's come for ye personally."

"Stop it." Hazel swatted at their teasing as she walked around their chairs and beds to meet Jim.

He picked up a candle lamp and led her from the ward into the cloister, leaving the door open just a crack to let the air in the ward circulate. The evening was dark, the moon and stars hidden by clouds. On the far end of the cloister, the hanging laundry made swishing sounds in the darkness.

They walked, in the bubble of light, to the bench, and Jim motioned for her to take a seat before sitting beside her. He set the candle lamp between them.

"Are you angry, Dr. Jackson?" Hazel asked. "I know today has been a bit disorderly, and I should have inquired about dietary restrictions before giving all the patients sweets. And the candles. I promise I will replace them. I just wanted it to feel festive."

"I'm not angry," he said.

"Are you certain?" she asked. She turned toward him, scooting around so her knees were close to touching his. She studied his face as the flame made shadows on her own. "You seemed distant today. Quiet. I hardly saw you at all after this morning."

She was right. Jim had found plenty to occupy himself with in his office, avoiding the wards as much as possible. He'd thought to protect himself by avoiding her, as if seeing her less would ease the pain of her eventual departure. The plan was a bad one, and he'd abandoned it after only a few hours. Staying away from Hazel was not only illogical but, in their confined circumstances, impossible. He'd come to the conclusion that he'd prefer to enjoy her company now and deal with the inevitable heartache when the time came. There was no use in beginning the pain early.

"I have something for you," he said, avoiding her question. He took a parcel from his coat pocket. "A Christmas gift."

"Oh." Hazel looked surprised and a bit apprehensive as she took the gift. He understood right away the impropriety of a man offering a single young lady a gift. Such a thing could be taken as a declaration or even an expectation.

"It is nothing . . . improper, I assure you," Jim said. "It is actually rather silly, but . . . well, open it; you will see." He was wondering if he'd made a mistake. It had seemed like such a good idea, but now that he was here, he felt a bit foolish.

Hazel untied the twine and peeled away the paper, tipping the matchbox toward the light to read the label. She shook it, realizing there was an object inside, and slid out the inner box. She looked closer, then turned it over, letting the object fall into her hand.

"It's a . . . a little . . . frog?" When she looked up, her brows were pinched together. She watched him, waiting for an explanation.

And now he felt even more foolish. "I carved it, you see. In Petersburg. The soldiers were in the trenches, and aside from the usual army illnesses, we could go weeks without so much as a broken fingernail to attend to in the military tents, so I took to carving, just for something to do. These tree frogs—they were everywhere, especially in the summer, and louder than you can imagine." He smiled at the memory. "At any rate, I've always considered this little chap here to be lucky, and I thought you might—"

"There were frogs in India as well," Hazel interrupted. "Sometimes we would find them in our water basin. There is even a temple dedicated to them in Lakhimpur." She clasped her hand around the carving. "I like it very much." A concerned look crossed her face. "I am sorry I don't have a gift for you—unless you enjoy ribbons."

"What you've done today is a gift," he said. He put the lamp on his other side and scooted closer to her, putting his arm around her and pulling her against him. "I get preoccupied with routine and procedure and often forget that the patients are more than bodies to be healed. What you did today reminded me that laughter and joy—hope—is as vital to human life as any medicine."

"It was only a bit of peppermint and a few pine boughs," Hazel said, folding her arms. "None of the patients would even be alive to enjoy them if not for your care."

The sound of singing came from the East ward, and Hazel sat up straight, which was extremely irritating. "I know this song," she said. She tipped her head, listening. "But the words are . . . they are singing 'Silent Night' in Spanish?"

Jim shrugged, wondering if she would return to lean on him again. "It sounds like it."

"Open the door wider," she said, pointing toward the West ward. She hurried to the East ward door, pulling it open so the music came out into the cloister.

Jim opened the other door, propping it with a rock. A moment later, the West ward joined in, singing 'Silent Night' in English.

Hazel's smile was wide. She came back to the bench, holding Jim's hand when he joined her. "Isn't that beautiful?" she whispered.

The singing continued, the familiar tune echoing off the stone walls and walkways as the patients sang the words in their own languages.

Hazel shivered, nestling closer to him.

"I can think of only one thing that would make this Christmas Day complete," Jim said, keeping his voice casual.

"What is that?"

"A mistletoe."

Hazel started, but she didn't pull away. She turned so that she faced him, looking as though she was thinking. She tapped her finger to her cheek and looked as if she were truly considering the problem. "I believe you're right, Dr. Jackson. A pity we don't have one."

"Do we need one?" he asked, seeing a teasing twinkle in her eye.

Hazel put her hand on his chest, her touch sending fire through him. "I imagine we will do quite well without."

Jim didn't need any more encouragement. He pulled Hazel against him, wrapping her in his arms and pressing his lips against hers. While their first kiss had been tender, gentle, this time, Hazel's response was not so unsure. Her lips moved with his, and her confidence was invigorating. He matched her energy with his own and wondered if he had ever felt anything like this before. Hazel hid her depth well behind her soft facade, and he considered himself a lucky man to be the one to discover just how much there was to this woman.

His heart pounded as he pulled away at last.

A quiet sigh escaped her lips. She shifted to rest her head against his chest, and her breath tickled his neck.

He leaned to rest his cheek on her head. The singing still sounded around them. Jim had forgotten completely about it. His heart felt full, and his skin was heated.

"Happy Christmas, Dr. Jackson," Hazel whispered. "And thank you for the gift."

Jim held her, tightening his arms around her, unable to come up with a response that would in any way tell her how he was feeling. It was a happy Christmas, the happiest he could remember. He pushed away thoughts of Hazel's inevitable departure and closed his eyes, treasuring the moment and wishing he knew how to make it last.

CHAPTER 15

Two days following Christmas, Hazel pushed a rolling tray filled with clean cups and pitchers of fresh water through the West ward. She glanced to the end of the row of beds and blushed when she saw Jim speaking with a patient. She'd begun calling him Jim in her thoughts, feeling it was entirely appropriate now that they had kissed twice, but she would never actually speak his Christian name aloud, especially not in the hospital, where the relationship of doctor and nurse was expected to be one of a professional nature only.

She poured a glass of water, helping Private Jenkins sit up so he could drink, and a memory came into her thoughts. On Christmas, when she and Jim had discussed how the patients' letters were to be posted, Hazel had mentioned taking them with her when she left. At her words, something had moved over Jim's face, something she could not explain in words, and it had filled her heart with both dread and a realization that he had feelings for her, as she had for him. True feelings. Her leaving was not something he considered lightly. If only . . . but, of course, nothing could come of their relationship. Jim's place was here, with the Red Cross Hospital, and Hazel's . . . she sighed. They were foolish to have let their feelings deepen as much as they had.

She helped the private lie back again in his bed.

"Is everything all right, Nurse?" the soldier asked.

"Yes, of course." She smoothed the sheets and moved on to the next patient.

Where *was* her place? As a child she would have said India, without hesitation. A month ago, she would have claimed London, among the members of the Blue Orchid Society. But now she didn't know where she belonged, only that she was doing what she was meant to, caring for patients, easing their pain, bringing hope when they despaired. It felt as natural to her now as breathing.

She poured water into another glass.

A blast sounded in the distance, followed by another and then another. Five more in quick succession. The water in the pitcher trembled. Gunshots sounded, and more blasts.

Jim rushed through the ward, calling to the nurses as he went. "Lucía, Hazel, Camila, with me. Bring your kits and report at the wagons!"

Hazel set aside the water glass and hurried after him, hearing from the footsteps behind her that the other nurses were following.

The sounds of battle continued, louder now that she was outside. She and the other two nurses climbed into the back of an ambulance wagon. Jim and Dr. Laurent lifted boxes of medical supplies inside, and before the nurses had even stowed them beneath the benches, the wagon started moving.

Lucía took three wool blankets from the boxes, handing one to each of the others. The women sat on them, having learned the hard way that if they didn't bring cushioning, they would be cursing the wooden seat before an hour had passed.

Hazel settled into her seat, wrapping her cape around her for warmth. She found a relatively comfortable position and settled in for another long journey into the mountains.

Beneath the canvas covering, she couldn't see anything aside from the road behind them. The other wagon was following at a distance with two orderlies on its bench. She wondered which nurses were riding in the bed.

They continued along, following the sound of the battle. The road became rockier, and through the opening at the rear she could see that one side of the narrow mountain road fell off in a cliff while the other rose up as a stone wall. The wheels rolled over a bump that made the entire wagon rock from side to side. The three women braced themselves, holding on to the bench and the side to keep from sliding from their seats.

More blasts sounded, this time much closer. The other wagon fell farther behind as the road became more difficult to navigate. Hazel could hear the doctors' voices but couldn't make out their words, which judging by their tone, she thought was for the best.

More blasts, more rocking. And now the road was higher on one side than the other. The nurses moved to the middle of the wagon bed, hoping to even out the weight distribution. One of the medical boxes started to slide, and Hazel held it in place with one hand. She gripped the wagon bench with the other to hold herself in place.

An explosion shook the wagon, sounding as if it were directly on top of them. The wagon jerked forward as if the mules had startled, tugging the wagon's occupants forward. An avalanche of rocks spilled down the mountain, covering the road behind them and cutting off their hopes of return as well as separating them from the other wagon.

Another blast came, but this one was different—a gunshot, and it was close. A man's voice followed. He sounded angry, as if he were making a threat.

Jim answered, his voice angry as well.

The nurses looked at one another, and Hazel could see fear in her companions' eyes. She looked toward the front of the wagon, where Jim and Dr. Laurent were, wishing she knew what was happening. Then she looked toward the rear and the exit, wondering what to do. Her airway constricted.

Breathe in . . . one . . . two . . . three. Breathe out . . . one . . . two . . . three.

More raised voices, Jim's and Dr. Laurent's among them. The sounds of boots scuffling over rocky ground and a whack as if someone had been struck.

Camila grabbed Hazel's hand, muttering a prayer.

Hazel's skin started to tingle, and the wagon bed began to shrink. *Breathe in . . . one . . . two . . . three. Breathe out . . . one . . . two . . . three.*

Before her panic came on fully, a man appeared behind the wagon.

Camila screamed.

The man pointed a rifle at the women, yelling words Hazel couldn't understand. Another man joined him.

Lucía spoke to them, sounding as if she were reprimanding them, and for a moment, the men looked ashamed.

A third man poked his head into the back of the wagon. He ignored Lucía and pointed to the boxes of medical supplies and the nurses' kits. By his tone, Hazel could tell he was giving orders.

He spoke one short sentence to Lucía, not waiting to hear a reply before he walked away.

"We are to follow him," she said to the others.

The men climbed inside, picking up the boxes.

Camila clamped Hazel's hand tighter, but the men didn't give the nurses a second look.

Lucía motioned to them, and Hazel and Camila followed her, stepping out of the safety of the wagon bed onto the mountain road. They walked single file along the edge of the steep decline to the front of the wagon.

Dr. Laurent and Jim stood there, surrounded by men wearing vests and berets. Each of the rebels carried a rifle.

Blood dripped from a cut beneath Jim's eye. He glared at the rebels, his expression dark with fury.

At a motion from their captors, the nurses went to stand by the doctors.

"Are you ladies all right?" Dr. Laurent asked.

"We're unharmed," Hazel said. She looked up at Jim. "Dr. Jackson, your eye." She offered a handkerchief.

"It's nothing." He shook his head.

"Who are these men?" Hazel asked, putting the handkerchief back into her apron pocket. "What do they want?"

"Zhey want us," Dr. Laurent said. "Or, at least, zhat is what I believe. Lucía will speak to zhem."

"Us? But why?" Hazel asked.

Camila still held on to Hazel's hand, and she was shaking.

"A trap," Jim muttered in English, still glaring at the men. "They lured us here. They knew we would follow the sounds of the battle." He turned away at last. "I don't believe they'll hurt us, but do not make them angry."

Dr. Laurent translated for Camila.

"Don't worry," Hazel told her, rubbing her friend's arm. "Dr. Jackson and Dr. Laurent will work this all out."

The man who had given the orders came toward them. He was lean with a long face and a shock of white hair beneath a red beret. He looked as though his skin had been carved out of wood.

He folded his arms as he spoke to Lucía, his tone leaving no room for discussion. Whatever he was telling her was an order.

After a moment, she spoke to the rest of them.

"Zhey intend to take us to zheir camp," Dr. Laurent told Hazel when Lucía had finished. "To treat zheir wounded."

"Surely they must know they would've received better medical care at the hospital," she said.

"Zhat is what Lucía told zhem." Dr. Laurent shrugged.

"They are afraid," Jim said. "These men don't trust easily."

Hazel thought of Mikel's father and how the prisoners were separated in the different wards. Even though the Red Cross Hospital was a neutral organization, they could not ensure a person's safety once they left. She pulled her cape tighter around her, shivering both from cold and from fear.

The leader called a command, and a group of men approached, carrying ropes and cloth bags. When they got near, Camila cried out, drawing back.

Jim stepped in front of the women and was shoved into another man, who pulled his hands together and bound them.

Camila cried out again when a bag was pushed roughly over her head.

Seeing one of the men approaching her, Hazel ran, but she made it only a few steps before the man grabbed her arm. She slapped at him and kicked his legs.

"Do what they say, Hazel," Jim yelled, twisting around. "Don't make them angry."

A bag was pushed over Jim's head, and immediately after, Hazel felt rough fabric on her own face and choked on the smell of damp burlap. The familiar prickling sensation moved over her skin. She could see only faint light coming through the weave of the bag. Her wrists were tied, and her back was shoved roughly with what felt like the butt of a rifle. The air inside the bag was thick in her lungs, but she forced herself to take in deep breaths. *Breathe in . . . one . . . two . . . three. Breathe out . . . one . . . two . . . three.* She squeezed her eyes shut, remembering what Nella had said weeks earlier on the train. *"Breathe, Hazel. You are needed."*

As she walked over the uneven ground, she could hear her companions' footsteps and breathing. Occasionally she heard someone stumble. Camila sounded like she was weeping, and Hazel wished she could reach out to her. What had happened to the mules and the wagon? Had the men just left the poor animals behind?

They continued on, and Hazel lost all sense of direction and time. She fell more than once, tripping over things she couldn't see, landing on her knees. Her bound hands could not be depended on to stop her from falling on her face, but someone was there to catch her shoulder before she fell completely forward and pull her roughly back to her feet. Her feet ached, her bruised knees hurt, and the smell of the bag was making her stomach sick.

The boots she wore were intended for indoors and gentle strolls along a beach, not the jagged mountain terrain. She felt each rock beneath her steps and sucked in a breath each time a particularly sharp one poked into the sole of her foot.

She stumbled along, trying to picture what they would find at the end of their journey. Her imagination conjured images of bleeding men lying on a rocky battleground, and in spite of her fear, she wanted to help them.

Eventually the terrain changed. Snow crunched beneath their feet, and they seemed not to be climbing any longer. When she fell again, her knees felt the cold. She reached out in the darkness, awkwardly grabbing the edges of her cape with her bound hands and trying to hold it tightly around her. Her thoughts turned to Camila and the others. Were they warm? Had Jim's cheek stopped bleeding?

It felt like hours had passed, but Hazel had no way of knowing for certain. Her legs were shaky from climbing the steep hills, and her throat was parched.

Just as she thought she couldn't take another step, she was halted with a forceful pull on her shoulder.

The bag was taken from her head, and she blinked against the sudden brightness, breathing in the fresh air that took her by surprise with its bite. Her hands were freed, and she rubbed her wrists, wincing at the skin rubbed raw by the ropes.

Her instinct was to sink down, to find a place to sit and rest, but she remained upright. She stepped away from the man who had bound her, moving closer to her companions. Each of them looked as tired as she felt. One of Dr. Laurent's trouser legs was covered in mud up to his hip, indicating he'd likely slipped as well. Camila and Lucía were standing next to him. They all appeared shaken but unharmed.

Jim came to her, touching the small of her back. "Are you all right, Hazel?" He spoke in a low voice, worry creasing his forehead.

"Yes." She studied the abrasion on his face. The bleeding had stopped and the blood dried. She didn't think he would require stitches, but it would leave a scar. And it definitely needed cleaning.

Satisfied that her friends were safe for the moment, Hazel turned and considered their surroundings. The group stood in an open field near a cluster of stone structures. She counted six of them. As she looked closer, she realized there was no road anywhere, and the structures were very small. Perhaps they were used for temporary sheepherder dwellings or some other similar purpose. She didn't imagine they were large enough for a family to live in.

The medical personnel were urged forward by their captors, and as the group approached the structures, she got a better view of the situation.

Canvas was strung between the little buildings, giving some small protection from the elements, and when she and the others were led closer, Hazel could see the shelter served as a makeshift hospital. She drew in a sharp breath as she tried to gasp the immensity of the task ahead of them. All over the ground beneath the stretched cloth, men and boys sat or lay on mats, each bearing a wound or an illness of some kind. There were dozens of them, and the sight was overwhelming.

She looked up to see Jim's face was drawn. His expression still bore anger, but there was concern as well. And determination.

He pointed to the boxes the men had brought. "Camila and Hazel, sort the supplies. See if there is additional material that can be used as bandages."

"Attend to the medication," he muttered in English to Hazel. "We have a limited supply."

She nodded her understanding.

"Dr. Laurent, you, Lucía, and I will determine who requires the most immediate attention and who can wait."

The long-faced leader stepped in front of them, speaking to Lucía and jabbing his finger as he pointed around the camp.

She replied in a calm voice, likely reassuring the man that they knew how to proceed and translating for Jim.

The three argued back and forth until Jim raised his voice. "Enough. Each moment we waste could mean the difference between a man's life and death. If you want our assistance, you must trust that we will do all we can to save as many of your people as we are able. Now, will you help us, or did you bring us all this way to argue?"

Lucía translated his words.

The leader scowled, but he stepped back, motioning for Jim to continue.

Jim nodded. "I need water, and it must be boiled."

Lucía translated, and the man shook his head as he replied. He folded his arms, his voice sounding decisive.

"There is a stream," Lucía told Jim, pointing beyond the structures. "But he said there are to be no fires. The smoke will announce their location to the Spanish Army." The corners of her eyes wrinkled as if she were asking Jim to understand.

Hazel realized how difficult it must be for her. These were her people, and yet she was treated as an outsider because of her relationship with the Red Cross Hospital. She was torn between her loyalty to them and her duty as a nurse.

Jim opened his mouth, ready to argue, but seeing Lucía's expression, he stopped, letting out a sigh through his nose. "Alcohol, then," he said. "To clean the instruments."

Hazel and Camila laid out a blanket and arranged the medical tools and supplies, making it easy to find the various instruments as well as see at a glance how many bandages, towels, and dressings were available.

The men who had accompanied them from the wagon stood guard, watching their movements, but they seemed more curious than anything. And Hazel imagined they were concerned for their friends.

She emptied a medical kit and filled it with the bottles of medication and chloroform, closing it and keeping it beside her. She glanced around the camp and saw there were men stationed around the edges of the tree line, their rifles at the ready. The sight made her insides tremble. She tried not to glance in the direction of those men, not wanting to draw further attention, but it was impossible to forget they were there, standing all around the camp, watching, guarding.

Once they had finished organizing the supplies, the nurses got to work. At Lucía's orders, some of the rebels converted one of the small structures into an operating room. Dr. Jackson and Dr. Laurent established which of the patients required surgery and in what order, and having the space and resources to perform only one surgery at a time, they took turns, with Camila managing the chloroform when sedation was needed.

With Lucía's help, the doctors directed men with stretchers, moving patients in and out of the surgery, putting patients with similar needs close together. Some they laid in the sunshine and others in the shade, making sure to keep those with any sort of illness away from the others.

Hazel and Camila cleaned and dressed wounds, treated burns with ointments and compresses, and placed cool towels on fevered brows. In between patients, they took turns cleaning instruments and washing bloody towels in a bucket of cold water. The towels were wrung out and laid over rocks in the sun, but they had little hope of drying before they were needed again. The guards continued to watch.

When a doctor wasn't in the surgery, he managed smaller procedures such as removing shallow shrapnel and stitching lacerations. Hazel and Camila took turns assisting.

It was well past nightfall by the time the last patient was tended to. Dr. Laurent and Camila helped a man with a fractured wrist, setting the bone and splinting it into place.

Hazel held a lantern and a pail of clean water as she moved among the patients. She noted with approval how they had been moved into orderly rows. She stopped at an outstretched hand and helped a young man lean forward and drink. Crouching beside another man, she poured the cool water onto a towel, returning it to his heated forehead.

Hearing a cry, she moved down a row, stopping beside a boy and kneeling beside him. He could have been no older than eleven. The boy was soaked with sweat, tossing on his mat and crying out in feverous delirium. Hazel wiped his brow, pulling over him the blanket he'd kicked away. The frigid air on his wet clothing worried her, and she considered whether it would be better to allow the cold to cool his fever or remove the wet clothes and cover him with blankets. She'd never tended to a feverish patient in the winter air before. She wiped his face with a cool towel, deciding to consult with one of the doctors, but as she moved to rise, the boy clasped her arm. His eyes were open now, and he stared at her. "*Ama?*"

Hazel didn't need a translation to understand the boy's word. In his state, he believed her to be his mother. She knelt back down, wincing as her bruised knees pressed against the hard dirt. "Hush, now." She spoke in a gentle voice, brushing the wet curls from his forehead. She stroked his cheek with a soft finger. "It will all be well. You need to rest, dear." As she had the other young man, Hazel helped him lean forward enough to drink.

"Ama," he said again much quieter. He closed his eyes, and his face relaxed.

Hazel covered him with the blanket, rising. She lifted the lantern and started when she illuminated the face of a man. It was one of the guards, and he stood very near, watching her closely. In the lantern light, she could see the man's face was tanned, as if he spent every moment of his life outside. He had a fresh scar beneath his jaw that was only partly covered by a bandanna tied around his neck. Small wrinkles spread from the corners of his eyes, as if he squinted often. Or perhaps they were from smiling. He was certainly not smiling now. He watched her with a curious gaze.

Seeing that she needed to move past him, the guard stood to the side, and Hazel scooted around him, hurrying to find Dr. Laurent to inquire about treating the boy with the fever. At the doctor's instructions, she kept the boy loosely covered and reapplied the cool cloth to his forehead.

An hour later, they repacked the medical supplies, covering the boxes with a section of oiled canvas to keep them dry. Jim carried the kit with the medicines, and the group of doctors and nurses gathered together.

Hazel gazed around, studying her friends and noticing how completely exhausted they looked. Camila seemed to be swaying on her feet. Lucía's blinks were long.

At a low table, they were given a piece of hard bread and some cheese to eat. Then the leader who had brought them from the road led them toward one of the small structures. He held a lantern, walking before them. Others followed behind the group, their footsteps sounding in the darkness. Hazel chewed the food gratefully, realizing she'd not eaten since early that morning.

The leader called out to another of the men, Ramiro, presumably telling him to open the door.

Hearing the name, Hazel looked up, studying him. Could this man be Jakinda's husband?

The man with the scar on his neck moved to obey, scooping up another lantern and moving to the structure's opening.

Other men urged the group closer to the door.

The scarred man pointed, directing them inside. Apparently that was where they were to be kept for the night. He gave the lantern to Jim.

One by one, the medical staff stepped inside. Hazel was the last.

"Ramiro?" She hesitated outside the doorway, asking in Spanish, "Are you Jakinda's husband?"

Ramiro turned toward her. He gave no sign that he'd understood, aside from the tightening of his eyes.

"Jakinda was my friend." Her voice cracked as she said the words. She put her hand over her heart. She couldn't even tell if he understood her attempts at Spanish but felt it was important for him to know that someone who cared had been with Jakinda during her last moments.

Ramiro pointed toward the doorway of the small structure. His meaning was clear; she was to go in.

"There was a letter," she said, making motions in the air of writing.

Someone pushed her from behind, and she stumbled inside.

Jim caught her before she fell, holding on to her arms until she regained her balance.

The floor of the structure sloped downward, reminding Hazel of a cellar. Perhaps vegetables were stored here. The space was dark and small, and she could hardly see the others in the shadows from the lantern light.

The door closed behind her, and she heard a bar dropped into place, locking it. The smell hit her almost immediately. A damp underground space—bodies too close together.

Tingling pricked her skin, and energy spiked into her toes and fingers. Her breathing came in gasps. Her stomach roiled, and the edges of her vision blurred. Hazel turned, blinded by her panic, and she scrambled for the door handle. "No, no, no." When she found it, she strained against it, pulling with all her might. "Please, no!" She screamed the words, hitting the door with her palm.

Around her, women and children were terrified and weeping as they hid in the darkness. Her chest was tight with fear.

"Hazel." Jim caught her arms again.

"I must get out . . . trapped . . ." Her teeth were chattering, making her words sound like they were shaking around in her mouth before coming out. She was shaking so badly that her legs gave out and her heart hammered. The panic carried her away, stealing her thoughts and leaving behind only terror.

CHAPTER 16

Jim helped Hazel sit down on the floor and lean her back against the wall as he sat next to her. Her breathing was irregular, coming out like sobs, and her body shook. He drew the lantern closer, setting it on the floor in front of them and lifting her face. Her eyes were wide, darting, unfocused.

Jim took her wrist, feeling her pulse. Her skin was cool and her heart rate elevated. "Hazel, look at me."

She curled in on herself, drawing her knees to her chest and wrapping her arms around them. "No, no, no." Her voice was high-pitched. She pressed her face to her knees.

Jim placed a hand on her shoulder. He could feel her trembling.

"What is it?" Dr. Laurent asked from the other side of the room.

"A panic spell," Jim replied. He'd seen a similar reaction in soldiers, even well after a battle had finished and the danger was gone. He'd seen the same look on her face when she'd come out of Jakinda's house with the baby and should have recognized it for what it was. Her face had been pale, with her eyes wide and darting, just like now.

Dr. Laurent spoke softly to the other nurses, explaining to them what was happening, and Jim scooted around to face Hazel directly. He rubbed her arms. "Hazel, look at me."

She shook her head. "I can't. I need to . . . get . . . out."

"Hazel." He held her shoulders. "I can help you. Will you let me?"

"Trapped." The word came out as a gasp.

Tears dripped onto her knees, and by the sound of her breathing, she was in danger of hyperventilating. "Focus on drawing air into your lungs," he said. "Then push it out. You must get your breathing under control."

"One . . . two, three . . ." Her breathing was uneven as she counted through her sobs.

"Breathe in slowly through your nose," he coached. "Then out through your mouth."

"One . . . two . . . three," she whispered. She blew out her breaths, counting again.

She was still shaking. Jim had dealt with such episodes before. He knew if the patient could focus on something, anything, other than the source of the panic, they might be able to calm themselves. Hazel had obviously learned some strategies for regaining control. He didn't believe she'd had to use them under such extreme circumstances, though, and feared she would find it more difficult here.

He shook her gently, getting her attention. "Hazel, look at me. Look at my face."

She lifted her gaze, drawing in a jagged breath and blowing it out.

"Tell me something, anything at all. What do you see before you?"

"Your collar," Hazel whispered. "There is blood on it." Her breath hitched.

"Good. What else?" Jim asked.

"A small mole." She breathed in and out. "Or a freckle, right near the corner of your eye."

"Keep breathing," Jim said. "In through your nose, then out through your mouth."

Hazel did as she was told. "Yes. My doctor—that is what he told me."

She seemed more coherent. Jim decided to keep her talking. "You've experienced these spells before, then?"

"Yes." She drew in a slow breath and blew it out. She was still shaking, but her voice sounded calmer. "Since I was a child." Her voice caught.

"Breathe," Jim said. He moved back around to sit next to her with his back against the wall and put an arm around her, pulling her against him.

She leaned a shaking head against his chest. "I'm sorry," she said. "I just . . ."

"No need to apologize," Jim said. He rubbed her back. "Keep your thoughts steady. Concentrate on your breathing."

After what he guessed was half an hour, Hazel's breathing at last grew calm and her shaking stilled.

"Hazel?" Camila's voice came from the darkness beyond the lantern light. "*¿Estás bien?*" She came forward, kneeling in front of them.

"Sí," Hazel said. "*Estoy bien.*" She sounded tired, her voice still unsteady.

Camila cupped her friend's cheek, giving her a reassuring smile, and bid her good night, nodding to Jim before returning to lie down beside Lucía.

Hazel shivered. Jim took a blanket from the pile the captors had left and wrapped it around her, then wrapped another blanket around his own shoulders. She leaned her head to the side, resting against his shoulder.

In the darkness beyond the lantern's light, they could hear quiet grunts and movements as their companions settled themselves for sleep. Before long, the nurses' deep breathing could be heard as well as Dr. Laurent's soft snores.

Hazel's head was heavy against Jim. He shifted his position the smallest bit, worried that if he extended his legs too far, he'd kick one of his companions in the dark.

"This is why I couldn't finish nursing school," Hazel said in a voice quiet enough that it wouldn't wake the others. "The panic spells. I never know when . . ."

"Have you any idea what brings them on?" he asked.

"Tight spaces, feeling trapped or crowded . . ." Her words came slower, drawn out as if she were falling asleep. "The episodes always end, but each time, I fear they won't, that this time will be different—that I won't survive."

Jim didn't answer. He listened as her breathing grew slow in sleep and thought of what she'd told him about Lucknow, the palpable terror she'd felt as women and children huddled together, not knowing whether they would at any moment meet their fate in the same manner as those in Cawnpore. For Hazel to relive that fear again and again . . . it must be unbearable. Jim looked up at the locked door and then down to the woman sleeping against his shoulder. He moved as slowly as possible, shifting her to lie on the ground, worried that if she woke, the reminder of where she was would set off another panic spell. One thought was at the forefront in his mind: he needed to get Hazel away from here.

He picked up the lantern and held it as he turned in a slow circle, studying the small prison. The space where his friends were sleeping was only about eight feet in each direction. Aside from the pile of blankets, there was some straw, a bucket of water, and the kit containing the medications he and Dr. Laurent had made certain to keep close. The building was made of stone with only the one door. There were no windows. A cold iron stove sat in one corner with a long pipe that rose up behind it. Jim studied where it met the slate roof. He couldn't reach the roof, but it didn't appear at all compromised—not even a crack—nor did any part of the walls. He thought for a moment that he could perhaps climb onto the stove and press up on the roof tiles. One may be loose. But he decided against the idea, knowing he'd certainly wake his companions from the sleep they desperately needed and the noise would draw attention from the guards outside.

He returned to the only empty spot on the floor, the small area where he'd been sitting beside Hazel. She had not moved, sleeping with the blanket still wrapped around her. Jim slid back down to the floor, leaning his shoulders back against the wall. He lifted Hazel, resting her cheek on his leg, thinking it was a better pillow than the hard floor. Cold seeped through his clothing from the stone, and he shivered, feeling a mixture of anger and desperation. He clenched and unclenched his jaw as he came up with and discarded different plans for escape. This was his team. They were here because of him. He'd led them straight into this trap.

He touched Hazel's forehead, glad that she at last felt warm.

There had been a battle, of that he was certain. And wounded men would be going to the Red Cross Hospital for care. His frustration made a tight ball between his shoulder blades. If only the Carlists realized the hospital was safe. If only they trusted the medical personnel. The men and boys he'd treated today would have a much better chance of survival in the hospital, yet here they were, lying on the dirty ground, exposed to the cold, their wounds infected.

He put out the lantern, not wanting to risk him or one of the others bumping it over in the night and igniting the straw. Then he rested a hand on Hazel's shoulder, hoping beyond anything that she would not wake in the dark.

Jim woke when a ray of light hit his eyes. A few small beams fought their way between the boards of the door, and one pierced through, shining right into his eyeballs. In the scant light, he saw Dr. Laurent was awake as well.

The older man splashed water from the bucket over his face.

Jim's worries about Hazel waking in the darkness were unrealized. She slept longer than any of them, not even waking when Jim moved away and put his rolled-up blanket beneath her head.

Camila and Lucía finger-combed their hair, straightened their nursing caps, and shook out their aprons before putting them on. Occasionally, the nurses glanced toward Hazel with worried expressions.

Jim scratched his cheek, wishing he had a razor. He splashed water onto his face and wet his hair.

They let Hazel sleep, doing the small bit of housekeeping that their sleeping space required—folding the blankets—in silence so as not to wake her. And once it was done, there was nothing more to do, so they sat back on the ground.

Jim was glad to see the others seemed to be well enough. He was proud of his team. Aside from some mud on their skirts and trousers, they looked every bit as professional as one would expect in the hospital.

"How long do you believe zhey will keep us here?" Dr. Laurent asked, picking a piece of straw off his coat.

"I don't know," Jim said. He glanced at the door. "I wonder how long they will remain at this camp. Surely they must be running low on supplies. And it is only a matter of time before the army discovers this place."

"Zhey have more camps, I am certain," Dr. Laurent said.

"The Carlists have hideaways all over these mountains." Lucía frowned, looking at the door. "I do not imagine they will stay here long. There is little cover, and there will be more snow. From the bits of conversation I overheard, I believe they intend to leave once the injured are well enough to be moved."

"Will they take us with them?" Camila asked. She tried to sound matter-of-fact like the rest of them, but there was a tremor in her voice. "When they leave, will they keep us as prisoners?"

"I don't know," Lucía said.

The men shared a look. The rebels weren't about to risk their camp being discovered, and releasing their prisoners might give the Spanish Army a hint as to where they were. The bags over their prisoners' heads had made that point clearly enough. Secrecy was their priority, and released prisoners were a liability—an unpredictable one.

Jim balled his hands into fists. If the women weren't here, he would find a way to take a gun. He'd fight, escape . . . but he couldn't put them in further danger.

He leaned his head back against the stones of the wall, trying once again to come up with a plan, anything that would keep his companions safe and ensure that Hazel never had to set foot in this dark prison again.

CHAPTER 17

A SCRAPING SOUND RASPED AT the edge of Hazel's consciousness, but she ignored it, not wanting to pull herself away from the warm floating of her dreams.

Hinges creaked.

Voices spoke.

Someone shook her shoulder.

"Hazel," Camila's voice broke through her sleep. "You must wake."

Hazel sat up, feeling disoriented. Her head was heavy, and her muscles ached. Probably an aftereffect of her panic spell last night. It was the worst she could remember. She blinked open her eyes, squinting in the light from the open door.

Her companions stood in the small dwelling with Ramiro, who was motioning them outside.

Camila helped Hazel rise.

Hazel swayed, pushing an arm against the stone wall to steady herself. The heaviness in her head turned into an aching pressure. She felt dazed. Seeing a bucket of water, she stepped over to it and splashed her face. The cold water helped wake her, but her head still felt too heavy. Her eyes were swollen, and every bit of her ached. Compared to sleeping on a stone floor, the monk's cot was luxurious. She found where her nurse's cap had fallen during the night and put it on, straightening her apron and brushing the wrinkles from her dress. She still wore her traveling cape.

When she stepped through the doorway, she crossed her arms against the cold, wrapping her cape around her. The frigid air made its way into her lungs, and she coughed.

Ramiro took a step toward her, twisting his shoulders just slightly to block her from the others in her group.

Hazel paused.

"*¿La carta?*" He took an envelope from his coat pocket. It looked worn, and the paper was dirty, as if it had been opened and closed often.

"Yes." She recognized the envelope and her own handwriting upon it. "That is the letter. Jakinda and I wrote it for you. I'm so glad you received it."

Based on his blank expression, Ramiro may or may not have understood her Spanish. He returned the letter to his pocket and stepped back, motioning with his head that she was to join the others.

"Come." He spoke the word in Spanish and pointed with his gun. They walked ahead of him to the low table where they'd eaten the night before. Bread, cheese, and some shriveled apples were upon it.

The sight of the food made Hazel's stomach feel sour. She looked away and tried not to smell it, pointing instead to the part of the clearing where the earth had been dug up in a mound.

Ramiro nodded his permission for her to go to the privy. Hazel's stomach sickened again, and she coughed at the smell when she got near, but that was to be expected.

Instead of returning to her companions at the table, she sat on a rock near them, holding her head.

"You should eat." Jim came to stand next to her.

"I'm not hungry this morning," Hazel said.

"You will need your strength."

She didn't reply. The talk of food was not helping her stomach settle.

Jim crouched beside her, chewing on a bit of apple. "How are you feeling?"

"A bit sore from sleeping on the ground." Hazel kept her voice light. "I imagine we all are."

"And . . . your other symptoms?"

"I am all right now."

He studied her face for a moment, then nodded.

"I am sorry," she said. "About my reaction." She turned her head to glance at him, the movement making her neck ache. "I must have frightened you all."

"Not frightened," Jim said. "But we were worried."

"It is embarrassing," Hazel admitted. "When a spell comes on, I have no control." She looked toward the table where the others were eating. "I didn't want any of you to know that I . . . that it happens sometimes."

"You have no reason to be embarrassed," Jim said.

She turned back to give him a smile before closing her eyes and resting her head in her hands. "I'm glad you were there," she said. "You made me feel safe."

"That is something you may count on, Hazel." Jim sat down on the ground by the rock, stretching his legs in front of him. "Always." He didn't say anything more, but in his silence she could feel affection, warmth. And she was comforted to have him beside her.

The group finished eating, but before they returned to tending the patients, Jim poured some of the alcohol over their hands and the medical instruments.

The men watching looked irritated at the waste of their perfectly good drink, but they did not stop him.

As she and the others returned to the infirmary beneath the canvas, the first thing Hazel noticed was empty places where patients had been the day before. Some must have improved during the night to the point where they had risen from their pallets and returned to duties around the camp. But others . . .

She looked around the clearing, seeing men digging at the far end. The sight made her heart heavy.

The camp had only cold water since the rebels still refused to light a fire, so Hazel gathered up some blankets and strips of bandages and took them to the stream. It was hardly more than a trickle of water, but it was frigid, and within a moment, Hazel's hands were red and numb.

She coughed again, and it made her lungs hurt. When she had rinsed the linens as well as she was able, she spread the blankets out on the ground to dry in the sun. She objected to the lack of sanitation but saw no alternative. Each time she bent over to straighten a corner or pull a bandage tight, her head swam. After a few moments, she sat on the ground. Her chest hurt, and she felt dizzy.

A few of the rebels came to join her, and seeing the task, they made quick work of spreading the remainder of the blankets and bandages. Hazel got to her feet, thanked them, and returned to the hospital tent.

When she stepped beneath the canvas, Jim called to her, and she joined him at the side of a patient. The man's neck and one side of his face were completely burned. Dr. Laurent had told Hazel the day before that the injuries had been caused by his rifle misfiring.

Jim was removing the bandaging from the day before, pulling the cloth carefully away from the skin. Even though they'd used ointment, the bandages still stuck to the skin, and the man winced as it was pulled away.

At Jim's direction, Hazel poured cool water over the bandage, loosening it enough that it could be removed completely.

Jim inspected the injuries, and once Hazel applied more ointment, he bandaged it again.

Hazel took the soiled bandages and the bucket of water and stood, swaying as she did. She dropped what she was carrying and coughed again, bending nearly in two. Her lungs felt tight and hot. Darkness speckled the edges of her vision, and she couldn't balance on her feet. She reached out for something to hold on to, but there was nothing.

Jim caught her before she fell. "Hazel, you're . . . you're burning with fever."

His voice sounded far away, and Hazel couldn't find the energy to respond before the darkness closed in.

CHAPTER 18

"DR. LAURENT!" JIM CALLED ACROSS the camp. He knelt to lay Hazel down in the shade of the canvas, snatching someone's rucksack from the ground nearby and putting it beneath her head.

Dr. Laurent rushed through the patients, coming to kneel on her other side. "What happened?"

"She fainted," Jim said, his fingers on the pulse in her nek. He counted the beats, frowning at their rapid speed. He felt the glands beneath her jaw.

Lucía and Camila joined them, bringing blankets and putting them over and beneath Hazel.

Hazel didn't react to the movement, her lack of response escalating Jim's worry. Her symptoms were much more serious than those of a simple cold or the aftereffects of a poor night's sleep.

Dr. Laurent touched Hazel's forehead and sucked in a breath through his teeth. "Such a fever. How long has she been zhis way?"

"I don't know," Camila answered. "She seemed tired and pale this morning."

"I believe I heard her cough earlier," Lucía said. "A dry cough."

Jim put the end of the stethophone into his ear, holding the bell against Hazel's chest and side. Her heart beat quickly and her breathing was shallow. He moved the bell, listening to different sections of her lungs. After a moment, he turned her over to listen to her back, and Camila assisted. In Hazel's right lung he heard crackling—the sound of fluid moving through the tissue—and in some areas nothing. Parts of her lungs were not receiving breath. He gave the stethophone to Dr. Laurent and loosened the buttons of Hazel's collar.

Dr. Laurent listened through the stethophone as well, his frown deepening.

Lucía brought towels and a water bucket, and the women bathed Hazel's skin, trying to cool her fever.

She shivered and began to cough.

"Zhe right lung," Dr. Laurent said somberly, listening through the cough.

Jim nodded, his gut sinking in dread. *Pneumonia.* For a moment, his worries overshadowed his thoughts, but he pushed them away. Now it was time for action. "The willow bark," he said, handing the kit containing the medicine to Lucía. There was no hot water to make a tea, so the soldiers had been chewing on the bits of wood to draw out the fever-reducing properties. "If she can't chew it, soak it in water and administer it cold."

Lucía nodded.

Camila wrung out a towel, placing it on Hazel's forehead. She picked up the nursing cap that had fallen off when they'd moved Hazel, then carefully put it in her pocket.

"She needs zhe hospital," Dr. Laurent said. His expression was grim.

Jim scratched his cheek, his worry growing. His friend was right. That Hazel was strong he had no doubt, but she was not used to the frigid mountain air, as the rebel men were. And he had no idea how it would affect her already serious condition if she were locked up again in the little shelter and suffered another episode of panic. He rubbed his eyes, trying to think of something, anything he could do to get her off this mountain. He glanced at the men around the clearing. Most had returned to regular camp activities, having decided the medical personnel didn't pose a threat of escape. The guard with the scar, Ramiro, stood near, watching them closely. Jim considered his chances of taking the man's gun. Could he overpower him? And then what? He couldn't carry an unconscious woman, protect his other companions, and flee from an entire band of men, especially when they knew the terrain and he didn't.

"Stay with her," Jim told Camila, glancing at the patients beneath the canvas. His best strategy was to make certain the injured were well cared for. "The faster the other patients mend, the faster we might be set free and can take Hazel back to the hospital. Send for me when she wakes."

Camila nodded, and Jim gestured for Dr. Laurent and Lucía to return with him to their tending to the other patients.

It was Hazel's cough that alerted Jim an hour later. She hacked for a long bout, her body convulsing.

When he reached her side, Camila was wiping the cool rag over her face.

Hazel's eyes opened, blinking slowly.

"How do you feel?" he asked, crouching beside her and taking her hand. Her skin was still hot.

"Hurts," she wheezed, starting into another spell of coughing. "Breathing," she said once she was able to speak. She moved as if she'd sit up.

"You need to rest," Jim said, pressing gently on her shoulders until she relaxed. He placed a hand on her cheek, his heart heavy as he felt her fever.

Hazel's eyes closed again.

"Did she drink the willow bark?" he asked Camila.

"Yes, but it was not strong. With the cold water . . ."

He nodded his understanding and opened the kit containing the medications, locating the bottle he was looking for. He shook it, holding it up to look through the opaque glass in the sunlight. There was only a small bit left. He took out a cup from the kit, poured a dose of the morphine into it, and handed it to Camila, motioning for her to administer it.

He stood, rubbing his face. His jaw was sore, and he realized he'd been clenching it. He had no fire, no way to heat water or keep Hazel warm, aside from blankets. He couldn't even count on the water being clean, not knowing how often, if ever, the buckets were washed or with what.

The routine continued throughout the day, Jim and the others tending to the patients while taking turns to remain at Hazel's side. The morphine helped with her pain, but her bouts of coughing happened more often, and Jim's worrying tightened his shoulders until they ached.

Evening fell, long shadows spreading across the clearing.

Jim and Dr. Laurent made a quick check of the remaining patients and returned to Hazel.

She was awake and propped up against a barrel. A lone lantern sat on the ground beside her.

Lucía was holding a cup for her to drink, and Camila wrung out the wet towel in the bucket.

"How do you feel?" Jim asked again.

Hazel opened her mouth to answer, but another spell of coughing took over, leaving her breathless. "Tired," she said at last.

"You should come out of the cold air," Jim said, helping her rise. He dreaded her reaction at returning to the small structure, but she couldn't remain outside.

Camila put a blanket around Hazel's shoulders.

The guard Ramiro stepped up to them.

Reflexively, Jim held Hazel tighter.

Ramiro glanced around as if making certain he couldn't be overheard. He leaned toward Jim. "You must go." He spoke in Spanish. "Take her." He lifted his chin toward Hazel.

Jim stared at him, not understanding what he was being told to do.

"Take her now." He moved closer, giving a small push with the barrel of his gun. "To the hospital."

Jim looked toward Dr. Laurent and the nurses. "I can't leave them."

"No," Hazel protested. "We can't do that."

"They will not be harmed," Ramiro said. "I swear it. You must go now."

Dr. Laurent pressed a medicine bottle into Jim's hand. "He is right. Zhe chance of your escape is better with only two."

"Come." Ramiro gave the command and left no room for argument. He started toward the edge of the clearing. "Come now."

Jim took a last look at Dr. Laurent and the other nurses, feeling an enormous rush of guilt. But if he did not get Hazel to the hospital . . .

"Go," Dr. Laurent urged.

Jim and Hazel followed Ramiro from the camp. Jim glanced over his shoulder, worried they would be seen, but the shadows were deep, and they were swallowed by the darkness almost immediately.

Hazel stepped along, keeping pace, but her movements were sluggish. She held tightly to his hand.

When they came to the tree line, Ramiro stopped. Jim could just make out his silhouette. "Follow the water." He pointed and turned to go back.

"The others," Jim said.

"They will be safe; I promise you."

"Thank you," Hazel said. Her breathing sounded labored.

Ramiro stopped, turning to look at her. A hint of moonlight gave a slight glow to his features. He inclined his head, his expression softening for an instant. And then he was gone.

Jim wrapped the blanket tighter around Hazel and led her through the trees, listening for the sound of water. He strained his ears, wondering if he'd hear a shout or a gunshot. His back itched as he imagined a bullet hitting him. Had their absence been noticed? Once it was, how much time did they have before the mountain was swarming with rebels searching for them?

He and Hazel found the stream and turned to follow it down the mountain. Occasionally the moonlight sparkled on the water, but they were mainly led by the sound. Hazel held on to his hand as they walked, but the farther they went, the more Jim was pulling her. Eventually, he supported her, his arm around her waist, taking careful steps in the darkness. She leaned heavily against him.

With every fit of coughing, he feared they would be overheard, but aside from their own noise and the trickling of the stream, the mountain was silent.

Another fit of coughing racked Hazel's body. She sat on the ground. "I . . . need to . . . rest," she gasped. "Just for . . . a moment."

Jim sat beside her. He looked back up through the dark trees, trying to remember if he'd ever heard of bears or wolves in these mountains. He wished he had a gun.

Hazel was shivering despite her fever.

Jim pulled the blanket tighter around her and rubbed her arms and back through the woolen fabric.

She coughed again, and Jim considered their options. He could move much faster on his own, getting to the hospital, he guessed, in a few hours and then return for her. But would Hazel be safe here alone? There was the risk that she would be discovered. But more worrying was her shivering. The fever had left her clothing damp, and the mountain was cold. Prolonged exposure could lead to hypothermia.

Her head leaned against him, but he couldn't let her sleep. "We must keep going."

She didn't complain, but he could hear her wheezing breath. She moved slowly, and Jim held her upright, pulling her along, making certain the path was sure.

They soon stopped again, sitting on a flat rock. Hazel slumped over, lying on her side and drawing her knees to her chest as she coughed. Jim could hear the pain in the sound. Her breathing was so shallow. He debated whether to give her more morphine, but decided it should wait. The medicine would make her too tired to continue. He stood and pulled at her arms, trying to get her to stand again.

"I can't," she whispered, her body limp. "I can't go on."

"You must," Jim replied, pushing any sound of worry out of his voice and speaking with certainty. "There is no other choice." He returned to sit next to her, pulling her against him and holding her in the circle of his arms.

She lay limply, her body hot. She gasped, taking shallow breaths. "Jim, I think I might die."

Her words punched holes in his determination, allowing terror to leak through. "You should have more faith in my abilities as a doctor," he said, thinking to distract her—and himself—with humor. But the joke fell flat.

"I really—" She gasped, pressing her palm to her breastbone. "My chest hurts so . . . badly . . . and I can't . . . I feel too weak to continue."

Jim turned her toward him, the bit of moon making her face barely visible. "You won't die. I won't let you. Do you understand, Hazel? You cannot think like that. You cannot give up. You mustn't." His voice shook, and he realized there were tears in his eyes. He cleared his throat, blinking them away. "We are close; I am sure of it. Once we reach the hospital, I'll be able to care for you properly. You must push on, just a bit longer."

The shadow of her face nodded, and Jim rose, drawing her up with him. He kept an arm around her waist, and she held his shoulder. They moved slowly, stopping when a fit of coughing overtook her, then continuing on.

When they stepped from beneath the trees, Jim saw the sky seemed to be a deep purple on one side, and over the next hour, it lightened until it was a lavender color. Dawn was near. They had been traveling for the entire night. The promise of morning gave Jim a newfound energy, and he stepped quicker, coming at last to the road.

"We're close, Hazel," he said.

"*Alto!*" a voice called out.

Fear turned Jim's blood cold, but it lasted only a moment until the speaker stepped onto the road and Jim saw he wore the deep-blue uniform of the Spanish Army. He nearly sagged in relief.

More soldiers joined him, coming out from beneath the trees. They must be guarding the road.

"Doctor?" the first man asked, pointing at Jim's coat.

"Dr. Jim Jackson, from the Red Cross Hospital." Jim pointed with his chin down the road toward where he knew the hospital was.

Hazel doubled over, coughing, and when her fit had passed, Jim lowered her to sit against a tree. One of the soldiers brought a flask of water, and Jim helped her drink. He gave her a dose of morphine, then laid her down, putting a fold of the blanket beneath her head.

She slept immediately.

Jim explained to the men what had happened, giving a description of where his companions were being held and pointing the soldiers in the general direction of the rebels' camp. He knew the rebels' lookouts would hear them coming before they got close, especially with the road blocked. Hopefully they would have time to move the patients to safety.

A wagon was sent for, and a soldier brought Jim a cup of coffee.

"There are sick and injured men at the camp," Jim told him. He turned to look squarely at the man who appeared to be the group's leader. "I trust you will act with honor, treating fairly your enemies who cannot fight."

"You have my word, Doctor." The man gave a solid nod before leaving with the rescue party.

Jim sipped the coffee, feeling the warmth move through his body, along with relief. They had made it. For most of the night, he'd worried they wouldn't, that they'd be caught by their captors or Hazel would be too weak to continue. He knelt beside her, touching her forehead. Her fever was still strong, and her breathing had not improved. The dread he'd ignored all night swelled until it nearly consumed him. His throat constricted with fear and his eyes burned. Pneumonia was a serious ailment with a survival rate much lower than Jim liked, and he knew her condition was only going to worsen.

He cleared his throat, pushing away his fear. If anyone were strong enough to fight this disease, it was she. And once he had her safely in the hospital, they would have a chance of conquering it.

CHAPTER 19

Hazel floated. Sometimes she heard voices. Fuzzy images came and went, and she didn't know whether they were real or dreamed. There were moments she felt very near to waking. But the last bit of effort required to push her completely awake was too much.

"Come, you must drink." The voice sounded like Camila's.

Hazel felt herself pulled forward and a cup pressed to her lips.

She sipped, tasting the cool water, and at last, her eyes drifted open.

"Oh, you are awake," Camila said and helped her lie back again.

The act of focusing made Hazel's eyes ache. She blinked slowly. "Camila, is that you?" Her voice sounded hoarse.

"Yes, it's me."

"But how . . . ?" she began, sorting through her memories. Camila had been left behind in the mountain with Dr. Laurent and Lucía. "It can't be you," she said. "I must be dreaming." She swallowed through her raw throat and closed her eyes again, every inch of her body hurting. "Or I have died," she muttered.

Camila laughed. "I hope not, because I think *I* am very much alive."

Hazel peeked through her eyelids again. Camila was still there, and she appeared to be counting Hazel's pulse.

"How?" Hazel asked. "How did you escape?"

Camila set her hand back on the bed. She took a thermometer from the side table and pressed it beneath Hazel's arm. "Once it was discovered that you and Dr. Jackson had gone, we were shut up in the little prison." She winced as she said the words, most likely remembering Hazel's reaction to the place. "In the morning, Spanish soldiers opened the door, releasing us, and we came out to find the entire camp had disappeared. They must have worried you would reveal the location." She drew out the thermometer, checking the reading and noting it on the chart. "Your fever is gone," she said, looking pleased.

"I'm so sorry we left you there," Hazel said. "We shouldn't—"

"You did exactly the right thing." Camila brought the cup of water again, helping Hazel sit up and drink. "If Dr. Jackson hadn't taken you when he did . . ." She shivered and crossed herself.

Hazel rested back into the pillow. The short conversation had exhausted her.

"Our adventure was not as romantic as books would have us believe, was it?" Camila said, returning the chart to the foot of the bed. "They never mention the cold or the fear." She pulled the sheet up, smoothing it.

"Or the smell of the privy," Hazel said. Her eyes were starting to close.

Camila laughed again. "Rest now. I'll tell Dr. Jackson you've woken. He has been very worried."

Hazel didn't hear her leave.

The next time she woke, Nella sat in the chair beside her bed, knitting.

"Nella." Hazel's voice was a croak. She cleared her throat.

Nella dropped her needles and leaned forward, grabbing Hazel's hand. "Oh, my dear, you're awake at last."

"I saw Camila earlier," Hazel said. "Was I dreaming?"

"No, it was really she." Nella smiled. "Everyone is returned, safe and sound. Now we just need you to regain your health, and it will all be just as it was."

Hazel glanced around, for the first time realizing she was in a patient bed, but she could not tell which ward. Curtains had been drawn around her bed as a protection to the other patients against contracting her disease. "Has anyone else become ill?" Hazel pointed to her throat to indicate her fear that she may have spread the illness with her coughing.

Nella shook her head. "No one." She picked up her needles and untangled the yarn, counting the stitches before she could continue. "You certainly had us worried, my dear. Such a fever, and the coughing . . ." She shook her head. "Poor Dr. Jackson. I've never seen a man in such a state. He went days without sleeping, until Claude finally ordered him to bed and gave him a dose of chloral hydrate to make certain he slept."

It took a moment for Hazel to realize Claude was Dr. Laurent. "Days?" She felt her cheeks color at Nella's words. She was sorry to have upset Jim so, but the depth of his concern made her insides feel warm and soft. "How long have I been ill?" She coughed, holding her chest and turning on her side as she did.

"You returned to the hospital four days ago," Nella said. She gave Hazel a handkerchief and helped her lie back. "Here, let me get you some water, dear."

"Thank you."

"The coughing is good," Nella said. "Should clear out your lungs and get you back to full health." She put a bit more optimism into her voice than was necessary, and Hazel could tell her friend was still worried.

She took a sip of the water and closed her eyes. It felt impossible to even imagine returning to how she was before. Everything ached, even breathing was difficult, and she was more tired than she'd ever been in her life—even after sleeping for four days. She vaguely wondered how much morphine she'd been given.

"Hazel, dear," Nella said, "there is something I hoped to talk to you about."

"Mmm?" Hazel tried to blink her eyes open, wanting to listen to her friend, but the warmth of sleep felt too comfortable, the darkness too inviting, so she stopped fighting and let it envelop her.

When Hazel woke again, the ward was quiet. She lay for a moment with her eyes closed, hearing only the usual hospital noises and knowing without looking that Jim was with her. Her heart rate picked up speed. She cracked one eye open. Night had fallen. A candle lamp sat on the table beside her, and in the chair where she'd last seen Nella sat Jim. His elbow rested on the table, and he held his forehead in his hand. He was fast asleep.

Hazel watched him for a moment, the candlelight moving over the planes of his face, making shadows around his eyes and highlights in his curls. She wondered how long he'd been there.

A cough pushed its way into her throat. Not wanting to wake him, she tried to hold it back, but it was no use. She rolled onto her side, facing away from him, and held herself tightly as the fit of coughing overtook her.

Jim was there in an instant, sitting on the bed beside her, his hand on her shoulder.

When the spell finished, she wheezed, pressing against the pain in her lungs. Her eyes were wet with tears.

"Hazel." He squeezed her shoulder.

The sound of her name thrilled her in spite of the circumstance.

"I'm sorry." She breathed in quick gulps.

"Sorry for coughing?" Jim said, a hint of a tease in his voice. He handed her a handkerchief. "Hardly something worthy of an apology." He helped her lay back onto the pillow and poured a cup of water.

"I'm sorry for disturbing you." She felt shy at his closeness, which was silly since they'd been much closer. She'd slept next to him in the little stone house, for heaven's sake.

"I heard you'd woken." Jim measured some medicine into the water and helped her drink. "And I couldn't bear to miss being here when you woke again." He brushed a strand of hair from her forehead.

She felt a ribbon of tingles where he'd touched her skin. His tone left her speechless for a long moment. There was so much emotion behind the words. "You look tired," she said at last.

Jim shrugged and smiled. "I'm entirely well."

She looked closer, seeing lines around his mouth and heaviness in his eyelids, but didn't argue. She yawned, and it turned into another cough. "I don't remember arriving back in the hospital," she said once she finished coughing. "We were in the mountains and then I woke here." She tried to find the memories, but there were only snatches, she couldn't tell which were dreams. "You brought me all this way," she said. "You saved my life." The frankness of her words made her blush, but they had to be said.

"Hazel, if anything had happened to you . . ." Jim swallowed, looking away. When he turned back, his eyes were shining.

His worry made her feel self-conscious and guilty for being the cause of it. It also made her feel like she'd been wrapped in a heavenly embrace, which was hardly appropriate for the situation. "Nothing will happen to me," she said. "I have an exceptional doctor." She took his hand, speaking in a light voice meant to lift the somber mood.

He squeezed her fingers in reply.

"Now, tell me what has occurred while I slept," she said, wanting to find a topic that would not upset him. "Has there been another battle? Has Captain Bryant's condition improved?" So much speaking left her gasping.

"We've acquired seven new patients from the battle a few days ago, and they were tended to by Dr. Ruiz while we were away. Captain Bryant improves each day. And . . ." Jim raised their joined hands and kissed her fingers, then set her hand back on the bed. He pulled up the sheets that had been crumpled with her coughing, straightening them. "Your doctor is ordering you to rest."

"I have slept for days," she complained, but her slow blinking betrayed her. The morphine was starting to work. She yawned and coughed.

"Tomorrow I will have Alona make you a special meal." The corner of Jim's mouth lifted in a teasing smirk. "Plain gruel."

Hazel made a face without opening her eyes.

"I'm going to take the light," he said. "Unless you need it." She could hear the implication in his voice. He wondered if waking in the darkness would cause her panic to return.

"You can take it," she said.

"Good night, Hazel."

"Good night."

She felt a soft kiss on her forehead and forced her eyes open. "Jim, I'm glad I came here."

He paused, his hand on the curtain. "I'm glad as well. There were times I feared we wouldn't find our way through the mountains."

"No." She fought against the sleep. "I'm glad I'm here in Spain. In the hospital. I'm glad I came here and glad I met you." The words left her exhausted, and the moment they were said, she dropped back into her dark slumber.

CHAPTER 20

Jim peered into the microscope lens, studying the blood sample, looking for the telltale shapes of bacteria. He worried one of the patients from the battleground the week before suffered from sepsis, and according to what he was seeing, his analysis was right. He blew out a tired breath.

A knock sounded on the door. "Dr. Jackson." Camila stepped inside. "There are some gentlemen here to see you—officers. They are English."

"Show them in." He made a quick note on the patient's chart and stood, coming to the door just as the men entered. They were indeed English officers. The pair wore red coats, and each held a black foreign service helmet, complete with gold insignia, beneath his arm.

The older man was clearly the superior officer, evident not only by the embellishments on his uniform—a general, if Jim was not mistaken—but also in the way he held his chin high, his eyes scanning the room with an air of authority. The general was slender with exceptionally straight posture, intelligent eyes, and a thick mustache waxed to a point on either cheek. He stood straight, confident in his own importance.

"I'm Dr. Jim Jackson of the International Red Cross." Jim inclined his head in greeting. "Please, come in and sit down. How might I be of service, officers?"

"Thank you," the general said. He glanced at his companion. "Our horses require water, Doctor. Is there somewhere the sergeant might tend to them?"

"Yes, of course." Jim stepped into the corridor, calling for an orderly. When the man arrived, Jim explained to him in Spanish what was needed, and the man departed with the sergeant, leaving Jim alone with the general.

Jim motioned toward a pair of chairs.

The general remained standing. "I beg your pardon; I have yet to introduce myself. General Sir William Ambrose Thornton." He tipped his head the slightest bit. "How do you do?"

Jim stared at the man, realizing immediately who he was. An unease twisted in his stomach as he realized the time he'd dreaded was here.

"I have come in search of my daughter and her traveling companions," General Thornton continued. "I have learned they were brought to this hospital after an explosion on the train track."

"You are Miss Hazel Thornton's father."

"Yes."

Jim pushed away his bleak thoughts and arranged his face into a pleasant expression. "You are right. Miss Thornton and her companions are here."

The man before him seemed to deflate, his stoic expression faltering as he closed his eyes and breathed a relieved sigh. "Thank the stars. And she is safe?"

"She is safe, but I must tell you, sir, your daughter has been very ill." Seeing the general step forward, his shoulders raised and his eyes wide, Jim held out his hands in a placating gesture. "She is recovering. Recovering well, actually."

The general stepped back, his posture relaxing. "And can I see her?"

Jim called into the hall, and when Camila came, she informed him Hazel was being bathed. He translated for the general, inviting him to be seated until she was ready to receive a visitor.

The general took a seat, accepting the offered sherry.

Jim braced himself, pushing out the words he knew he must say. "I believe Miss Thornton lives with relatives in London?" The general nodded, and he continued. "I would recommend that she return as soon as she is able to travel." He swallowed the emotion that swelled in his throat. "Hospitals are filled with people and disease, and pneumonia leaves a patient weak and susceptible to reinfection. Our supplies here are delivered irregularly, and once a medicine is depleted, there is no guarantee of when more will arrive."

"I can believe it," General Thornton said. "Blasted inconvenient to travel around here. It took days to find a coach, and the nearest train station is nearly thirty miles away over mountain roads." He set his glass on the table between the chairs. "But she will recover."

It was not a question, but he looked to Jim as if he expected confirmation. "If she continues as she is now, she will recover. But, General, there is always the chance—"

General Thornton held up a hand, stopping the words, and Jim wondered whether hearing them would be too difficult or whether he simply would not allow himself to consider the alternative. "She's a strong one, my Hazel. Endured a lot for one so young. An exceptional woman."

Jim nodded, pleased at the man's assessment of his daughter. He completely agreed with it. "We have been very fortunate to have her," he said. "You may not know that she has worked here as a nurse these past weeks. She has been well trained and has a certain instinct for the work."

"Gets that from her mother," the general said. "You never met a gentler woman. Always helping. Always concerned." He stared ahead, seeming to be lost in a memory. "One day she'd be making a warm compress for a neighbor's toothache, and the next she was cleaning and stitching up a boy's scraped knee." He smiled with fondness. "She was a healer, but more than that, people just wanted to be near her. Something special about her. She gave comfort to the sick and infirm."

The man could have been describing Hazel exactly. "Miss Thornton is quite the same."

The general shook himself from his musing. "I beg your pardon. Has she had enough time now, do you think?"

"Why don't we find out." Jim led him down the stone passageway to the wards.

The general appeared suitably impressed with the converted monastery, studying the high ceilings and doors they passed. "I've seen hospitals all over the world, but this is truly a sight. What a magnificent building." He looked approvingly at the doorway into the ward, noting the thick stone around the archway and the heavy wooden door.

"Miss Thornton," Jim called out when they reached the curtains around her bed. "You have a visitor."

"A visitor?" Hazel's voice was both tired and surprised. "Please, bring them in."

He pulled the fabric aside, holding it as the general entered.

Hazel sat up in the bed, propped up with pillows. She was writing in what looked to be a journal. Her hair was damp and freshly washed, the small hairs around her forehead and cheeks curling as they dried. She had changed from her hospital clothes to her own nightclothes, a gown with a high lace neck and ribbons on her sleeves. She set down her pencil, squinted for an instant, and her expression lit up as if she'd stepped out into the sunlight. "Father." She clasped her hands, then held out her arms. "Oh, Father, you've come." Her voice was heavy with emotion.

The general went to her, sitting on her bed as they embraced.

Hazel laid her head on her father's shoulder, tears falling on her cheeks. "You're here at last," she said.

Her father pulled back, holding her hands as he looked at her. "Oh, my dear, you are very pale. And so thin."

"I am much improved." She waved her hand as if to push away his worries, then looked toward the doorway. "J—Dr. Jackson, can you believe my father is here?"

Jim smiled his acknowledgment. He stepped inside the curtain, and feeling as if he needed a reason for being there, he picked up her chart, looking over her noted vital signs.

"I have missed you," Hazel said to her father. She leaned back on her pillows, smiling but looking very tired. Washing her hair and changing clothes had clearly worn her out.

"And I you." The general straightened, moving to sit on the chair beside her bed. "I am so sorry about Christmas. This has all turned into quite a mess, hasn't it?"

Hazel shrugged. "It hasn't been all bad. I've been a nurse here, Father, just like I always hoped to be."

"Very good. And you'll be able to be a nurse once you've returned to London."

Hazel frowned. "Perhaps." She stretched out the word, looking at Jim, then back at her father. "The Red Cross is in need of more nurses, you know. There is much to be done here."

"We can discuss all that once you're safely home in London and fully recovered."

Hazel's frown deepened. "But I—"

"Excuse me." Jim broke into the conversation before Hazel turned it into an argument. It was obvious she did not want to leave. He needed to convince her it was the right thing to do for her health, but he preferred to do it privately. The constriction returned to his throat as he thought about saying goodbye.

"Miss Thornton needs to rest. General, I imagine you're anxious to see Captain Bryant as well." Jim held open the curtain.

"I'll return soon, my dear," the general said. He kissed her forehead and followed Jim out of the curtained area.

They walked toward the other end of the ward. Captain Bryant's bed was at the very end, where the light was less severe on his headaches. Once they were nearly there, Jim called Lucía over, introducing her to the general.

When she heard the man was Hazel's father, Lucía's eyes widened with interest.

"Lucía is our head nurse," Jim said to General Thornton. "After you visit with the captain, she will show you and the sergeant to your sleeping quarters and send for a meal. I imagine you are tired and hungry after your journey."

"Thank you, Dr. Jackson." The general glanced back at the curtained area. "When will my daughter be ready to travel?"

"Soon," Jim tried to say, but his voice made no noise. He cleared his throat and tried again. "Soon." It must be soon.

When Lucía and the general left, Jim returned to Hazel's bed and stepped back through the curtains. Her eyes were closed, but she opened them when he entered.

"How is your pain?" he asked.

"It is manageable," Hazel said. "As long as I don't cough."

He nodded. The morphine could wait, then.

Hazel looked toward the opening in the curtains. "My father seems determined to take me away from here."

Jim let out a breath. "I recommended to him that you should return to London. Your recovery could take months, and this is not the place for it."

Hazel stared at him, the hurt in her expression hitting him like a blow. "You're sending me away?"

"Not at all," he said. "But London provides the best chance for a successful recovery."

She blinked. "I thought that I . . . that you . . . we . . ." Her voice softened to a whisper. She swallowed and then coughed deeply. "I should like to be alone now, Dr. Jackson." She turned onto her side, facing away from him.

"Hazel."

"Please . . . I don't want to talk anymore. Please just go."

He stepped back through the curtains, kicking himself for how he'd managed to botch the explanation. There surely were a hundred other ways to deliver the news, to convince her that it was the only way, that the decision was made with her health in mind. Now not only was Jim about to lose the woman he loved, but thanks to his inability to express his feelings without sounding like an utter fool, she would leave without knowing how he felt. That, at least, he could remedy. He rubbed his eyes and walked back toward the office, knowing he could not remedy the feeling of his heart breaking apart.

CHAPTER 21

Hazel lay still long after Jim was gone. She wished she could just fall into a deep sleep and forget everything, but contrary to each time she'd closed her eyes over the past week, she lay painfully awake now, her stomach hard and her heart aching as she repeated Jim's words again and again in her mind.

She'd been so certain he would be on her side, that once he heard that she was to be taken to London, he would convince her father that she should stay—or at least ask her to return once she was well. But he hadn't argued for her. He'd been the one to insist she leave. He hadn't wanted her to stay.

The frustration at having everyone else dictate her life was making her itch with vexation. She finally had what she'd always wanted: the chance to be a nurse, the opportunity to decide her own future, and of course, a person she loved with whom to share it. But it was being taken away, and Hazel had no say in the matter. And Jim. Knowing that she would leave him behind, that whatever had been growing between them, whatever might have come of it, was over made her heart ache.

Feeling as though she needed to be doing something besides wallowing in self-pity, she decided to speak with Nella. Not wishing to walk through the hospital ward in her nightclothes, she wrapped her sheet around her, holding the corners in her fist. That, at least, felt a bit more appropriate.

She peeked through the curtains, praying she wouldn't encounter Jim, but the ward was quiet.

Within only a few steps, Hazel felt winded. She steadied herself on a bed frame and then continued on. Earlier, when Camila had taken her to the washroom, she'd insisted on Hazel using a wheeled chair. Hazel had thought it excessive, believing herself entirely capable of walking the short distance, but now that she'd gone no more than twenty feet and could hardly catch her breath, she realized the wisdom in the precaution.

After a few stops to rest, she arrived at Nella's bed, but she found it empty. Had Nella been moved? Or was she simply away from the bed? She looked around to the other side. The travel bag was there, with an unfinished knitting project sitting on top.

Satisfied that it was the right bed, Hazel sat, leaning back against Nella's pillows, her strength entirely expended by the short walk. She closed her eyes.

"Well, this is a pleasant surprise." Nella's voice pulled Hazel out of her doze.

She sat up. "There you are, Nella. I worried you'd been moved to a different bed."

"Still here," Nella said. "Though, I am getting rather anxious to be doing something besides sitting all the time. I've knitted enough socks and scarves to supply the entire hospital and then some." She chuckled. Using a cane, she stepped around the bed and sat in a chair.

"Nella, my father is taking us away," Hazel said. "I don't want to go, but we must, and I . . . I wish it were not so."

Nella sighed, shifting in her chair. She fidgeted with the edge of the bedsheet, flicking it with her thumb. "Hazel, dear, I meant to speak with you about this earlier." She released the sheet and clasped her hands together. "I have something to tell you."

From the nervous way her friend was acting, Hazel worried something terrible had happened. "What is it? Is something wrong?" She looked down at Nella's ankle.

"No, not at all," Nella said. "But it is going to . . . change things." She took a breath and let it out. "I'm not returning to London with you."

This was preposterous. Had the doctors decided she was unable to travel? "Because of your ankle?" Hazel asked. "Surely it has healed enough."

"It is not because of my ankle. I . . . I am to be married." She said these last words softly, almost shyly, as if she were telling a secret she hoped Hazel would be pleased to hear.

It took a moment for the words to make sense. Hazel stared at her friend, and then she lifted her gaze to where Dr. Laurent was writing in a chart a little farther down the ward. He wasn't looking in their direction, but he was close enough to hear their conversation. His ears were bright red. She looked back at Nella. "You are marrying Dr. Laurent?"

"Yes." Nella's face broke into a radiant smile. "I wanted to tell you before, but you were ill and then you kept falling asleep and—"

"Nella, what glorious news. I am so happy for you." Hazel leaned forward, pulling her friend into an embrace. The news really was wonderful, but it settled strangely inside her, as if it didn't fit where it should have. She was, of course, pleased for her friend, but she also realized she would very likely never see her again. And there was something else, a longing that she soon recognized as envy.

"I am happy as well," Nella said. "Splendidly so." She looked toward Dr. Laurent, meeting his gaze with a glowing expression.

He smiled in return, his cheeks coloring.

"He is wonderful, isn't he?" Nella sighed.

"He certainly is," Hazel said, tamping down her feelings of jealousy. "And when is the wedding to be held?"

The very corners of Nella's eyes tightened in a wince. "Since you are to be leaving so soon, we are hoping to arrange it for tomorrow or the day following. I would be very pleased to have you there."

"I wouldn't miss it, naturally," Hazel said, speaking in a voice that she forced to sound cheerful. *So soon.* Her father must be planning to leave within the week, perhaps even within a few days. She glanced toward the far side of the ward, where her curtained bed waited, and she felt tears pricking at her eyes. Her throat was swelling. "I should return," she said, swallowing as she maintained her pleasant expression.

"Oh yes. You look very tired, my dear." Nella called out to Dr. Laurent, and a moment later, the man brough a wheeled chair.

Hazel rose, but before she sat in the chair, she embraced Nella again, kissing her cheek. "I am truly so delighted, Nella." She squeezed Dr. Laurent's arm. "And congratulations to you as well, Doctor."

She somehow managed to keep her smile in place, holding in the wave of emotions as Dr. Laurent thanked her with a grin and delivered her back to the other side of the ward.

Once she was alone in her bed behind the curtains, she pressed her face into her pillow and let the tears come.

The next day, Hazel sat on the cot in her bedchamber. She held her head in her hands. The effort of getting here had drained her energy.

Nella's luggage had at last been removed from the room, leaving only Hazel's trunk and travel bag, Captain Bryant's portmanteau, and a hatbox.

She tipped over, lying on her side, and watched the candle's flame, remembering the first time she'd come into this little room. She'd been so nervous and determined to prove herself, especially to the irritable Dr. Jackson. She thought of the day she'd brought in an extra lamp and opened her Christmas gifts. She glanced at the little carved frog watching her from the table and felt a strong ache.

Once she had regained enough strength, she pushed open her trunk and took out a gown she deemed suitable for a wedding, then stockings, a corset, a bustle, a hat, and shoes. She set it all out on the bed, dreading the effort it would take to put it all on, especially the corset.

She moved to close the lid and saw the embroidered shawl Dahlia had given her. She knew Nella had nothing fancy to wear. This was just the thing to make her feel like a bride. Hazel took out the shawl and refolded it, setting it on the trunk's lid.

A fit of coughing came on, and she bent over, holding her arms around herself until it finished. She breathed heavily.

"Hazel? Are you in there?"

She recognized Jim's voice. "One moment," she said and dug through her trunk, finding a dressing gown. She put it on before she answered.

Jim held a candle lamp. He glanced past her into the room. "What are you doing?"

"I will not attend a wedding in my nightclothes," she said.

"I see." Jim said. He glanced into the room again. "I'd hoped to talk to you if you have a moment."

Hazel stepped aside, opening the door to admit him.

Jim entered, closing the door behind him. He set the candle lamp on the trunk and turned to face her. "Hazel, I must apologize to you. I realize it came as a surprise, your father's arrival and the plans for your return to London. We—I did not consult you, and the manner in which I delivered the news was insensitive, to say the least."

"I don't want to leave." The words came out of their own volition, and she felt silly. She sounded like a petulant child. She glanced up at him.

"I know," Jim said. His expression was very serious, his forehead furrowed. "Hazel, if there were any other way—"

And then she was in his arms, holding on to him as if he were a life raft.

His arms wrapped around her, their warmth, his familiar smell, the feeling of just being near him making the prospect of leaving nearly unbearable.

There was so much she wanted to say. Jim had given her a chance to become what she'd dreamed of. He'd encouraged her, taught her, trusted her. She wanted to tell him how much these weeks had meant to her, how they'd changed her. She wanted to ask him to promise to write letters or plan for him to visit in the summer. But she said none of it. The words hung heavy in the air around them, unspoken. This moment felt final. A goodbye. And for that, there were no words.

She held him tighter, as if doing so would dull the ache inside her.

At last, they separated.

"Hazel, I—" Jim swallowed hard. He pressed his lips together tightly. "Promise me you will get well."

She nodded, not trusting herself to speak. This moment was likely their last opportunity to be alone together.

He kissed her then, a soft kiss without the hesitance, the questions, or passion of before. This was a farewell kiss. A last kiss.

The ache in Hazel's chest grew and had nothing to do with her illness. She did not know if she could bear it.

CHAPTER 22

The wedding was a quiet ceremony, performed by padre de Leon in the cloister. Dr. Laurent and Miss Westbrook had chosen the late afternoon because it was the warmest hour of the day, but there was still a sharpness in the winter air.

The nurses had brought every chair they could find, and all of the hospital staff and most of the patients were in attendance. Dr. Laurent was well-liked in the hospital, as was his bride.

Jim sat beside Dr. Ruiz, and he glanced regularly—without meaning to—to where Hazel sat with her father, the sergeant who had accompanied him, and Captain Bryant. She wore a pale-green gown with an excessive amount of fabric and ruffles in the skirt. Her hair was pulled up beneath a small hat adorned by a cluster of roses and a few feathers. At her neck was the brooch she'd worn the first day he'd seen her—a blue flower surrounded by swirls of metal.

Her face was paler than usual, making the periorbital dark circles beneath her eyes appear even darker, and she had lost weight during the worst days of her illness. But none of these factors detracted from how lovely she was. Jim directed his attention back to the ceremony, but it was difficult.

Hazel coughed a few times in the cold air, but the long fits she'd suffered from days earlier seemed to have passed. Her father kept a close watch on her, moving her shawl up onto her shoulders when she shivered.

Once the vows were said, the atmosphere of the cloister became one of celebration. Laurent grinned as he looked at his new bride, and she beamed back at him.

Jim approached the newlyweds, taking Dr. Laurent's hand in a firm handshake. "Congratulations," he said, clapping his friend on the shoulder. "I am very happy for you."

"Thank you, my friend." Dr. Laurent's grin was impossibly wide.

Hazel embraced the new Mrs. Laurent. "Such a lovely bride," she said. "Nella, you are glowing."

"Thank you, my dear." She tugged at the shawl around her shoulders. The garment appeared to be silk with elaborate embroidery.

Jim did not know much about gentlewomen's clothing, but he could tell it was much more delicate than the practical chocolate-colored dress she wore.

"It is much too elegant for me," her friend said, blushing.

"Hardly." Hazel straightened the shawl. "It suits you. I believe you shall have a very happy life, Nella."

"I believe I shall," her friend replied, taking her husband's arm and smiling at him.

Dr. Laurent's eyes were soft as he gazed at her.

Jim took a step back with Hazel, feeling as though they were intruding on an intimate moment. Their gazes met, and he tipped his head toward the couple and widened his eyes.

Hazel smiled, looking tired.

"Perhaps you should sit down," Jim suggested.

Hazel took his offered arm, allowing him to lead her back to the chair beside her father.

The general was deep in conversation with the sergeant and Captain Bryant.

The captain shaded his eyes with his hand, and Jim imagined the sun must be making his head ache.

Jim sat on the other side of Hazel. "You don't have to attend the banquet," he said. "They will understand."

"It is my last night here," she said. "And my dear friend's wedding. I am not going to miss it."

Jim nodded. He'd known what her answer would be, and he tried to remind himself to treat her like a friend instead of a patient. But it was difficult. If she was to recover, she needed to rest as much as possible. "Your brooch," he said to distract himself. "I believe you wore it the day you arrived as well. Is that . . ."

"An orchid."

"Ah." He looked closer at it, noticing its distinctive shape. "I've never seen a flower that color."

"It is . . . ," she began, then seemed to consider. "It is a symbol. Something special to my friends and myself." A small smile pulled at her mouth.

"A symbol of what?"

"Sisterhood, friendship, strength in womanhood . . . the sorts of things men find tedious, I imagine." Her tone sounded flippant, but there was a hint of uncertainty in what she was saying. Her friends were important to her, and he could tell she was watching to see how he'd respond, whether he would discount what she said as insignificant or whether he would be interested.

"You haven't told me about these friends," he said. "What are their names?"

"Sophie, Vivian, Elizabeth, and Dahlia," Hazel responded. She touched the brooch. "Dahlia gave one to each of us."

"It is very unique," he said. "Beautiful."

"It is a reminder," Hazel told him. "The day we met, we made a promise together, a pledge, I suppose, to follow our dreams." She looked past him, her eyes unfocused, as if she were remembering. "I promised I would finish my nurse training."

"They sound like excellent friends, if they encourage you this way."

Hazel's expression was pensive. She folded her gloved hands in her lap, glancing to the other side of the cloister.

Instead of the lines of laundry that usually stood there, tables had been arranged in the garden. Alona and the other nurses were rolling out carts filled with food from the kitchen. Jim had sent to Santa Rosa for sherry, and the bottles clanked together as their cart rolled over the uneven ground.

Jim excused himself and went to assist, carrying chairs and lifting trays. As he worked, he considered what Hazel had said. He'd not thought of what her life had been like in London, not in any great depth. He'd vaguely imagined that she attended balls and dinner parties where only the most perfunctory subjects were discussed. He was pleased to know that she would return to friends who cared deeply about her. But the thought that sat heaviest was the realization that she had been ready to give all of it up: her friends, her dream, her life in London. She'd wanted to remain in Spain—with him—and knowing she would be leaving such a rich life behind, with deep friendships and plans for her future, made her willingness to sacrifice everything all the more valuable.

He glanced to where she sat next to her father, and he knew more than he knew anything that he was in love with Hazel Thornton. And he had no doubt that she loved him in return.

Hazel had left the next day.

Jim and the other members of the medical staff had come to the front of the hospital to bid her farewell, and then they waved as the carriage drove away.

He hadn't said anything profound. He couldn't think of anything that hadn't already been said and couldn't find any words that felt right.

In the end, he'd clasped her hand and, under the watchful gaze of her father, thanked her for her service to the International Red Cross and reminded her to drink often and rest.

That was it. He'd actually spent more time bidding farewell to Captain Bryant.

He sighed, sitting on the steps in front of the hospital's entrance. Weeks had passed since Hazel had tearfully embraced the nurses and Mrs. Laurent, since she'd taken a last long look at the imposing facade of the monastery before holding her father's hand and climbing into the waiting carriage, and still Jim could not shake off the gloom her leaving had caused. It was as if a light inside him had been extinguished.

He'd been irritable with the staff, curt with the patients, and restless, pacing late into the night. Surely this despondency could not last.

He rested his elbows on his knees, staring at the road leading away from the hospital.

The day after Hazel had departed, Camila had brought him the small drawing, telling him she'd found it in Hazel's bedchamber. Whether she'd left it deliberately or not, Jim assumed he'd never know, but he treasured the image and often found himself staring at it late into the night, long after his lamp was extinguished and he could no longer see it in the darkness.

The front door creaked open, and Jim recognized Dr. Laurent's footsteps as he came down the stairs to sit next to him.

"Ah, zhere you are, my friend. I hoped for an opportunity to talk."

"Looking for marriage advice already?" Jim asked dryly.

Dr. Laurent chuckled. "Ah no. I am still in zhe phase of zhe . . . how do you call it? Zhe honeymoon?" He stretched out his legs in front of him and leaned back. "In truth, I hoped to offer some advice to you if you are willing to hear it."

Jim shrugged.

"My friend, it is time to stop punishing yourself for your brother's death."

Jim blinked, turning to face the man. He had not expected such a direct statement from the amiable man, and the words infuriated him. "I beg your pardon?" he said sharply.

Dr. Laurent did not appear at all put off by Jim's anger. "Jim, you deserve happiness."

"I'm not happy?" He snorted.

"Are you?" Dr. Laurent spoke the words softly.

The genuine compassion in his voice deflated Jim's anger. "I don't know," he said. "And I don't think it matters. A patient's health doesn't improve or decline based on his doctor's cheerful temperament."

"Would you care to hear my diagnosis, Dr. Jackson?" Dr. Laurent asked, joining his hands across his chest.

Jim raised his brows and lifted his hand, indicating that Dr. Laurent could say whatever he wished.

"You are here, at zhe Red Cross Hospital, because you hope to prove something, even if it is only to yourself. You hope to make it right, what happened to Teddy. To atone. You believe you must save as many people as you can, each one a penance for zhe most important one, zhe one you were not able to save."

Jim frowned, not liking how close his friend's words came to ringing true. "And you consider yourself an alienist now?"

Dr. Laurent shrugged. "I say only what I see."

Jim pointed with his thumb at the doors behind him. "These people need me. I do what I do to save lives, not to make up for what happened to Teddy." He cleared his throat, embarrassed by the rush of emotion the mention of his brother's death caused.

"Oui, my friend. And you do it better zhan anyone I have ever met." Dr. Laurent sat up, his face becoming more animated. "But you do it at zhe expense of your own life."

Jim stared ahead at the road through the mountains. The trees cast shadows across it, as if to hide any indication of who had come this way and who had gone. Jim wondered if, once he was gone from this life, any memory would remain of his ever having been here.

"Zhere are lives to save in London, you know," Dr. Laurent said.

"Ah, now we get down to it." Jim was defensive. "You are saying I should go after her."

"I am saying that life is short. And you deserve happiness." Dr. Laurent pushed himself to his feet, patting Jim's shoulder as he left him. "Let zhe past go."

Jim remained on the hospital steps long after Dr. Laurent had gone. He pondered what the man had said, fearing it was alarmingly close to the truth.

CHAPTER 23

THE MOOD WAS FESTIVE AS the five members of the Blue Orchid Society clinked together their champagne glasses.

In true Dahlia Lancaster style, the party had been a success. The food was delicious, the conversation lovely, and the decorations . . . Hazel smiled, glancing up at the banner strung above the French doors.

Congratulations, Nurse Hazel Thornton!

The words were painted in large black letters, with small red crosses around the edges of the sign. Dahlia had invited all of their families and some of the other nursing school graduates, and even Captain Bryant had come for a short while. But now the hour was late, the other guests were gone, and it was just the five of them—exactly the way Hazel wished to celebrate, with those who loved her best.

The women took seats on the various sofas and chairs in Dahlia's parlor. Vivian sat beside Hazel on a sofa. Elizabeth leaned back in a leather armchair on one side, and Dahlia and Sophie sat in a divan facing them.

Servants moved about quietly, cleaning up the remains of the celebration.

"It was a wonderful party, Dahlia," Hazel said. "Thank you."

"It's not every day a young lady graduates from nursing training," Dahlia said. "An accomplishment like that calls for a celebration."

"We are so proud of you, dearest," Sophie said.

"Hear, hear," Elizabeth said. She raised her glass to make a toast. "To a bright future of lanced boils and fat leeches."

Hazel and her friends laughed and raised their glasses, joining in the toast. She sat back on the sofa, feeling content and warm, which could partly be attributed to the champagne. Her eyes traveled around the room, revealing flashes of pleasant memories: all the times she and her friends had visited together, laughed, wept, shared secrets . . . but there was one secret Hazel had kept to herself. She hadn't told them about Jim.

Of course, she'd mentioned him when she'd described all that had happened in Spain, but those intimate moments—the stolen kisses, the embraces—she kept them locked inside her heart, wanting them for herself alone.

A familiar ache squeezed inside. She'd heard nothing from Jim in the months since she'd returned. Not that she'd expected to—even if he had tried to write, the postal system was unpredictable—but it still hurt to have lost not only him but the hopes of what could have become of the two of them. It was the loss of a future together that hurt the most.

Sophie set down her drink on a low table and crossed the room. "We have something for you." She took a wrapped package from a cupboard and presented it to Hazel.

Hazel pushed away her sad introspection and sat up straight, setting the box on her lap.

The other women shared excited glances and leaned forward.

Hazel pulled off the ribbon and floral paper and opened the box. Inside, nestled in the box's felt lining, was a new modern stethoscope. "Oh, thank you," Hazel gasped, touched by the gift. She didn't know of any nurses who owned their own medical equipment. The instrument would be very valuable in her new position at the Hospital for Women.

Vivian leaned over to look into the box. "It is the latest model, a binaural version that improves diagnosis by auscultation. See here, the bell attached to the rubber tubing enhances the acoustic performance. And the tips at the other end insert directly into your ears to decrease sound interference." She pointed to the various parts as she spoke. "May I?"

"Yes, of course." Hazel could see that Vivian was itching to examine the stethoscope. She grinned as her friend inserted the ear tips and pressed the bell to her own chest to listen.

"This was all so very gracious of you and so thoughtful." Hazel waved her hand to indicate the room as well as the gift. "It was not so very long ago that we were doing the same thing, a party and gifts. I am very spoiled."

"It's been nearly four months since you left for Spain," Dahlia said. "High time for another party, in my opinion."

"And look at all that's happened since then," Sophie said. "Look at everything you've accomplished and all the adventures you've had."

"You completed nursing school," Dahlia said, holding up a finger.

"You survived a train explosion," Sophie added, widening her eyes as if she still could not believe something like that could happen to a person she knew.

"You were kidnapped, held prisoner, and rescued," Elizabeth pointed out.

"You survived pneumonia," Dahlia said seriously.

"You fell in love." Vivian moved the stethoscope bell to her ribs, listening through her corset as she coughed. After a moment she glanced up, realizing the room had gone quiet and the others were all staring at her.

"Oh, was I not supposed to mention it?" Vivian grimaced. "I'm sorry. I didn't realize it was a secret."

"It was a bit obvious," Elizabeth said.

Hazel's cheeks burned as she thought back through every conversation they'd had about her journey. She'd been so careful never to mention anything that might give even the slightest hint about her feelings for Jim. "How?" was the only question she could think to ask.

"The way you speak about Dr. Jackson," Dahlia said, her voice kind. "You mention him often, but you seem to be holding something back whenever you do."

"And your eyes become . . . *dreamy*." Elizabeth exaggerated the word dramatically. "Rather like those two." She cocked an eyebrow and pointed between Sophie and Vivian, both of whom were engaged to be married.

"It's nothing to be ashamed of," Vivian said. "Emotions are natural."

"It's true," Hazel admitted. "I'm sorry I didn't say anything about it earlier."

"We knew you would tell us when you were ready," Dahlia said. "Your feelings must still be very tender."

Hazel sighed. "I thought—it's silly, I know—but I hoped he would come, that he would leave the Red Cross Hospital behind and one day knock on my door."

"Why should he have to be the one to do it?" Elizabeth frowned. "Because he's the man? You have just as much of a right to make the decision about your future as he." She drank the rest of her champagne in one swallow, setting down the glass and leaning forward. Her eyes were intense, and they held a mischievous glint. "If you want to be with this Dr. Jackson, you should go to him."

"Elizabeth!" Dahlia put a hand over her mouth, shocked by her cousin's words.

"It is hardly proper, dear," Sophie said, shaking her head and lifting her brows high, as if to convey to Elizabeth that she should not put such ideas into Hazel's mind.

"Why not?" Elizabeth asked. "Because she is a woman?" She scoffed.

"I can't simply get on a train and return to the Spanish mountains," Hazel said, feeling a nervous tingle in her belly.

Elizabeth shrugged. "You did it once before."

"But there were . . . circumstances then."

Elizabeth shook her head. "You should not have to wonder, to wait helplessly, just because Society tells us that a woman should not be the one to initiate a relationship." She spread her arms wide. "Look at all you've accomplished, Hazel, all you've endured. You are strong and intelligent and entirely capable of choosing your future. You should not have to depend upon a man to choose it for you."

Hazel's heart banged into her ribs. She thought of how her father had always made decisions for her, how he'd shipped her off her to London in the first place, sent for her to come to Spain, then brought her home when she'd not wanted to leave—all the times plans for her life were made without even asking what she wanted. What if she did make this decision on her own, choose her own path? Did she dare?

"Why do men have to make everything so difficult?" Elizabeth muttered, blowing an exasperated sigh that made her lips puff out.

"If you did go," Sophie began, and then she held up her hand before a shocked-looking Dahlia could interject. "Can you be certain . . . would Dr. Jackson be . . . pleased to see you?"

"I believe he would." Hazel shook her head. "I know he would. He loves me; I'm sure of it." *Can I do this?* Hazel's heart still pounded. She imagined Jim's face when he saw her. The smile that showed a flash of teeth and made lines spread from the sides of his eyes.

Vivian moved the stethoscope bell to listen to Hazel's rapid heartbeat. "It sounds as though you are considering it," she said, smiling.

The others laughed, and just like that, Hazel had made her decision.

They all moved to the floor, scooting close to sit around the low table.

Dahlia brought paper and dipped a quill into an inkpot. "Ladies, shall we make a plan?"

"I cannot travel alone," Hazel said.

Dahlia wrote the words *traveling companion* on the page.

"I may have an idea about that one," Sophie said, looking thoughtful. "Mimi would love an opportunity to travel, but she will insist on bringing her dog, you know."

Hazel nodded, thinking how diverting it would be to make the journey with Sophie's eccentric grandmother.

"Mr. Thomas is familiar with train schedules and routes," Vivian said, offering the assistance of her fiancé's man of business.

Dahlia made the note *train schedule*.

"I will need to give my apologies to the Hospital for Women and somehow convince my uncle," Hazel said, her nervousness changing into something more akin to anticipation. "And I must pack some practical shoes this time."

Dahlia noted each item.

Hazel looked around the circle at her friends, excitement making a humming in her ears. "I'm really doing this," she whispered.

"You're really doing this," Elizabeth said, taking her hand and squeezing. The others joined hands as well, reminiscent of that first night in the Marquess of Molyneaux's library, and the mood turned bittersweet as Hazel realized she was leaving her friends again—these women, who were the core of all she was, her strength. She blinked at the tears that came to her eyes, knowing that no matter where she went, where her passion for healing took her, these four women would be behind her, and that knowledge gave her the courage to do the impossible.

CHAPTER 24

Jim watched through the window as the train pulled into St. Pancras railway station in London. Even in New York City he'd never seen so many people in one place.

He came down the steps onto the platform and was immediately engulfed by a crowd. The sound of many of the people around him speaking English was a change he hadn't anticipated. Some people hurried past, others embraced loved ones, welcoming them home, or wept as they bid them farewell. Jim made his way along the platform, holding his hat with one hand and his traveling case with the other. He had only the one piece of luggage, making a stop at the train's baggage car unnecessary.

As he moved into the station, he considered his next steps now that he'd finally arrived. His immediate instinct was to go directly to Hazel's house. But he realized he'd been traveling for over a week and should first find a place to wash and change his clothing. He needed to find a room anyway and had a list, given to him by the new Mrs. Laurent, of boardinghouses in neighborhoods that were reputable but not too costly. She had also provided letters of introductions to various hospitals, and Dr. Laurent had written glowing letters of recommendation.

Leaving the Red Cross Hospital had taken longer than he'd anticipated once he'd made up his mind to do it. He'd waited nearly a month for his replacement, a Dr. Blanchet, and had spent another week training the man.

He was frustrated the process had taken so long. But he was here now, and just being so near to actually seeing Hazel quickened his footsteps.

In the noise around him, he thought he even heard her name spoken as he passed by. He paused but realized he was being foolish. In his eagerness to be with her, he'd surely imagined it.

Jim glanced toward where he'd thought the sound had come from, and he saw a group of young women standing together on the platform.

A man pushed past him, hurrying to catch a train, and Jim caught his balance.

He glanced again at the women, tipped his hat, and continued on. But an uneasiness settled into his thoughts. There was something . . . and an instant later he knew what it was. He spun, coming back to the young ladies.

"Excuse me, miss."

The woman he spoke to turned toward him. She was slender with dark hair and intelligent eyes. And just as he'd thought, on her lapel was a brooch exactly like Hazel's. When he glanced at the others, he saw they all wore them as well.

"I'm sorry to bother you, but are you Miss Hazel Thornton's friends?"

The woman blinked. "I beg your pardon, sir?"

"Your pin, I . . . Miss Thornton wears the same brooch, and I—"

"How do you know Miss Thornton?" Another of the women asked. She was shorter with light-brown hair. She put her hands on her hips, appraising him with a suspicious scowl.

"I beg your pardon. My name is Dr. Jim Jackson. Hazel worked with me at the Red Cross Hospital in Spain."

Eight eyes stared at him, and at the same time, they all went wide with panic. The sight made him uneasy.

Then the four women spoke at once.

"Dr. Jackson?"

"You are here!"

"Hazel is returning to Spain."

"She is already on the train!"

"We have just bid her farewell."

"You are just moments too late."

It was all a jumble of words, but his mind somehow managed to make sense of it. "Which train?"

In a synchronized motion, the women pointed as a train let out a blast and started to move.

Jim dropped his traveling case and ran.

Now he was the one pushing through the crowds. He skirted around a pile of trunks and dodged a porter wheeling a crate, moving as fast as he was able. He ran alongside the train, ignoring the yells of conductors and police.

The train was picking up speed, windows moving past, and in one, he saw her.

"Hazel!" He called out her name, and she looked directly at him, her mouth forming an *o*. A burst of speed pushed him the last few feet to grab on to a railing, pulling himself up onto the landing, where he found himself face-to-face with an irate attendant.

"Stop!" The man grabbed Jim's arm, pulling him away from the edge of the train landing. "Dangerous business, that." He motioned with his eyes to where the earth sped past them. "I'll need to see your ticket, please."

"I'm sorry," Jim said. "I don't have one, but I'll be happy to—"

The man's grip tightened, and he frowned. "'Fraid I'll have to detain you, sir. Report you to the officials in Ashford." He shook his head as if he were very disappointed. "Train jumping is a punishable offense." He pulled Jim inside the train car.

"Wait!" At the sound of Hazel's voice, the men turned.

She hurried down the train's passageway, followed by an old woman wearing a very fine gown and carrying a parasol in the same way a Viking might carry a battle-ax. In her other hand was a rope leading a very fat, very annoyed-looking pug.

"Jim, what are you doing here?" Hazel asked when she reached him.

"I came to find you," he said. "I'd hoped to come sooner, but . . ." He held out his hands as if to say, "Here I am."

"I was going to Spain to find you," Hazel said. Her cheeks were pink, all traces of illness gone, and a charming smile lit her face.

Jim's stomach flopped over. He couldn't look away.

The old woman put a hand on her heart, smiling widely. "My, isn't this a pleasant turn of events." She glared at the attendant until he released Jim's arm, then stepped back, pulling the dog to the side of the passageway, and pointed with her parasol. "Go on, now, you two. Into the compartment." She scooted around them. "I'll work things out with the attendant."

The pair stepped into the compartment, and Jim closed the door, cutting off the sounds of arguing between the woman and the attendant in the passageway, which had apparently caused the dog to begin yapping.

"Jim." Hazel pointed out the window to where she'd seen him running beside the train only moments earlier. "I can't believe you—"

He cut off her words when he kissed her, holding her tightly against him. Her soft lips, the smell of her skin, the way she sank into his arms all reaffirmed that coming to London was the right decision. *She* was the right decision.

Hazel kissed him back, her arms going around his waist. "I've missed you," she whispered against his lips.

The sound of the door scraping and a throat clearing made him pull away.

The old woman was back with her dog. She looked between the two of them and moved around them, sitting on the compartment's bench, and motioned for Jim and Hazel to sit on the bench facing her. The dog jumped to sit beside her.

Hazel and Jim sat as well.

"I haven't introduced you," Hazel said. "I apologize. I was . . ." A blush spread over her cheeks. "Yes, well, Dr. Jim Jackson, meet Lady Mather. She is my traveling companion. And, of course, Mimi, this is Dr. Jackson, my . . ." She blushed again.

"A pleasure, my lady," Jim said, inclining his head.

"How do you do?" Lady Mather said.

Jim took Hazel's hand, squeezing it.

"Well, you two, it appears our trip to Spain will not happen after all," Lady Mather said. "Pity. I'd rather hoped to practice my Spanish." She squinted, looking at them thoughtfully. "But it would be a waste of a perfectly good holiday if we were to just turn around and return to London, don't you think?"

Jim and Hazel looked at one another, unsure of what to say.

"I wonder," Lady Mather continued, "should the pair of you care to spend a few days in Paris? Quite a romantic city—museums, musical performances, if you're interested in that sort of thing. And you could spend some time becoming reacquainted."

"I think . . ." Hazel glanced at Jim, and seeing his nod, she smiled. "I think that sounds lovely."

"Dorrit loves Paris, don't you, my dear?" Lady Mather patted the dog's head.

Dorrit scratched her ear, not looking particularly partial toward either destination.

"Then, it's settled," Lady Mather said with finality. "Now, if you'll excuse me, I am ready for my nap." Her lips smirked the slightest bit as she leaned her head back and closed her eyes, one hand resting on her little dog.

"Paris. What do you think of that?" Hazel said in a quiet voice.

"It matters not at all to me where we go. As long as I am with you, Hazel, my darling, I am where I am meant to be."

This time, it was Hazel who kissed him, sending a light feeling flooding through him until he thought he might rise off his seat and float out of the train.

The remainder of the journey passed very happily, especially since their chaperone found endless excuses to leave Jim and Hazel alone, and they, in turn, found pleasant ways to spend their time together, many of them including quiet moments and secret kisses.

What he had told her on the train was true. It did not matter whether they were strolling through a Paris museum or imprisoned in a rebel camp or working in a surgical theater. When Jim was with Hazel, he was home.

HISTORICAL NOTE

The Carlist Wars were a series of Spanish Civil Wars in the late nineteenth century. After King Ferdinand VII's death, the country split, supporting different claimants to the crown. The Carlists supported Don Carlos, a younger son of a previous king. They were religious and traditional and worried when the Spanish parliament appointed an Italian duke to rule the country that their way of life was in jeopardy.

The Carlists rebelled in Catalonia and in the Basque region, occupying towns and creating a temporary state. They used guerrilla warfare to defy the Spanish Army.

The International Red Cross was established in 1859 in Geneva. It received legal backing when the Geneva convention was created. The mission of the Red Cross (and Red Crescent) was and is to ensure humanitarian care for all victims of armed conflicts and natural disasters, no matter their religion, race, ethnicity, political beliefs, or country of origin.

AUTHOR'S NOTE

Before I began this project, I spent some time considering what exactly I wanted to say. What is important enough to me that I'm willing to spend an entire series exploring it? What have I learned, or what do I want people to know or to reexamine in their own perceptions?

Still looking for a direction, I read quite a few books and watched some movies, and after a while, I began to notice a trend that was so contrary to my own experience that I was surprised I'd never realized it before. It involves how women's relationships with one another are portrayed in fiction, especially in romantic stories, and it's something I'm guilty of in my own writing. Women are often represented as rivals, either to provide competition for the main character in vying for the same man's affection or simply to give the main character someone to compare herself to. Other times, they are underdeveloped secondary characters the heroine confides in when she wants to talk about the hero.

Neither scenario quite reflects my own experiences. From the moment I was born, my mother, sisters, grandmothers, aunts, cousins, friends, and teachers cheered for me, encouraged me, and offered advice as I grew up. And now I still find myself surrounded by strong, intelligent, supportive women in every area of my life. Women are my friends, my mentors, and my heroes. I turn to them when I'm hurting or unsure or happy, and time and again, I've been bolstered and comforted and inspired by my own Blue Orchid Society. The women I know are complex and interesting and filled with wisdom. And that is what I hope to represent in this series—the sisterhood that's often overlooked in stories but so prominent in the lives of real women.

I love the time period of this story. The industrial revolution was changing the way people worked and lived. Florence Nightingale was instructing nurses, and women were being admitted to colleges and inheriting property. Colonies were pushing back against English expansion. The suffrage movement was growing in both England and America. Women were working as detectives in the Pinkerton Agency and starting to get credit as writers and teachers.

It feels like such an exciting time, and such a turning point in history, and I wanted my characters to be smack in the middle of it, navigating these modern developments and adjusting to a changing world.

So this book is meant as a tribute to them—the women who came before—and to us, the women who follow in their footsteps. And to the sisterhood that has marched along throughout history, often silently and unnoticed, and shaped our world.

ABOUT THE AUTHOR

Jennifer Tolman Photography

JENNIFER MOORE LIVES WITH ONE husband and four sons, who produce heaps of laundry and laughter. She earned a BA from the University of Utah in linguistics, which she uses mostly for answering Jeopardy questions. A reader of history and romance, she loves traveling, tall ships, scented candles, and watching cake-decorating videos. When she's not driving carpool, writing, or helping with homework, she'll usually be found playing tennis. Learn more at authorjmoore.com and on Jennifer's social media.

Facebook: Author Jennifer Moore
Instagram: jennythebrave